NOT WITHOUT YOU

A.P. WATSON

not without you

By Your Side Series: Book Three

a.p. watson

Not Without You

First Edition.

Published in the United States of America.

ISBN 13: 978-0-9888019-4-3

Edited by Tamara Beard of Wrapped Up Writing

Cover Design by Regina Wamba

Formatted by A.P. Watson

 Created with Vellum

For Heather,

Because no one ever tells you no.

chapter one

white

W HITE. THAT WAS THE color that reigned supreme in places like this, places promising all the enlightenment that follows a higher education. Frankly, I would rather be surrounded by any other color in the crayon box. Yes, that meant puke green, sunshine yellow, and even the bright orange screaming at us from every inch of campus. In my opinion, anything was better than white. White was the color of a blank canvas, a stark reminder of the creative sabbatical my soul was currently taking.

"Why do you look like your grandma just flipped you off?"

The sound of Wren's voice threw me out of my train of thought.

"Because I hate this class. Anything not related to art is a waste of my time."

"Yeah, that might be true, but everybody is required to take Probability & Statistics."

"And the *probability* of me passing this class is slim, so as you can see, no further instruction is needed," I quipped, sticking my tongue out at her.

She flung her long copper locks over her shoulder and plopped in the seat to my left, pulling out a spiral notebook and a green pen. She was feeling sassy today, and that was an incredible sign. If I had to deal with everything she'd been through the past few weeks, I would have curled up in a ball and flipped the world the middle finger. But not Wren. She was a damn force to be reckoned with.

Placing my hand on her arm, I gave it a little squeeze. Instantly, her body stilled. Although I didn't reveal my thoughts, my gesture meant she could count on me. It meant she wasn't alone.

"Thanks, babe," she whispered, setting her hand on my knee. "You're the best."

"Ditto, babe."

To my right, I could just make out the form of the hot blond guy who had been staring at me for half the class on Tuesday. Not that I hadn't done my fair share of staring. My eyes had wandered in his direction more than a couple of times since the start of the semester. After all, no harm ever came from looking. He stepped closer, intent on occupying the empty chair next to me.

"If you're going to sit there, you'd better have a good handle on what the hell is going on in this class," I stated. My less-than-stellar performance on our first test meant I needed to get my ass in gear if I had any hopes of making it through this class with my GPA intact.

"You mean you don't?" he asked, humor evident in his tone. "Because you seem like the type of person who has a handle on everything."

I glanced up at him. Most of the time whenever a guy hit on me, I would dismiss them with little more than a wave of my hand. But his comment had more than piqued my interest. His shaggy blond hair and golden skin tone were *so* much hotter than I remembered. "Oh," I whispered with a smile, "you're good."

He sat down next to me, sliding a pen out of the pocket of his jeans. "That's what I hear." And Hottie was apparently telling the truth, because when he opened his notebook, the first test we took slid out, landing in my lap. "Sorry." He leaned in my direction.

But I was too quick for him. I grabbed the paper, completely at a loss for words, which was really fucking rare for me. *Holy hell.* Hottie got a ninety-six? "Look, we got the same grade!"

Wren snickered at my exclamation, trying her best to keep from laughing, since Professor Leigh had already started passing out the attendance roster.

"Really?" asked Hottie.

"Yeah, if you reverse the numbers on your test, that's what I got."

The bitchy chick who always wore a red headband turned around to glare at me. "Shh," she spat, holding her finger over her lips.

"Oh, shut up. It's not like we're going to use this fucking bullshit in everyday life." My retort either offended or shocked her, because she scoffed at me before spinning back around. God, I hated that fucking headband.

"That girl annoys the shit out of me," Wren mumbled.

"Me too, babe."

"Eh, she's just pissed because she got the second-best grade in the class," Hottie said.

"That seat is yours for the rest of the semester if you want it."

"I may hold you to that. And my name is Ryan Evanston, by the way." He held out his hand for me to shake.

Crystal blue eyes met mine—the color so pure and pristine my fingers twitched with the need to recreate it.

Well, *fuck*.

For some people, sexual dry spells ruled their existence. For me, my artistic dry spell was worse than being stranded in the Sahara without a canteen. Sure, I'd been creating art projects for school, but my desire to paint—to let the world fall away and just create—had been non-existent. Wren believed I was uninspired, and she was probably right. But here, at this moment, all I wanted to do was paint those eyes.

Eventually, I slid my hand into his, noting the warmth radiating from his flesh. "Terayn Andrews."

"And you?" he asked, leaning toward Wren.

"Wren Williams," she answered.

"Nice to meet both of you."

"Likewise," I muttered for both of us.

Professor Leigh droned on for what felt like an eternity. So the guy had his passions, and they all happened to lie within statistics, but that still didn't warrant the need for him to subject each of us to said passions. Alas, the board of this higher education establishment somehow feels we will benefit from taking a statistics course. And it was a load of freaking bull too.

I tried to concentrate on the sound of Leigh's voice, but my brain was only capable of withstanding so much torture. I copied down a few notes from the lecture, but my willpower was obliterated by the color periwinkle. My hand had been twitching since I caught sight of those blue eyes. Pulling a few colored pens from my purse, I decided to let my fingers do their bidding.

Line after line flowed together, forming a perfect representation of the human eye. That iris and the multitude of colors it possessed were astounding. I used not one but three different blues in order to capture the intricacy of the hue. And I still wasn't done. Something about his expression when he had looked at me caught my interest. It needed to be captured too. Now, the drawing had a set of eyebrows to accompany those eyes.

A sharp elbow to my side pulled my attention from the growing portrait in front of me.

"If you keep at it, you're going to wind up drawing a full portrait," Wren whispered in my ear.

"What?"

"And you might want to stop before you get to Hottie's body."

"Fuck," I muttered, the momentary enchantment his eyes had cast over me finally breaking.

I scrambled to cover the drawing that had now taken up over three-fourths of my notebook paper, but my efforts were too late. Hottie had already caught sight of my sudden artistic breakthrough.

He pointed to my drawing. "You're really talented."

"Thanks. Art major, so I have a bad habit of doodling all the time."

"I like it."

I swept a strand of hair behind my ear and glanced at the clock. Thank God, this hell pit of a class was nearly over. I was in the middle of straightening my papers when a page full of notes landed right on top of my stack.

I glanced to my right, staring at Hottie, or rather, Ryan. "What's this?"

"Notes for today's lecture."

"Don't you need these?" I asked.

"Not really. This class is almost fun for me. I'm double majoring in corporate finance and business."

"Holy shit."

He laughed, turning that blue gaze on me. "That's one way to put it."

"Thank you for the notes."

"No problem."

To my left, I could just make out Wren's body stiffening. Her phone was clutched in her hands, and she squeezed the plastic case dangerously.

That couldn't be good. I glanced at her and the phone. A text from Liam lit up the screen.

Fuck that fucking jackass.

Even after all the shit he had pulled on her birthday, he was still trying to fuck with her life. I was just about to throw my arm around her when she stood and bolted from the class. I grabbed my stuff and flew after her, ignoring the astonished stares of our fellow classmates. The moment I reached the doorway, my head turned in either direction. Wren was at the end of the hall, clearly fighting back tears. The girl didn't cry. In fact, the only time I'd seen her cry—other than at my mother's funeral—was on her birthday last week when she caught Liam fucking his ex.

I approached her with caution. "Hey, babe. Talk to me about it?"

She shook her head, water shining in her brown eyes. "I am so over him and all his bullshit! Why can't he just leave me the fuck alone?"

Her raised voice garnered a few curious stares. Not thinking, I grabbed her hand and pulled her into what I thought would be an empty room. Instead, we were met with a wall of urinals. Oh well, it would do.

"What is he doing now?"

"Trying to apologize. As if I would even take his lying, cheating ass back."

"The nerve of that fucker."

"Hey! This is the men's restroom!" A guy I'd never seen before held the door open, staring at us in shock.

"Ask me if I care," I replied, glaring at him with nothing but hatred in my eyes.

"But—" the guy began.

"Find another restroom. This one is occupied." Hottie from our statistics class loomed over the guy. All right, he wasn't just another pretty face. He had some nicely muscled arms to back up his threat.

"My mistake." The guy scurried away a second later.

"Are both of you okay?"

"Wren?" I questioned in a soft voice.

"Not really," she replied, her fingers twisting around a long strand of her hair. Her eyes were glued to the floor, but the faint trace of tears still lingered on the curves of her cheeks.

"I see." He nodded, looking thoughtful as he shoved his hands in the pockets of his jeans. "You guys hungry?"

"Yeah," Wren answered.

"I could eat," I added.

"My Jeep is parked right outside this building. Why don't I take you guys to get something to eat?"

I looked to Wren so she would know this was her call.

"Okay," she muttered.

He held the door open for us while Wren and I filed out of the men's restroom. The three of us exited the building, stepping out into the overcast day. Yesterday was nearly seventy degrees. Today, it was barely above fifty. I really wished Tennessee would decide what the hell it wanted to do with the weather.

Hottie drove us to a diner not far from campus. I'd always been told not to get in the car with a stranger, but Ryan put off nothing but good vibes. He had opened and closed the car doors for Wren and I, and he even held open the door to the diner. Everything in my gut informed me he was a nice guy.

We slid into an empty booth just as our waiter arrived. He handed each of us a menu and a glass of water before he scurried away, stating he'd be back in a minute to take our order. I sipped on my water, watching Wren out of the corner of my eye.

"Do you have any more classes today?" I asked Ryan.

"Nope. I'm free. What about you two?"

"I've got art history tonight at seven but that's it."

"I'm done too," Wren stated.

"And you're an art major. What about you, Wren?"

"Nursing. I'm still getting a few requirements in now, though."

"That's awesome."

"What about you?" she asked. She'd been too distracted by Liam's earlier message to hear Ryan's answer in class.

"I'm double majoring in corporate finance and business."

"Damn. Guess that explains the A you got on the first statistics exam."

"If either of you need help in that class, just ask. I really don't mind."

"Thanks," she answered.

"I think I'm the only one who really needs the help," I added.

Wren grinned, nudging me with her shoulder. "Numbers so aren't your thing."

"I'm tragically left-brained."

No sooner than the words left my mouth, and our waiter popped up out of nowhere to take our order.

"Alright. What can I get y'all to eat?" He turned in my direction first, awaiting my order.

"I'll have a burger with a side of onion rings."

He jotted down my order. "And for you?"

"I'll have two pancakes and a double side of bacon."

"Oh, we stopped serving breakfast at noon."

Wren's expression dropped at his words. It was only two in the afternoon. I figured this place served breakfast all day, and she must have too. She picked the menu back up, scanning through the lunch dishes.

"Give her whatever she wants," Ryan ordered, pulling out his wallet.

"I wish I could, but we stopped serving breakfast two hours ago."

Ryan set a fifty-dollar bill on top of the guy's order pad. "Surely a few pancakes and two sides of bacon won't be too much trouble, right?"

"It's okay! I'll just order something else," Wren said.

"Nope, you want pancakes and bacon, and you'll get it." Ryan's voice wasn't angry, but it did err on the side of being extremely dominant. And I kind of liked it.

"Two pancakes and two sides of bacon it is," the waiter agreed, scribbling on his pad.

"We really appreciate you being so accommodating," Ryan stated.

"And for you?" the waiter asked.

"A burger with a side of fries and a strawberry milkshake."

"Okay. I'll have that out to you as soon as possible."

"Thank you," Ryan answered, collecting all the menus to hand back to the waiter.

"Thank you so much for what you did, but you didn't need to do it," Wren said once our waiter was out of earshot.

Ryan shrugged, acting like it wasn't a big deal. "You

seemed like you weren't having the best day, so it's the least I can do."

"Thank you," I added, staring into those sapphire eyes.

"It's nothing."

"I really do appreciate it," Wren replied.

"Happy to help. Besides, what kind of diner doesn't serve breakfast all day?"

"I was thinking the same thing!"

I nodded, completely in agreement with Wren. "I thought it did too. Kind of weird that it doesn't."

"I suppose next time we eat out, it'll have to be at Street City Grill. They serve breakfast all day."

"Bacon should always be served all day."

"I agree wholeheartedly." Ryan smiled at her. "So, how long have the two of you been friends?"

"Since we were six," Wren and I answered in unison.

Ryan nodded. "I can tell."

"This copper-haired beauty is my number one babe." I slid my arm around her neck and squeezed tight.

"No boyfriend?"

"What the hell would I want one of those for?"

"I don't mean to put down my own gender, but you're probably better off without one," Ryan joked.

"No kidding," Wren agreed.

"Look, I'm not one to pry, but if you want to talk about whatever has been making your day so shitty, feel free to get it off your chest."

"I appreciate the thought."

"It's either about relationship or family troubles. And while I'm well-versed with the latter, I'm also a good listener if you ever need to vent about it."

Wren gave him a slight smile. "Thank you. I'll definitely keep your offer in mind. It might be nice to have a guy's perspective on everything."

"Relationship trouble then," Ryan muttered more to himself than to Wren and me.

"What was that?" I asked.

"Sorry, I figured it was guy trouble, but I didn't want to pry."

"Oh," Wren breathed. "Yeah, it is."

"Figures. Men are dicks most of the time."

"Oh, so you're gay?" I questioned. The way Ryan had been staring at me in class led me to believe he fell to the charms of the female population, so I couldn't help but be curious.

I blamed his eyes.

"What?" His eyebrows pinched together as he shifted his attention from Wren to me. "I'm not gay."

"If you are, we don't care. Actually, it will probably make us like you more."

"Sorry to burst your bubble, but I like pussy."

His reply caught me off guard. Those periwinkle irises held my gaze for a second before tearing through me like a damn power drill. "Um, I-I . . ." What the hell was I even going to say? I was not the type of woman to be at a loss for words, so this development was pretty strange for me. And Hottie's looks were definitely responsible.

Wren burst into a fit of laughter beside me. "Oh my God! You made her blush! Jesus Christ, Ter, I don't think you've blushed since ninth grade." She leaned across the table and held out her hand, giving Ryan a high five. "You are crass and awesome! We can be friends."

Ryan licked his lips and grinned like the freaking Cheshire cat. "Happy to have your approval."

Thank God, my embarrassing moment was cut short by the arrival of our food. Our waiter placed a plate in front of each of us before scurrying away.

"Bacon!" Wren bounced with glee as she shoved a strip of crispy goodness into her mouth.

"In the world of Wren, bacon makes everything better," I explained.

"I can see that. And in the world of Terayn, what makes everything better?"

Usually, that answer was painting and Wren's mom making me a chicken pot pie. But with my creative hiatus seeping into every part of my being, I was going to have to settle for baked goods. "Wren's mom makes the best chicken pot pie I've ever had in my life."

"So, it makes everything in your life better?"

"Pretty much." I shrugged my shoulders and shoved an onion ring in my mouth as I watched Ryan devour his burger. "And what makes everything in your life better?"

"Foodwise? A burger and fries. Not foodwise, I guess hitting the gym. It's a good way to burn off steam."

"We can tell."

Wren snickered beside me, quickly shoving a bite of pancake into her mouth.

"Thank you?"

"Was that meant as a comment or a question?" I asked Ryan.

"Both, I guess."

"Fair enough."

We finished the rest of our food, and I couldn't help but be thankful for the distraction Ryan had given Wren. Her life had been turned upside down, so any excuse to forget the shit storm Liam had brought on her? I was all for it.

Although, the part of my brain continuously stressing about my future career as an artist was thankful for the distraction as well.

chapter two

blue, blue, blue

"UGH," I HUFFED, UNLOCKING the door to my dorm room. Usually, I loved art history class, but today, the three-hour lecture felt like cruel and unusual punishment. My focus was wrecked, and I blamed the super attractive owner of a pair of blue eyes. A glance to my right informed me that Brooklyn and her boyfriend were already sitting on her bed and watching a movie.

Shit.

I nodded to them and tossed my messenger bag on the floor. If the boyfriend was over after ten, that meant I'd be sleeping with my headphones on again tonight. Falling asleep while listening to Deftones was an art form in and of itself. But I much preferred listening to their music than the sounds of my roommate and her man humping. Fuck this dorm. Tomorrow, I'd remember to snag a key to Wren's new apartment. Even if she was at work, at least I could sleep in peace. When Liam fucked up her world last week, I tried everything I could to get out of my dorm situation, but unfortunately, I was locked in for the semester.

On-campus housing was factored into my scholarship, but if I sweet-talked my dad just right, maybe he would be cool with me moving into Wren's place.

Grabbing a pair of yoga pants and a tank top, I headed into the bathroom Brooklyn and I shared with the room next to us. Four girls sharing one bathroom made for an interesting arrangement, but luckily, it wasn't occupied. After scrubbing my hair and body, I coated every inch of skin with my favorite lotion and got dressed. I prayed there was still enough time to slide on my house shoes and grab my bag before Brooklyn and Joe lost any clothing. Last week, I almost got a full-frontal view of Joe's junk. And that is one show I'd rather not see again.

I raced back inside my room and grabbed my slippers, messenger bag, and phone at the speed of light. I didn't even bother covering my feet until the door was shut behind me. Then I walked down to the first-floor common room, praying it would be empty.

Despite being a dormitory, Lucille Langford Hall was still a beautiful building. Thick columns outfitted the front of the structure and the common room was drenched in dark mahogany wood. A flat-screen television occupied the far left corner of the room, a couch and two armchairs huddled around it, and a table and chairs by a fireplace sat on the right side. The other half of the large space housed an air hockey table and a ping-pong table. Thankfully, I had the whole room to myself. I plopped down at the table and spread out my statistics book and the dinner I'd picked up from Subway. I tried to avoid cooking in the kitchen on our floor after almost setting fire to macaroni and cheese the first month of the semester. To be honest, it took skill to be that shitty at cooking, and I happened to be excellent at it. Setting my phone and a bottle of water next to me, I dug in to my six-inch spicy Italian sub and a bag of chips. As I ate, I decided to send a quick text to check on Wren.

Me: *Hey babe, don't let me forget, but tomorrow I need to get a spare key to your new place. I'm sick of listening to Brooklyn and Joe screw, so I figured I could crash at your place while you're at work.*

Wren: *I'm so sorry they're going at it again, but we will get you a key tomorrow! Feel free to crash at my place any time you want!*

Me: *Thanks babe! You the best!*

I accompanied my text with a string of hearts and other emojis.

Wren: *Welcome! And you know how I feel about too many emojis.*

Me: *Whatever, you know you love me.*

Wren: *True. Well, things just got hectic here, so I better let you go. I'll see you tomorrow. Love you!*

Me: *Love you too!*

Taking a sip of water, I cracked open my book and removed the notes Ryan had given me. I hadn't noticed it at the time, but his name and number were scribbled at the top of the page with a short note.

If you ever need help studying, just give me a call.

The tips of my fingers rubbed over the words several times. Part of me expected the message to be a figment of my imagination, but when I removed my hand, his words were still there. Well, damn. His words from the diner rang in my head for the fiftieth time today. *Sorry to burst your bubble, but I like pussy.* I wasn't the type of person who embarrassed easily, if at all. And two semesters of drawing the naked human form only further instilled that nature. But there was something so casual and sincere about Ryan's reply that wrecked my composure.

Perhaps it was because I wanted to introduce him to that part of my anatomy.

Fuck.

Sighing, I flipped over the notes and began reading over the chapters we had covered in class earlier today. I was three pages in when I decided to throw in the towel. The book might as well have been written in Greek for everything I could understand from it. I turned the notes back over and chewed on my thumbnail. It was already after eleven on a Wednesday night. Chances were he had an early class and wouldn't reply anyway. Before I could second-guess myself, I typed out a quick message and pressed send.

Me: *What the fuck is the Kirkwood approximation? And further-more, are we sure it's part of the English language? Because I can't understand a single word of it. This is Terayn, by the way.*

I stared at the screen feeling like the biggest idiot on the face of the earth. He was acing this class, so why the hell would he want to spend time teaching a dunce like me? The initial answer my brain concocted was that he was a player trying to get into my pants. Not that there was anything wrong with that. I didn't do relationships. Well, I didn't do a lot of casual sex either, but if that floated some-one's boat, then who was I to judge? But the way Ryan had acted around Wren and I, along with the way he had made sure she got her pancakes and bacon, rebuked that answer entirely. I was about to pursue another line of reasoning when a reply lit up my phone.

Ryan: *I promise the Kirkwood approximation is written in English. But yes, it can be a tricky concept. Are you going over today's lesson?*

Me: *Yes, but I have no idea what I'm reading.*

Ryan: *Do you need some help? I can come explain it if you want.*

If I chewed on my thumbnail any harder, I'd draw blood. Giving in to defeat, I decided to accept his offer. I had to pass this class. It was a required course, and once I made it through, I'd never have to think about the Kirkwood approximation ever again.

Me: *I would actually really appreciate some help if it's not too much trouble. I live in Langford Hall and I'm downstairs in the common room. If you come to the main entrance, I'll buzz you in.*

Ryan: *Sounds good. Be there in fifteen.*

Sure enough, fifteen minutes later, I was letting Ryan into my dorm building.

"Hey," he said, breezing past me.

I caught a whiff of his cologne as he came inside. And Jesus, it smelled delicious. "Hey."

"That's your stuff on the table, right?"

"Oh, yeah." I stepped in front of him, taking note of his attire. He had on a zip-up hoodie and a tight pair of track pants. His hair looked damp as he ran a hand through the blond locks. He had that quintessential surfer guy thing going on, like he belonged on the walls of an Abercrombie & Fitch store.

He scooted one of the chairs next to mine and took a seat. "So, where do you want to start?"

"You pick. It's not like I understand any of it anyway."

"Alright," he replied with a laugh. "Let's start with my notes and then we can use the book if there is something we need to look at in depth."

I nodded. "Okay." I glanced down at my thin tank top and wished I hadn't skimped on wearing a bra after my shower. And going back up to my room to grab a hoodie was absolutely out of the question. I'd be avoiding that fucking room until at least four.

I listened as Ryan went over the first page of notes. He explained a few of the concepts, taking his time while covering the Kirkwood approximation. I was actually beginning to understand some of this shit, which to me, was a miracle. But as we reached the second page of notes,

I was finding it hard to focus. I'll never understand why the buildings on campus are boiling in the summer and freezing in the fall and winter, but I guess that was my scholarship money hard at work. Rubbing my hands over my arms, I tried to ignore how cold I was and shifted my attention back to Ryan.

"You're freezing. If you want to grab a jacket from your room, I'll wait down here."

"I appreciate the thought, but there is no chance in hell I'm going back to my room."

"Why is that? Is everything okay?"

"Yeah, but my roommate has her boyfriend over and I'd rather not walk in on them screwing."

"Oh."

"Yep. I've tried to talk to her about it, but it hasn't gotten me anywhere. I fall asleep listening to Deftones most nights."

"Deftones?"

"They drown out the sound."

"I see. I figured you and Wren were roommates."

"God, I wish! That would be awesome! I'm going to get a key to her new apartment tomorrow, though, so whenever she's at work, I'm gonna sleep at her place."

"She works nights?"

"Yeah, she works as a tech at the hospital."

"That's cool," he answered, removing his jacket. "Here, put this on."

"I'll be fine. I'm not that cold. Don't worry about it."

"You have goosebumps all over your arms."

I glanced at my fair skin, noting the raised bumps covering my flesh. "I'm okay."

Ryan shook his head and draped his jacket over my shoulders. The fabric was still warm from when he'd worn it, and I was hit with the scent of his cologne once more.

"Thank you," I said, sliding my arms through the long sleeves.

"No problem."

When I looked up, his blue gaze was fixed on me, and for the second time today, my fingers itched to draw him. Too bad he wasn't one of the models we were required to sketch in class last semester. My hands would've had a field day recreating the lean muscles in his arms and chest.

"So," he began, leaning toward me, "do you want me to go over discrete probability distribution again or do you think you've got it?"

"One more time, if you don't care."

"Of course."

I sighed loudly, feeling more like an idiot with every passing second. "I'm sorry. I'm sure you feel like you're wasting your time."

"Hanging out with you is the furthest thing from a waste of my time."

"Are you trying to butter me up or something?"

"Maybe . . . Why? Is it working?"

"Maybe."

His deep laugh filled the otherwise empty room. "Good to know all my efforts aren't in vain."

"Speaking of, I really appreciate everything you did for Wren today. She's been through hell the past few weeks, and I know the three of us hanging out today was the most fun she's had in a while."

"I'm just glad I could help," he replied. "Was her ex a douche or something?"

"That's putting it mildly."

"I figured as much."

"It's not my story to tell, so that's the only thing I'll say, but yeah, Liam is a fucking douche nozzle."

"Relationships can be hell."

"Sounds like you've had firsthand experience."

"Something like that. I definitely know how it feels to be treated like shit."

I set my hand on his arm. "I'm sorry," I replied with a light squeeze.

"It is what it is."

"True that. Relationships aren't worth the trouble if you ask me."

"So you're anti-relationship?"

"Just romantic ones. They only lead to trouble."

"I agree," he said, catching me off guard.

Most guys that I told about my aversion to relationships reacted one of two ways. Ecstatic because they thought it meant I was down to screw or frustrated as they tried to convince me that I do, in fact, believe in love. Both kinds of reactions annoyed the shit out of me. If I wanted to screw a guy, I would. And it's not that I don't believe in love, it's more along the lines that I don't like the effect it has on people. Love can ruin you, and I've lived through the destruction it can leave behind.

My head tilted so that I could get a better look at him. "I thought you said at the diner you only have experience with family troubles."

"Well, watching all the shit my mom went through gave me a good perspective on relationship issues."

"What kind of shit?"

"Thought we were supposed to be focusing on statistics?"

"You're right." I usually wouldn't let such an attempt at diverting a conversation slide, but the tone of his voice stopped me from pressing the subject any further. "Impart your wisdom on me, teach."

"I'll try my best," he countered, clearly teasing me.

"Hey!"

His smirk informed me that he was very amused at my expense. "Only joking."

After two hours of incessant studying, I actually felt as if I'd learned something. Ryan was a good teacher, and he understood these concepts inside and out. Not to mention, the guy had the patience of a saint. When it came to stuff I didn't understand, I tended to get frustrated pretty quick, but Ryan took his time explaining everything to me. He never once tried to rush me through something, and in my book, that earned him extra brownie points.

"You know more than you think you do," he said, stretching out his arms.

"I'm glad one of us is confident in my knowledge."

"We can study again this weekend if you want."

I licked my lips and stuffed the notes he'd given me into my textbook. "I'd like that."

He grinned at me, the gesture barely crinkling the outer corners of his eyes. "Just let me know when. I'm free all weekend."

"Okay, I will," I replied in a quiet voice. When he stood from the table, I realized I didn't want him to leave. "Would you like to stay and watch a movie with me?" I motioned toward the corner with the flat-screen TV.

"I don't want to bother you."

I grinned and made my way to the couch. "If I thought you were a bother, I never would've asked."

"Alright, movie it is."

"Awesome."

I sat on the left side of the couch, my heart practically vibrating in my chest as he sat next to me. His arms stretched along the back of the couch, one resting behind my back. My spine stiffened. I wasn't sure why, but his close proximity felt much more intimate than should be possible.

"Are you still cold?" he asked. He leaned toward me, his hands rubbing up and down my arms as if he were trying to instill warmth in my body.

In that moment, cold was the last thought in my mind. "Nope, not cold at all." In fact, I was really fucking hot, and I had half a mind to share that heat with Hottie next to me.

"I'm not going to start hitting on you, if that's what you're worried about."

"I know that."

"Do you?"

"Well . . . Why did you come up to me in class today?"

"I'm guessing men hit on you quite frequently, right?"

"Yes, and it gets really old after a while. I mean, I've stopped having conversations with them because it's just easier to wave them away."

He laughed, and the sound filled my ears like music. "I came up to you because I could hear you bitching in class Tuesday and I died laughing. I thought you were hilarious, and I wanted to get to know you better."

"That's acceptable."

"Glad I have your approval," he said, the corners of his lips turning upward.

Picking up the remote for the television, I flipped through a few channels. "Anything in particular you want to watch?"

"Lady's choice."

I scrolled through a few channels before coming to a stop on one of my favorite movies, *The Goonies*. "Is this okay with you?"

"Of course. Who doesn't love this movie?"

"We can be friends," I announced in a matter-of-fact tone.

"Oh, you've just now decided this?"

Settling back into the couch cushions, I shrugged. "I've kind of been thinking about it all day."

"What sealed the deal for you? Was it the fact I told you that I liked pussy?"

My skin hummed as if it'd been set on fire. What the hell was it about this guy casually uttering the *p*-word that made my composure go to shit?

"Oh my God!" I smacked his arm and pulled my hair over my shoulder to hide my blush. "What is wrong with you?"

Ryan leaned toward me until his lips were mere inches from my ear. "So many things."

"Obviously."

"You're not really complaining."

"Give me a minute and I'll fix that."

His laughter filled the room, echoing off the walls. "I figured as much."

We watched the remainder of *The Goonies* without much conversation. Silence had the ability to make some people uncomfortable, but I reveled in the quiet. Wren and I didn't need to talk every single second of the day, and we would often sit for hours without uttering a word. Somehow, I felt the same kind of companionable silence with Ryan as he didn't seem to feel the need to force a conversation.

By the time the credits finished rolling, it was already after three in the morning.

"What time is your first class tomorrow?" I asked.

"Not till noon. Yours?"

"Ten."

"That's not too far away. I'll leave so you can get some sleep." Ryan moved to stand, but I stopped him by latching on to his wrist like he was a coveted set of Old Holland oil paints.

"Would you stay a little longer?" The words spilled from my lips before I even had a chance to contemplate what I was asking him.

He nodded, settling back into the leather cushions. "Yeah, of course."

"If you want to leave, you can," I replied, immediately second-guessing my question. "It's just nice to not be alone all the time. Whenever Joe comes over to play doctor with Brooklyn, I'm left down here by myself for hours on end."

"And Wren works a lot."

"Yeah, she has an apartment and school stuff to pay for. The woman is a boss. She works her ass off."

"She seems pretty awesome."

"She's the best."

"Have you thought about trying to get another roommate?"

"Believe me, I've exhausted all possibilities in that area. My scholarship includes on-campus housing, and since we're in the middle of a semester, I'm locked into my room situation like a woman wearing an eighteenth-century corset."

"I'm sorry. That really sucks."

"Eh," I replied with a shrug. "It's not your doing."

"You know what we could do?" When Ryan faced me, his perfect periwinkle irises sparkled with mischief.

"What?"

"Give your roommate a taste of her own medicine."

"What do you mean?"

"You said she and her boyfriend are always having sex—"

"You want me to have sex with you?" I asked, practically shouting my question. Heat warmed the apples of my cheeks. I felt as if Jackson Pollock had splattered me with red paint, because I knew my blush had to be as clear as day.

"You didn't let me finish."

"Yeah, I know, because you were propositioning me for sex."

"No, I wasn't. Will you just listen to me for a second?"

I released a heavy sigh and prayed to God above that Ryan hadn't noticed how flustered I was. "Fine."

"I said we should give her a taste of her own medicine. And what I meant is we should pretend like we're having sex to get back at her," he explained. "Some discarded clothes, a few moans, and everything covered by a blanket, and she'll be the one bolting out of the room as fast as she can."

My eyebrows arched nefariously. Hottie was a legit scheming mastermind. It was now my turn to look like the damn Cheshire Cat. "You know, I think you may be onto something here."

He shrugged. "Somehow, diabolical seems like the best choice when it comes to you."

Flipping my raven hair in a manner that would've made me a shoo-in to act in a Pantene commercial, I touched my hand to my chest. "You understand me," I said in the most drawn-out debutante voice I could muster.

"I do what I can."

"Are you free tomorrow night by any chance?"

"Yeah."

"Friday means Joe will be over at seven. Think you can swing by after six?"

"I can do that."

"Awesome. We're putting this idea in motion."

"Sounds like a plan."

"We should go over a few things first."

"Naturally," he agreed.

"Are you going to be okay with getting half naked with me?"

Ryan slid his arms along the back of the couch. "Shouldn't be a problem."

"And you have to pretend to be really into me."

"I can definitely manage that," he replied with all the confidence in the world.

Picking the remote back up, I began flipping through the channels. "Good."

"Can I ask you a question?"

Something about the tone of Ryan's voice forced me to look at him. It was as if all his usual mirth had evaporated into thin air.

"Yeah? What's wrong?"

Blowing out a deep breath, he asked, "You said you stay down here a lot by yourself, right?"

"Yeah, but only at night. Sometimes I suffer through the weirdness upstairs, but for the last three weeks, I've been sleeping down here most of the time."

"But the doors lock and everything?"

"Oh yeah. You have to have a key card to get in."

"Has anyone ever bothered you down here?"

I shook my head. "No. I'm usually the only person that hangs out down here. Every now and then, people come to play games, but no one stays. Why do you ask?"

"You're probably going to think I'm being ridiculous, but something about you staying down here by yourself, where drunk dumbasses—girls and guys alike—can just stumble through, doesn't sit well with me."

"You haven't even known me for twenty-four hours and you're already concerned about my safety?"

He gave a noncommittal shrug. "It's the way my mom raised me. Always treat women with respect, never force them to do anything they don't want to do, and make sure they know they're safe with you."

He repeated the principles by heart, as if he were reciting some kind of sacred proclamation straight from his memory.

"She did a damn good job with you."

"I like to think so," he agreed.

"I won't be staying down here once I get a key to Wren's new place. Rest assured, I'll be safe behind the locked doors of her apartment."

"Good."

"You're not leaving until I'm back in my room, are you?"

"Nope."

"I figured as much."

Tucking my feet underneath me, I relaxed against the soft couch cushions. A chill began to creep over my muscles. I pulled Ryan's hoodie tighter around me and absorbed the warmth of the soft fabric.

"I knew you were still cold," Ryan said, pushing to his feet. "Wait here. I'll be right back."

"Okay, but take this so that you can get back in." Holding out my key card, I felt the tips of his fingers brush against mine as he took it.

In the few minutes he was gone, I continued searching for something to watch. At this time of night, there wasn't much on except for infomercials. But after a few more clicks of the remote, I stopped on *The Golden Girls*, chuckling at the antics of Dorothy, Rose, Blanche, and Sophia.

If Wren and I don't cause all kinds of trouble in a Floridian retirement community one day, I'll die of shock . . . and disappointment.

"Hey," I said, watching as Ryan approached. "That was pretty fast."

"I told you I'd be right back." He unfolded a fleece blanket and wrapped it around me.

"Thank you."

"You've been freezing all night. I should've gotten it hours ago."

"I was fine."

"No, you're stubborn."

I rolled my eyes. "Whatever," I scoffed.

"Never said I didn't like it."

Ryan and I sat on the couch, our shoulders touching as we watched *The Golden Girls*. With the combination of his shirt and blanket, I was entirely surrounded by his scent. I breathed it in as sleep beckoned and my eyes began to close.

chapter three

amber sunrises

"TERAYN." A VOICE SOFTLY uttered my name, the sound fading as my mind refused to wake.

"Nope," I murmured.

"It's almost nine," a masculine voice said, louder this time.

My eyelids popped open like some kind of crazed jack-in-the-box. Beautiful streaks of amber bathed the room around me in light. The tips of my fingers pressed against something hard. Where the hell did I fall asleep? Rubbing my hand along the firm surface, I sat up and came face-to-face with Ryan.

"Oh!" I jumped, my attention was quick to take note of our intimate hold on one another. The hard surface I'd been using as a pillow was Ryan's chest. Apparently, we'd fallen asleep on the leather couch in the common room. Pushing off the fleece blanket, I discovered I was lying on top of him. My legs entwined with his, giving off the appearance of a living Celtic knot.

God, his body felt nice pressed against mine.

Great. Not only did I have the itch to draw every single line of this guy's body, but I also wanted to touch each inch of it. Blaming the irrational thought on lack of sleep, I began the complicated process of unwinding myself from Ryan.

"You passed out just after four."

"Did you sleep at all?"

"Yeah. I woke up just a few minutes ago."

Combing my fingers through my hair, I moved toward the opposite end of the couch. "Sorry, I didn't mean to be on top of you."

I swore under my breath. Eloquence was not a trait I possessed this early in the morning, especially not before a few cups of coffee.

He grinned, his blue eyes sparkling as he studied me. "Trust me, I'm not complaining."

"Thanks for staying with me last night. You didn't have to do that."

"I wanted to. Besides, I wasn't about to leave you down here alone. You would have frozen to death."

"Nah," I countered, "I've got ice water in my veins."

"Is that so?"

"Yep."

"Must be why you were shivering so much then," he mused with a grin.

I sighed dramatically and rolled my eyes in a perfect circle. "Fine, I was being stubborn. Are you happy now?"

"Extremely."

"You said your first class was at noon?" I asked, unzipping his hoodie.

"Yeah. It only lasts forty-five minutes though. I've got two classes back-to-back and then I'm done for the day."

"That's nice." I handed off his jacket with a nod. "My

class this morning is also only forty-five minutes, and thank goodness, it's the only one I have today."

"And then you're going to see Wren?"

"Yeah."

Ryan stood from the couch and stretched. The bottom of his T-shirt lifted a bit, and I could just make out the V-shaped grooves in his hips. After taking Anatomy & Physiology, Wren probably knew the technical name for those babies, but I always referred to them as panty droppers. Something about those lines made the composure of level-headed girls go to shit, and I'd be lying if I said they hadn't almost gotten me in trouble on more than one occasion.

Jumping off the couch before Ryan could catch sight of my drool, I folded the blanket and shoved it in his direction.

"Well, I should probably go get ready for class, but thanks so much for all your help last night. I truly appreciate it."

"It's no problem. Like I said before, if you want to study some more this weekend, just let me know."

"I will."

"And tonight, we'll have our fun with your roommate," he stated in a suggestive tone.

"Oh, yeah." Somehow, I'd pushed the memory of our plan from last night out of my brain. "So, I'll see you tonight around six thirty?"

"Wouldn't miss it for the world." Ryan winked at me, making me feel every bit like a hormonal schoolgirl. He gathered up his hoodie and blanket before exiting the common room and stepping out into the sunshine.

I gathered up all my stuff in record time before sprinting upstairs. Thankfully, the room Brooklyn and I shared was empty. After throwing on some clothes, I twisted my hair into a complicated fishtail braid and then started on my makeup. Being an artist had its perks. My hands were steady from years of painting, and now, I could draw on winged eyeliner with the skill of a practiced surgeon. After a quick swipe of cherry lip balm, I switched out my statistics textbook for my drawing pad, charcoal pencils, erasers, and ridiculous assortment of felt-tipped pens. Seriously, the people at Hobby Lobby knew me by name due to the amount of art supplies I'd purchased from them in the past few years.

Sliding on my Uggs, I flung my bag over my shoulder and headed to the art annex. Along the way, I decided to shoot Wren a quick text.

Me: *Hey, I know you're probably still sleeping, but I'm gonna grab some food after class is over and then swing by your new place. Also, I have things to tell you!*

With that, I tossed my phone into my bag and sprinted across campus to make it to Intro to Visual Arts without being tardy.

By the time I reached the lecture auditorium, the majority of the seats were still vacant. People always seemed to skip Friday lectures more than any other day. I guess that's because most everyone wanted to start their weekend early, but I actually enjoyed this class. All right, so I enjoyed every class that wasn't statistics, but that was just my art-obsessed brain at work. Seriously, I commended Ryan for being able to double major. The guy was smart, impressive, and ridiculously attractive—a lethal combination.

I pulled out a pen and notepad, forcing myself to focus on the lecture that was starting. My mind needed to be distracted from Ryan and the fact we would be pretending to have sex this evening. At the time, it had sounded like a great plan, but was getting physically close to Ryan a smart move for me?

Exhaling, I stilled the thoughts addling my brain. Ryan had confessed he wasn't a fan of romantic entanglements either. So there was absolutely nothing for me to worry about. This whole scheme was about enacting some revenge. That's all. Putting pen to paper, I lifted my gaze to the projector at the front of the auditorium and began scribbling notes.

However, I only managed to write a single sentence before I felt a tap on my shoulder. As I glanced behind me, I came face-to-face with Keith. The only reason I was even on a first name basis with this guy was because he was one of those dudes who couldn't take *no* for an answer.

He flashed me a bright smile. Despite being a jerk, the guy did have nice teeth. But that was the only thing he had going for him. He'd already asked me out at least five times this semester—much to my disappointment. It was almost as if he expected me to change my mind. Yeah, fat chance in hell, dude.

"Are you having a good week?" he asked.

It was fantastic until you decided to ruin it for me.

"Yeah." I stuck to a one-word reply, because it was the only thing I trusted myself to say without screaming at him to fuck off.

"I'm glad." He answered with another million-dollar smile, but little did he know, his charm had zero effect on me. "I feel like it's been forever since I've seen you."

My eyes rolled like a damn hamster wheel at his comment. Cue my gag reflex. Did this asshole honestly believe that was a good pick-up line? "Trust me, forever wouldn't be long enough," I muttered under my breath.

"What was that?"

"Nothing. Just ready to focus on the lecture."

"Well, while I've got your attention, I just wanted to ask—"

"For the love of all that is holy, the answer is *no!*"

"But you didn't even know what I was going to ask."

Call me evil, but I chuckled at his attempt to save face. "Yes, I do. And it doesn't matter how you phrase it or where you offer to take me, the answer will always be no."

"Damn."

"I'm not interested in dating—anyone." With a loud huff, I snapped my head forward and focused my attention back on the images that were being displayed at the front of the auditorium.

For the next forty-five minutes, I wrote furiously and without interruption. My consciousness slipped into the realm of art. Illustrious shapes of dazzling colors and mediums passed before my eyes. This was the world I loved, the one I lived for.

I'd always enjoyed drawing and painting, but after Mom passed, I tried to paint my pain away. It's almost comical how the word *paint* is *pain* with the letter *t* tacked on to the end. Perhaps that's part of the reason why I was able to delve so fully into expressing my creativity. The world and everything in it fell away whenever I put pen to paper. Creating was my solace, the one way I felt reprieve from losing the person I loved most. Dad and I managed, but he was never really the same without her.

Truth be told, neither was I.

That's not to say we let despair rule our existence. There was laughter; there were good days and bad. But things were invariably different. My dad had lost the love of his life, and that kind of loss takes its toll. It's the reason I distanced myself from the idea of love—it's the only guaranteed way not to get hurt.

Even though I loved creating art, my passion for it had diminished as of late. And I wasn't the only one who'd noticed. Several of my professors had commented on the lack of desire in my latest assignments. I'd always prided myself on thinking outside the box. I wasn't afraid to take risks with my paintings. The bigger the risk, the bigger the reward, but that mentality had no doubt faded. I was uninspired. And for an artist, there was no worse plight.

It seemed as if only a minute had passed when the lecture ended and everyone stood to leave. Knowing Wren would be a bit more agreeable to being woken up if I brought food, I headed over to a nearby bakery and grabbed a bag of bagels and some juice before making my way over to her new apartment.

Her new place was only a five-minute drive from campus. It was a miniscule studio apartment, but it felt like the Four Seasons compared to my dorm room. Much to my elation, Wren answered the door on the second knock.

"What?" she asked in an irritated tone.

"I'm sorry I woke you up, but I brought bagels."

Her eyes lit up at the mention of food. Snagging the bag out of my hand, she ushered me inside. "Good. I'm starving and I haven't had a chance to make a grocery run yet."

Plopping on the mattress in the center of the room, she stared up at me. "I set out a spare key for you on the counter. Feel free to come sleep here any night you want. I usually come home late in the morning."

"Thank you so much. I slept in the common room again last night."

"Yikes."

I watched as Wren grabbed two cinnamon bagels and slathered each with an unhealthy amount of cream cheese. Holding one out for me, I accepted it with a smile. "Thanks."

"I hope you know I'm going to eat this and then go back to sleep."

I laughed. "I figured as much. I didn't get a lot of sleep last night, so I'm going to lie down with you."

I watched as she washed down a large bite with a swig of orange juice. "Oh, your text said you had things to tell me. What is it?"

"Umm," I mumbled, tucking a strand of hair behind my ear, "well, I was forced to evacuate the dorm room because Brooklyn and Joe were playing doctor."

She pretended to gag at my reply. "Fuck, I'd leave too."

"So, naturally, I headed to the common room."

"Naturally."

I took another bite of my bagel and sucked down half the bottle of orange juice. For some reason, I was almost nervous to tell her that I had hung out with Ryan last night. Which was ridiculous, but here I was, fumbling over what words to force out of my mouth. "And because I had nothing else to do, I decided to study some statistics, but I got absolutely nowhere. I mean, honestly, what is the damn point of that class? Like what kind of life skills are we learning from that course?"

"Who knows? Personally, I think it's all a money racket. Like, what book costs two hundred dollars? It's a damn scam."

"True that, babe," I replied. "So, Ryan gave me his notes from class and left his number on them. He said to let him know if I needed help studying, and since I was failing by myself, I decided to text him."

In an instant, Wren was all smiles. "You like him."

"I do not! I like his brain."

She rolled her eyes. "Yeah, okay."

"Didn't think someone so tired could muster up that much sass."

"It's a talent," she countered smugly.

"Getting back to the story, he hung out with me in the

common room and we studied all the notes from yesterday's lecture. Surprisingly enough, Ryan is a great teacher and I actually understand some of the things Professor Leigh has been talking about."

"That's awesome."

"I know! I have to pass that class to keep my scholarship."

"And school sure ain't cheap."

"Nope."

"So . . . y'all studied?"

When you've been friends with someone long enough, you learn to read their tone of voice or interpret their implications. My bestie was low-key asking if anything physical happened between Ryan and me. And truth be told, I loved her for it. She would always be there to give me a high five after I make out with a hot guy at a party or bail me out of a horrific blind date. The girl was an absolute gem.

"We studied for a few hours, and then we watched a movie together."

"Did you ask him to stay?" she questioned.

"Maybe."

"You so did. You find him intriguing because he made you blush."

I groaned at her insinuation. "Ugh, I shouldn't have said anything at all."

"You texted me because you were excited about hanging out with him and wanted to tell me about it!"

I stared at her shrewdly. "What is it going to take for you to forget this?"

"So, so much."

"Whatever."

"In the years we've been friends, I've only seen you interested in a handful of guys, and even then, it was because you thought they were hot or had a nice body. You've never showed the slightest amount of interest in someone, even Blake, and y'all dated for a year."

"I tried to like him."

"I know, babe," she replied with a sigh. "You just can't let yourself get that involved."

"What are you talking about? You and I are totally involved," I countered in an attempt to lighten the conversation.

"Yeah, but we don't sleep together."

I feigned shock as I motioned toward the bed we were both occupying. "The evidence disputes your claim."

"You know what I mean!"

"Do I?"

My question earned me another sassy eye roll. "If you ever find a man who can handle all that attitude housed in your body, you need to hold on to him with a death grip."

"Geez, now you sound like your mother."

"Don't even get me started on that woman."

"What? Your mom is the best!"

"She's all about using college as a means to find a husband and all that Southern nonsense."

"I suppose the majority of people do meet their spouses in college," I stated.

"And when have we ever followed the majority?"

"In high school when we plucked our brows within a centimeter of their existence."

Wren cringed at my reply. "Never again."

"You got that right." I glanced around at the blank walls of her apartment. "Are you planning to decorate this place?"

"I'd like to, but I really don't have the time right now. Work is eating into all of my free time."

"Yeah, you work all the damn time now."

"I gotta eat."

"True. I can decorate it for you if you want."

"That would be amazing! Have at it."

"Yay! I'll get started this weekend!"

"Well," she replied with a yawn, "I'd love to stay up and chat, but I'm beat. I'm going back to bed."

"Same here." Pulling off my shoes, I slid underneath the covers next to her. "Night, babe."

"Night."

chapter four

red lace

I AWOKE IN WREN'S bed a few hours later. The thick curtains were pulled over the windows, bathing the entire space in darkness. It was almost five, and I still needed to get ready to see Ryan. Because Wren was fast asleep, I skipped the goodbyes and snatched up the key she'd left for me on the counter.

Overall, her apartment was small. The kitchen was barely large enough for one person, but it was so much better than her living with Liam. Even before she had caught him cheating, she hadn't been happy for a long time. That knowledge weighed heavily on me. All I wanted was to see her happy again and that meant being there for her in any way I could. Wren had always been there for me, especially after I lost Mom. Her strength and love instilled some life back into my heart—life that cancer had all but taken away. Now, it was my turn to take care of Wren. And there was something I could do to cheer her up. I could decorate her apartment and make it look beautiful for her. Wren deserved all the happiness in the world, and it was my job to remind her of that.

It didn't take long to get back to campus. As I trudged up the steps to my dorm, I couldn't help but question the plan Ryan and I had devised. It was ingenious, there was no doubt about it, but would pretending to sleep with him only make me want to do the deed more?

I didn't have much time to ponder my predicament, because my phone was buzzing in my pocket. Seeing the call was from my dad, I answered quickly.

"Hey, Daddy."

"Hey, angel. How was your week?"

"It was good. What about yours?"

"No complaints here. You know the office stays busy, but I'm so used to it I don't notice."

"That's good."

"How's Wren doing?"

"About as well as can be expected, all things considered. You know how she is though."

"Yeah. If there is anything I can do, you'll give me a call?"

"You know I will."

"Your favorite holiday is coming up. I sent you a few things in the mail, so be sure to look out for them."

"I will, thanks."

"So, any news about the big art show? I know you said the other week they would announce the featured artists sometime soon," he said.

"It should be the week after Thanksgiving, I think. Tickets should go on sale sometime next month."

"Let me know when so that I can come see your work."

"I don't even know if any of my paintings or projects will be featured yet."

"I do," he answered with complete confidence.

That was my dad. He always had faith in me and my

abilities as an artist. According to him, there wasn't a shadow of a doubt that I could make a living off my artwork.

I only hoped that one day I could be as confident as he was.

"Thanks, Daddy."

"You can do anything you set your mind to, remember that."

"I will."

"Will Wren be at the show too?"

"Yeah," I replied. "She is planning on being there, so I'll be sure to get both of you tickets."

"I'm really looking forward to it."

There was a lightness to his voice I hadn't heard in a while. Dad always put on a good show. He had a great job and friends, but most people didn't realize how much sadness still lingered inside him. Losing the love of his life had left a deep wound on his soul, and while it had healed, the scar would always remain.

And I knew exactly how he felt, because my scar was in the same place, right across my heart.

"And I'll also be home for Thanksgiving. Wren and I are going to drive back together."

"Okay, I'll let Shelly know we'll be there again for the holiday."

"One of these years, I'm going to talk Wren's mom into cooking chicken pot pie instead of the traditional roasted turkey." Wren's parents always invited dad and I over to spend the holidays with them. Their invitation came the first year after mom passed, but now it was like a tradition for all of us. We were a patchwork family of sorts.

My dad chuckled at my declaration. "Shelly's cooking is only second to your mother's. No one can make a peach cobbler like she could."

"Agreed."

"Well, angel, I won't keep you any longer. I just wanted to check in and see how you were doing."

"Thanks, Dad. I'll talk to you later."

"I love you."

"I love you too."

I slid my phone back into my purse and made my way down the hall. One of the girls who lived in the room next to mine smiled at me as I passed. I may not have known her personally, but sharing a bathroom with an utter stranger, well three strangers to be exact, bonded us in a way most people wouldn't understand. You're never more vulnerable than when you're in the shower—it's the sole reason horror movies love to trap their victims there.

And needless to say, we've all walked in on one another while in the buff several times this semester.

Hurrying to my room, I discarded my stuff on my bed and grabbed my robe, a towel, and my razor. I still had a meeting . . . an appointment . . . a whatever the hell it was . . . to get ready for, and I didn't intend to smell like a barn full of cows.

I was in and out of the shower within minutes, and I made sure to shave every part of my body that needed it. Not that I was expecting anything to happen between Ryan and me, but pretending we were going to have sex meant we would have to be in some sort of state of undress in order to convince our audience. And I had no intentions of being anything less than prepared. Glee filled my stomach as I thought of the look on Brooklyn's face when she caught Ryan and me together.

Once I was back in my room, I dried my hair and touched up my makeup. My next challenge was deciding what kind of undies to wear. My undergarments would set the tone for this whole charade, and truthfully, I wanted to look good. No, not *good*. That adjective wouldn't suffice. *Hot* is the descriptor I was after. Because, after all, I needed to match Ryan.

Red.

That was the color I needed to wear. It was the color of lips, of lust, and Wren always said I looked amazing in it. Rushing to my dresser, I rifled through my panty drawer in search of the lace set I'd bought at Victoria's Secret last year. The tips of my fingers caressed the delicate lace with affection. It had been an impulse purchase. I had bought this set with the intention of wearing it for someone, but as luck would have it, I hadn't met any guy worth my time. Even if tonight was just an act, I could still show off my lingerie. It had been benched for way too long, and now was the perfect time for it to see some action.

I changed into those panties and bra like a superhero sliding on their cape. A rush of confidence ignited in my bones. I wasn't the type to bathe in self-doubt, but that didn't mean I had no insecurities. That was simply a part of being a woman, of being human.

My phone lit up just as I finished covering up the MVP in the scheme Ryan and I were about to put on. Brooklyn's text covered my screen, letting me know that she was on her way back to the dorm. Typically, that was code for vacate the premises or witness the magic of Joe and me humping. Since I had no intentions of doing either, I didn't even bother to reply.

Ryan would be here any minute, and now that I was ready, nervous energy simmered in the pit of my stomach. It bubbled like the contents of a witch's cauldron.

Every inch of my skin became warmer by the second. This wasn't going to work. There was no way I could fake arousal if I was drenched in sweat.

Fake? Yeah, keep dreaming, bitch, the snarky part of my

brain cackled. With those periwinkle eyes watching me, there wouldn't be a damn thing to fake. There was only one solution I could think of to help ease the tension coiling in my gut.

And that was vodka.

I tossed back my fourth shot as I heard a knock at the door. Discarding the bottle of vodka and glass in the drawer beneath my bed, I sprinted to the door.

Ryan stood in the hall, dressed in a pair of black jeans and a tight V-neck. He looked freaking edible. "Hey."

"Hi!" Grabbing his hand, I jerked him inside. "I thought you were going to call me when you were outside."

"I was, but another girl let me in. I told her I was here to see you, so she opened the door for me."

"Oh, okay. And you had no trouble finding my room?"

The sound of Ryan's laughter filled my ears. "Nope, no trouble. The rooms are numbered, after all."

"Smart ass," I mumbled. My comment was met with more laughter. "Well, Brooklyn just texted me and said she'd be back in a few minutes, so we don't have much time."

"Alright. Do you want me to sit down?"

"Can you do something for me first?" I asked innocently.

"Sure."

"Can you lift up your shirt for a second?"

"Why? Is something wrong with this shirt?" He lifted the bottom half of his T-shirt, showcasing the most cut set of abs I'd ever laid eyes on. "Should I have chosen a different one?"

One, two, three, four, five . . . six. Yep, all six of those babies were there, just as I suspected. "No, that shirt is perfect," I replied with a giggle. Vodka coursed through my bloodstream, fueling my laughter.

"Are you feeling okay?"

"I feel great."

"Something seems off."

"Nothing is off . . . yet."

Ryan motioned me forward with a simple curl of his finger. "Come here."

"Why?"

Bending toward me, he moved until his mouth was almost on top of mine. Sucking in a deep breath of air, he stared at me in shock. "Are you drunk?"

"No!"

"Terayn."

"I had a few shots. I am buzzed, not drunk. There's a difference."

"And why did you think you needed to get buzzed?"

"I was nervous! Plus, I get really loud when I've been drinking, so I thought it would add some dramatic flair to our performance."

"You're nervous?"

"What? I'm only human."

"I'm nervous too."

"Really?"

"Yeah," he answered with a laugh. "Would you mind if I had a drink too?"

"Not at all!" I retrieved the vodka and shoved the bottle in his hands. "Drink up."

"Thanks." Ryan turned the bottle upward and chugged. After a few seconds, he stopped and handed back the vodka. "Now, at least we'll be on an even playing field."

"Good!"

"Just so you know, I'm not going to try to take advantage of the situation or anything. If you want to stop or if something makes you uncomfortable, let me know."

"You're a gentleman," I said with a smile.

"I try to be."

I sat on my bed, patting the spot next to me that was covered with my pink comforter. "Sit down."

"Okay, what now?"

"How am I supposed to know? This is your plan!"

"Kissing?"

"You want to kiss?"

"It's either that or strip down to our underwear."

I gulped and stared at him. Both options sounded like heaven to me. My tongue moistened my lips as I couldn't help but stare at his mouth. Something in my gut informed me I was going to enjoy kissing Ryan a little too much. Since Mom passed, I've kept my heart closely guarded when it came to love. I'd never fallen for someone, never wanted to, but Ryan seemed different. He wasn't like all the other guys I'd encountered, and the thought was terrifying.

"Underwear it is," I stated.

"You're sure?"

"Kissing seems really intimate, don't you think?"

"Depends on what part of the body is being kissed." He snickered and pulled his T-shirt over his head.

"Huh?" I was in *so* much trouble. Because the first body part that came to mind was the damn *p*-word. I gawked at Ryan as he stripped down to a pair of black boxers. He was lean and muscular in all the right places, and the quick glance I'd gotten of his abs was just the tip of the damn iceberg. The man could give Michelangelo's *David* a run for its money.

"Not going to leave me out in the cold, are you?"

His question was a frank reminder that I still had to talk to him and form coherent thoughts. Drooling over him like a brainless zombie wasn't doing me any favors. "Wouldn't dream of it." I wasn't one to be shy, but my fingers trembled as I removed my tank top. I eased out of my jean shorts until the only articles of clothing I still wore were my matching bra and panties.

"That's a great color on you."

Glancing down at the red fabric, I fought the sudden urge to cover myself up. "Thank you." The sound of a key jiggling in a lock distracted me from Ryan's ridiculous body. "That's her!" I whisper-yelled. "Quick!"

All rational thinking flew out the window as I jumped on top of Ryan. Much to my excitement, his strong arms caught me with little effort. And every ounce of anxiety I felt melted away the moment our skin met.

"Hi," he whispered, grinning like a damn fool.

"Hi."

"Do you trust me?"

"Yeah."

"Alright, just follow my lead."

We crashed on my bed, our bodies intertwining like ivy. Before I could even register what was happening, Ryan's mouth dropped to my abdomen. His tongue met my navel briefly before trailing all the way up between my breasts.

"Oh my God," I moaned, my back arching off the mattress. This may have been all for show, but there was nothing false about the way I responded to his touch. "Please don't stop," I called out loudly.

Why on God's green earth did I think it was a good idea to take multiple shots of vodka before taking off my clothes with this man?

That same snarky part of my brain was all too eager to reply. '*Cause you're an idiot.*

Reaching over me, Ryan pulled a small packet out of the pocket of his jeans. He ripped it open with his teeth just as the door flung open. Brooklyn stood in the doorway, her eyes instantly locking on Ryan and me. The entire scene—two lovers in a state of undress spread across a bed as a shocked bystander approached—was like something straight out of my art history textbook.

I'd never brought a single guy to our room all semester, so her shocked response at seeing a half-naked man straddling me was glorious.

"Oh . . . I, I didn't realize—"

I didn't even attempt to mask my glee at the wonderful shade of crimson covering Brooklyn's skin.

"Do you mind giving us some privacy? We're in the middle of something here," Ryan announced with the most devious smirk I'd ever seen. "Unless, you'd rather stay and watch, that is."

"No!" she squeaked. "I'll just leave and come back later."

"What do you think, babe?" Ryan asked, bending to kiss my neck. "Three or four hours enough time?"

Rubbing my hands down the length of his chest, I bit my lip as I stared up at him. "Whatever you want."

"I fucking love it when you say that." In the blink of an eye, Ryan flipped me over and spanked my ass. I yipped at the gesture, quickly breaking into a grin. The line between fact and fiction, reality and fantasy, was almost non-existent. And I loved every fucking second of it.

The realness of our charade worked in our favor.

"Oh, God! I'm so sorry!" Brooklyn cried, fumbling with her keys. I'd never seen her look so flustered, and I reveled in the sweet taste of revenge.

"Lock the door on your way out," Ryan ordered with complete authority.

Well, *hell*. I always liked it when a guy knew exactly what he wanted and how to get it too.

He slid off the bed and reached for his jeans. The

moment his hands left my flesh, I sighed. That felt too real, too incredible to be pretend.

But it was pretend, and my body needed to get in line with my brain.

"I think it's safe to say she bought it," Ryan stated, spinning to face me.

"Yep. Well played, sir."

"Believe me, it was my pleasure, dear lady."

I shimmied into my jean shorts, taking note of the way Ryan watched. "The spanking was a nice touch."

"I didn't hurt you, did I?"

"Not at all," I answered.

"Good. I'm going to remember that."

"For what?"

He shrugged, the fire in his eyes unmistakable. "For the future . . . you know, just in case."

My fist collided with the side of his arm. "You would."

"Can you blame me?"

"Well, when you phrase it like that, I guess not."

Picking up the unused condom, Ryan pulled a few more foil packets from his back pocket. "Got any lotion?"

"For what?" I questioned, staring at the unrolled condoms suspiciously.

"To plant evidence."

"Huh?"

I handed off my vanilla-scented lotion and watched as he squirted a little in each condom. Then he added a few drops of water, mixing the solution together. "Looks pretty convincing, doesn't it?"

"Holy crap. You're like an evil genius."

Grinning from ear to ear, he planted our "evidence" in various locations on the floor.

"There. Not only did she get kicked out of her room

and get a taste of her own medicine, but she'll have to do something with those too."

"Hell yes!" I gave him a high five and finished tucking in my tank top. "Wren and I are keeping you."

"Sounds good to me."

"So, what should we do for the next three to four hours?" I asked, nudging him with my elbow.

"Liked that, did you?"

"Don't get full of yourself."

Leaning in until we were practically plastered to one another, he whispered, "Come on, you know I was good."

Breathing in his cologne, I willed myself to speak. "Never said you weren't."

Ryan broke away and collapsed on my bed, his arms stretching behind his head. "So, you wanna watch a few movies and then grab some food?"

"Sounds like a plan to me." I handed off the remote and positioned myself next to him. "You pick the flick this time."

"Alright." Ryan accepted the remote, his eyes glued to the television sitting on a dresser near my bed. "Can I see some of your artwork?"

"What?"

"You're an artist, and really good too, from what I saw of the sketch you were working on the other day. I just want to see some of your drawings or paintings."

"Oh . . ." My attention shifted to the sketchpads littering my side of the room. "I have a few projects I've worked on this semester, but nothing really stellar. I've sort of lacked the inspiration to create lately."

"I can inspire you if you want."

It was an innocent suggestion, but my skin flushed to match my panties anyway. "Huh?"

"Your drawing from class yesterday. I mean, those were my eyes, right?"

Damn. Wren hadn't stopped me soon enough, it seemed. "They're a very nice, complex shade of blue. What was I supposed to do?"

"I wasn't exactly complaining, Ter."

"Oh, so I'm Ter now?"

"Just a few minutes ago, I spanked your ass like you were a naughty schoolgirl. I think pet names are only appropriate."

"Whatever you say, Ry." Sighing heavily, I wondered what the heck I was supposed to do if Ryan kept calling me out on my shit. He knew I'd been drawing his eyes, and if I wasn't careful, he'd find out that my hand had been set on rendering his entire face. "Here," I said, snagging a sketch pad and placing it in his hands. "If you really want to see some of my art, I guess you can look at that."

Ryan sat up, his fingers turning to the first page. "Wow." He traced a couple lines of my sketch. "This is amazing."

I chuckled slightly. "It's just a flower."

His gaze locked on to mine. "It's beautiful."

"You can have it if you want."

"Really?"

I motioned around the room. "It's not like I don't have plenty of drawings. Besides, you can consider it payment for helping me get some revenge on Brooklyn."

"You don't owe me anything for that. I was happy to help."

"Even still," I replied, leaning over to tear the sketch out of the pad. As I removed the drawing, my shoulder brushed against his chest. Such a miniscule gesture shouldn't have been capable of eliciting such a heavy response. His breath poured over my flesh, amplifying our close proximity. Every hair on my body seemed to stand on end, and it felt like I was hurtling right for the danger zone at a speed that would've made Kenny Loggins proud. "I want you to have it."

"Thanks."

"So . . . what did you want to eat?" I asked, steering our conversation to safer grounds. What the hell was I thinking? I'd known this guy for a single day and I was acting as if he'd gotten under my skin. I didn't let anything with a penis dictate my happiness. It was the only way to live. Just look at everything Wren had been put through in the last month. Was I completely coldhearted? No. I believed in love, believed it was a gift to some and toxic to others. And I had no hesitations about which group I fit in to. Love and loss were mere breaths apart from one another. Caring for someone on that level was simply toxic to my well-being.

And it always would be.

"Ter?" Ryan's voice sounded from far away. "Does that sound okay to you?"

"Huh?"

"I asked if you were okay with ordering a pizza."

"Oh! That sounds fine."

"Is everything okay?" he questioned, leaning toward me.

"Everything is perfect."

My heart hammered inside my chest like a freaking woodpecker as he continued to study me. "Your face got a really serious look for a second."

"I was just trying to decide what kind of pizza toppings I wanted."

He wasn't buying my reply for a second. "If you ever want to talk about it, I'm here."

"And if I don't?"

"I'll still be here . . . trying to figure out what the hell you want on your pizza."

Unable to help myself, I rolled my eyes. "Pepperoni and banana peppers."

Ryan grinned and whipped out his phone. "I can make that happen."

chapter five

golden locks

"RUN, RUN, RUN!" I shouted at the television.

"It's too late." Ryan snagged a slice of pizza from the box I held on my lap. "She's done for."

"Why is it that the women in these movies always go back to the house? I mean, logistically speaking, that is the last place you should go."

"I suppose because without a helpless victim or two, the plot would really drag."

I considered his comment for a moment before replying. "I never thought of that before."

Ryan shoved the pizza in his mouth, practically consuming the entire slice in a single bite. "Think about Halloween for a second. If you take away all the killing, all you have is a whack job Peeping Tom lurking about in a discount mask."

"Geez, that would be more boring than sitting through statistics class."

"Statistics class is fun."

"Yeah, for you and your math-oriented brain."

"Okay, so what kinds of classes are fun to you?"

"I enjoyed my drawing class. They brought in live

models and let us study the human form so we could properly sketch it."

"That sounds awesome. How do I volunteer to be one of these models?"

"Huh?" I asked, panic shooting through my throat. I coughed and reached for the cup of soda sitting nearby.

"Come on. It will be fun. You can have your sketch pad and pencils, and I'll sprawl out on a couch with the heart of the ocean hanging around my neck."

As a southern woman, I was well versed on the topic of manners. But my grandmother would have shuddered in shame if she had witnessed the act of me spraying my drink all over Ryan.

"Oh my God! I'm so sorry." Setting down my cup and the pizza, I rushed to find a towel. "Fuck. I can't believe I just spit all over you."

"It's fine, Ter."

I dabbed Ryan's face and chest with a towel, but his shirt was soaked. Jesus, I just had to spaz out and spew my drink all over him. Apparently, Ryan and my nerves mixed about as well as baking soda and vinegar.

Been there, done that. And let's just say Mrs. Harper never let me do another science experiment in her class ever again. My so-called volcano erupted worse than Mt. Vesuvius. All right, so maybe I put a little extra stuff in there that the internet recipe didn't call for, but I blame Sean for giving me some of his firecrackers. And Wren for encouraging me to use them.

"Let me grab my hair dryer really quick."

"It's just a shirt." Ryan stood and pulled the garment in question over his head. "I'll just hang it up for a bit and let it air-dry."

Don't look at his body. Don't look at his body. I repeated the mantra in my head over and over again, but the second my eyelids parted, my attention fell to his abs. Personally, I blamed all the pheromones we woke up during our little charade. My body wasn't quite on the uptake like my brain.

"Do you want to wear something of mine?" I inquired. "I have a few old sweatshirts that might fit you."

"I don't know if you've realized this about me or not, but I am a guy. It's normal for us to go without shirts."

"Well . . ."

"Also, I tend to run warm, so it's not like I'm going to get cold or anything."

"Such a smartass." I huffed louder than I intended.

"Why?" he questioned with a grin. "Am I making you uncomfortable?"

"I'm perfectly comfortable."

"Right."

"Shut up."

"Level with me for a second, Ter." The feel of Ryan's fingers against my arm almost made me jump out of my skin. "Do I make you nervous?"

"That's ridiculous. Why would you make me nervous?"

"I mean, I understand why you were nervous before because of all that stuff with Brooklyn, but now, you seem just as nervous."

"I hate to burst your bubble, but I'm not nervous," I countered, feigning confidence and flipping my hair for good measure. I sent a silent prayer to the big man upstairs in the hope that Ryan would buy the front I was putting on.

"Come here." When that damn finger of his curled forward, I all but snapped to attention.

"Absolutely not."

My defiance only reaffirmed his determination. "I've got a theory I want to test."

"Well, too bad."

Ryan grinned at me in a way that informed me I was in serious trouble. The dorm was nothing more than a twenty-by-twenty-foot concrete block, so there wasn't exactly a means of escape. "You're going to make me work for this, aren't you?"

"That's where you're wrong, Ry. I'm not making you do anything." My words may have been as sweet as sugar, but my tone indicated pure venom.

My first instinct had me sprinting to my left and seeking shelter on top of Brooklyn's bed. I would brave the inevitable DNA samples coating her mattress in order to escape the half-naked, *p*-word slinging hottie in front of me.

But Ryan could see right through my ploy. He followed suit, and before I knew it, both of those chiseled arms were wrapped around my waist.

"Ter, Ter, Ter," he said with a heavy sigh. "You just had to make me work for this."

"You can let go of me now." I squirmed like a greased pig as I tried to free myself.

"You grinding against me like that isn't helping your situation."

My gasp was filled with as much shock as a pastor hearing someone drop an *f*-bomb in the middle of Sunday morning service. I didn't know what I was expecting though. I'd set him up for the perfect response, and Ryan delivered.

"You are crude and nasty!"

"I thought we already established that yesterday," he whispered in my ear.

"Ugh, do you always have to be so superior all the time? Really, Ry, it's not becoming at all." If I had expected his arms to loosen, I was sorely disappointed.

Instead, Ryan's arms squeezed tighter and pushed my boobs toward my chin. "Umm . . ." I began before losing my courage.

"What's wrong?"

"If you squeeze me any tighter, I'm going to be able to use my tits as a pillow."

Over my shoulder, I could sense Ryan's gaze dropping. His attention slid over my skin like velvet. Warmth from his body seeped through my thin tank top, and just as I was beginning to get used to the embrace, he apologized and backed away. Like me, Ryan seemed to be impossible to embarrass. But much to my surprise, the apples of his cheeks flushed with a color equal to that of my panties.

"So, you can be embarrassed. I was beginning to think such a thing wasn't possible for someone like you."

Ryan scoffed at my teasing comment. "Maybe there is more to me than what meets the eye."

"I figured that out the moment you told me you had a double major."

His lips tipped up on the left in a lopsided grin. "Impressed you, did I?"

"You're exasperating, has anyone ever told you that before?" I asked as I collapsed on my bed once more.

"You'd be the first."

"Somehow, I find that rather impossible."

"Alright, you caught me. My mom tells me that at least three times a day."

I snorted and chewed on another slice of pizza. "Can't really say I'm surprised by this revelation. Where do your parents live?"

"My mom lives in Chattanooga. We used to live in Florida, but she had to relocate for work."

"That explains it."

"Explains what?" he questioned.

"You're surfer boy thing."

"Excuse me?"

I rolled my eyes and watched as he sat beside me. "Your look. If I didn't know any better, I'd think you stepped out of an Abercrombie & Fitch catalog."

He chuckled quietly. "Ah, that's what you mean by surfer boy thing."

"Yep. And what about your dad? Where does he live?"

"Somewhere else," he spat.

There was no mistaking that tone of voice. Whatever emotions Ryan held for his father weren't warm or fuzzy. "There's a story there."

"Yeah. One I'd rather not get into."

"I feel you on that. I only have a dad."

Ryan's head tilted to meet my gaze. A sense of under-standing played across his features, as if we were kindred spirits. "There's a story there." His voice was soft, all traces of contempt flushed away.

"One I'd rather not get into as well," I answered, repeating his earlier reply.

When he nodded, golden locks of hair tumbled into his line of sight, and before I even knew what was happening, his arm curled around my body as he pulled me in for a hug. This time, I wasn't nervous at the thought of being close to him. Instead, the only thing filling my body was comfort. And the feeling was better than I had ever imagined.

My parents had shared this kind of comfort with one another. They drew reassurance in one another's presence, and I couldn't help but wonder how much my father missed it. Like most fathers, he sought to protect me from the pain life can cause, but losing a loved one was impos-sible to prevent. The fact he never moved on after Mom passed only reaffirmed the belief that allowing yourself to be vulnerable would only result in heartache. Even if you were loved unconditionally, the day would come when that connection would cease to exist.

"I'm not good at the serious stuff," I confessed, my voice not much louder than an exhaled breath. It wasn't typical for me to be so forthcoming, especially not where my mom was concerned, but talking to a stranger could almost be liberating. Ryan didn't really know me. He wasn't privy to all of the intricate layers that my mind and soul were comprised of, and because of this, it was easy to utter the truth. If he wasn't familiar with all my faults and virtues, then Ryan couldn't judge me.

"Neither am I."

Three words were all it took for me to realize I was in the presence of someone more than just a kindred spirit.

And deep down, I didn't know whether to be horrified or relieved.

chapter six

black lines and smudges

UNFORTUNATELY, WREN WAS WORKING another long stretch this weekend. But even if she couldn't take a break from work, I could take a few things off her to-do list. Decorating her new place was my way of helping her start this new chapter of her life. She needed a fresh start, and I would ensure she had it.

Liam and his bullshit be damned.

"What about this?" Ryan asked. The decorative pillow he held up seemed out of place in his hands, but much to my surprise, the guy had great taste. I hadn't expected his offer to help decorate Wren's apartment, but who was I to turn him down?

"I like that one! It's very pretty . . . and girly."

Ryan tossed the pillow into the buggy with a triumphant grin. "I'm very in touch with my feminine side."

"I've noticed," I teased. "I mean, what guy would willingly venture to Bed Bath & Beyond in their spare time?"

"Well, in all honesty, I came for the company."

I turned my head and feigned interest in a small vase on the shelf next to me. Per usual whenever I was around Ryan, my cheeks filled with heat. I really needed to get my dang emotions in check. Maybe I could blame the excess hormones in my birth control?

"So, did our scheme last night work in your favor?" he asked in response to my silence.

I picked up the vase I was trying to distract myself with and added it to the numerous items littering the buggy. "I'd say it was beyond successful. I haven't seen Brooklyn since she bolted from the room. Last night was the best sleep I've ever had at the dorm."

Ryan held up his hand for a high five. "Nice."

Slapping my palm against his, I grinned. "We are masters of deception."

"This is true, and if we ever need to repeat our scheme, just let me know."

"I will," I replied. "So, what about you? Do you have any awful roommates you need to play a prank on?"

"No roommates from hell on my end. I'm lucky enough to have an apartment all to myself."

"Geez, you are lucky!"

"Some of us are just born awesome."

My eyes rolled in a dramatic fashion. Honestly, those damn things had a mind of their own sometimes. "If you're awesome, then what am I?"

"Incredible," he answered without skipping a beat.

"Ha."

"You don't believe me?"

"Not even for a second."

"Why?"

I stopped the buggy in the middle of a crowded aisle. "Because you don't even know me." I was pretty sure that my tone was wavering on the side of being bitchy, but

Ryan's comment had caught me off guard. I mean, what did he know about me?

"You're spending your weekend buying things to decorate your best friend's apartment in the hopes of cheering her up. Such a selfless act is pretty incredible, if you ask me."

"It's not that selfless."

"Maybe you don't see it that way, but I do."

"Whatever."

"Are you always this stubborn?"

"I know no other way."

"I figured as much." Ryan playfully knocked his shoulder into mine. "So, what else do

we need to get for Wren's apartment?"

"Some candles, a throw blanket, and I wanted to pick up a few groceries as well. She hasn't had much time to go grocery shopping because of work and school, and I don't want her to be without food at the apartment."

"Sounds like a plan. You want to grab a bite to eat before we head over to her place?"

"Yeah. That's a good idea. It'll be best if we go over to her place after she's left for work so that we won't be in her way," I replied. "Also, you know how to do guy things, right?" I didn't have the slightest idea how to work a power drill. There were pictures I wanted to hang up for Wren, and undertaking that task by myself was sure to result in disaster. Part of being a responsible adult was knowing your limitations; at least, that's what Dad always said.

But as soon as I asked my question, Ryan's eyebrow quirked. If I had drawn the mischievous expression on his face, I'd be selling prints of my work to women all over the country. "There are lots of *guy things* I can help you with."

"I didn't mean it like that!" The sound of my voice

earned us more than a few curious glances from people nearby.

"Then I'm going to need you to explain what you meant."

"I meant using a power drill and hammer to hang things! Jesus!" My palms cupped my cheeks as I tried and failed to hide my embarrassment. "I wasn't talking about *your* power drill."

"Got me all excited for no reason," he teased.

"I'm going to say this again, but you're extremely exasperating."

"If you keep saying things like that, I'm going to develop a complex."

I picked up a fleece blanket and some lavender-scented candles before placing them in the buggy. "Ugh," I groaned. "Let's finish up before I decide to uninvite you to my decorating party."

Ryan faced me and held his hand over his heart. "I promise to be on my best behavior."

"Does that promise actually mean anything?"

My question earned me a wink and a smirk. "I guess you'll just have to wait and see."

By the time Ryan and I finished eating and picking up supplies from the grocery store, it was almost nine. Granted, we did spend two hours at the restaurant engrossed in our conversation. Despite his devilish charm, Ryan was very easy to talk to. Even if we had avoided all emotional topics, there were still plenty to discuss. And much to my surprise, we had a fair bit in common, to the point that I could see Ryan being the perfect addition to the dynamic duo of Wren and me.

"Can you hand me that guy tool?"

I groaned as I set a hammer in Ryan's palm. "Never going to let me live that down, are you?"

He plucked a nail from his mouth and held it against the wall. "Not if I can help it."

"I was afraid of that."

"You could always bribe me to forget."

I waited until he was finished with the nail before answering. "Alright, name your price."

Those periwinkle irises surveyed every inch of my body before meeting my gaze. "Are you sure you want me to?"

"Well, not now."

Laughter poured from his mouth and filled the empty apartment. I never thought it was possible for a laugh to be sexy, but it seemed as if Ryan had been specifically created to blow all of my preconceived notions out of the water.

"What were you just thinking?" he asked.

"What?"

"I want to know what you were just thinking about."

"You're very demanding."

"You've no idea," he countered with a smirk.

"I hope you're also accustomed to disappointment, because I'm not telling you."

"Not even if I beg?"

"Absolutely not!"

"Ah, sweet victory."

I stopped arranging the slew of sequined pillows on Wren's bed and spun around to face him. "Excuse me?"

"I don't know if you've noticed this about me or not, but I thoroughly enjoy getting under your skin."

A fire ignited in the depths of my soul. Two could play at that game. Sure, Ryan may have affected me, but it was time for me to see if the feeling was mutual. "Yeah, I've come to realize that." In a fraction of a second, my brain concocted a ploy to turn the tables on his annoying ass. "Oh, you have a string from one of the pillows stuck in your hair."

Ryan ran a hand through his hair. "Did I get it?"

"No, it's still there," I replied with a slight laugh.

This time, he shook his head from side to side. "What about now?"

"Nope."

"Damn."

"Sit on the bed and I'll get it out for you." Ryan did as he was instructed, and the moment his ridiculously sculpted derriere hit the mattress, I moved to stand in front of him. Leaning forward until my cleavage was the only thing in his line of sight, I slowly raked my fingertips through his blond locks.

All right, so maybe what I was doing was more like massaging his scalp than trying to untangle a string. But Ryan didn't need to be privy to that bit of information.

"Umm . . ."

"Dang, this string is really knotted in your hair." Wanting to increase our proximity, I pushed closer, forcing Ryan's knees apart.

"Ter—"

"Hold on just a second. I've almost got it." When the tip of his nose pressed into my rack, I knew I'd hit pay dirt. It wasn't that I was trying to suffocate him with my boobs, but I wanted him to be completely aware of their existence.

In an instant, Ryan's hands fastened around my waist. He carried me across the room and set me down before putting ten feet between us. "Forget the fucking string."

"Did I do something wrong?" I questioned in the most innocent tone I could muster.

"Nope. I need to use the restroom. I'll be right back."

"Okay." The second I heard the door slam shut, I smiled in victory. It seemed Ryan wasn't too keen on getting a taste of his own medicine.

While he was indisposed, I finished straightening the pillows and started setting out all the candles. When he returned a few minutes later, it was my turn to smirk.

"Are you feeling okay?"

"I'm fine."

"Did you get everything taken care of?" I made sure to pointedly glance at Ryan's crotch as I posed my question.

The look Ryan gave me was teeming with shock. "Excuse me?"

Unable to control my amusement any longer, I burst into a fit of laughter. "Just so you know, Ry, I enjoy getting under your skin too."

"Okay, I'll give you that one. You got me."

"I didn't just get you . . . I got you good."

"Yeah, yeah," he added with a sigh. "So, you seem to be a big fan of lace."

"Huh?" My attention dropped, and sure enough, I caught sight of my bra poking out of my shirt.

Today's color was pink.

"I'm a big fan of it too."

"Believe me, I know." Snagging a pillow, I flung it in Ryan's direction.

"You're the one who practically shoved my head down your shirt! What was I supposed to do? Not look?"

"No, my goal was to get your attention."

"This feels a lot like entrapment."

Grinning from ear to ear, I took a couple steps in his direction. "If you're having such shameful thoughts, then maybe you need to get right with Jesus."

"Maybe you should help me." The words spilled from Ryan's lips as he lunged in my direction. One second, my feet were planted on the ground, and the next, I was draped over Ryan's shoulder like a fur stole.

"You're beyond help!" I shouted, my reply teeming with laughter.

"Forgive me, but you don't sound like you hate it up there." His hand squeezed my thigh, holding on to me as he spun in a circle.

"It's terrible." More laughter sprang from my lips.

"You have a very strange definition of terrible."

I slapped his ass as hard as I could, my lungs burning with the need for air. "Sanctuary," I called out with a laugh. "I claim sanctuary."

"I thought that only worked with the church."

"Have you no mercy?"

"For you?" he questioned with a smirk. "I have more than you know."

After what seemed like an eternity, I felt Ryan's hands shift to my waist as he set me back on the floor. My palms pressed against his chest as I searched for balance. When I lifted my gaze to meet his, I felt like I was floating with no stability in sight. His eyes brimmed with heat, an unspoken suggestion of the things that could happen next if we so chose.

Breath poured from my lips as I exhaled. A vision of our arms tangled around one another danced inside my mind. But passion was swiftly replaced with panic as I considered the gravity of our situation. Giving in to this moment would be the equivalent of walking through a field littered with land mines.

There was no way I would walk away unscathed.

"Terayn?" The way he said my name demanded my attention. His mouth was curled into the sexiest grin I had ever seen in my life. That smile was accompanied by his perfect eyes. And the desire to recreate it seeped all the way into the depths of my bones.

"I want to draw you!"

"Come again?"

"I have to draw your expression . . . right now."

"Okay," he replied slowly.

I dashed to my purse and withdrew the sketch pad and set of charcoal pencils I always kept with me. When I turned to face him once more, Ryan looked to me for instruction.

"Just sit on the couch over there." I pointed to the left and watched as he sank into the soft cushions. Wren's place was nothing more than a tiny studio apartment, but with all the decorations we had added tonight, it was starting to feel like a home.

"How is this?"

"Perfect," I replied, turning to a clean page.

His mercurial smile froze for me as my hand flew across the paper. Lines and smudges of charcoal melded together, forming Ryan's facial features.

Drawing Ryan forced me to take note of all the minute details of his face. The subtle changes in his eyes as he regarded me were captivating—some expressions playful, some serious, all Ryan.

An hour passed and then two. I must have sketched him at least half a dozen times, and to my surprise, my hands ached for more. The creative sabbatical I'd been lamenting over for the past few months had all but dissipated. For so long, I had lacked inspiration. It was impossible to create while living in a vacuum, after all. But at that moment, my creative well was overflowing with excitement.

And it had everything to do with the man sitting in front of me.

Completely lost in the creative magic of focusing on a current project, I had forgotten the existing world until Ryan's voice demanded my attention.

"Do you ever draw yourself?"

Smudging a line of charcoal with my pinky, I glanced at him. "Huh?"

"Do you ever draw pictures of yourself?"

"Like a self-portrait?"

"Yeah."

"No. Why would I do one of those?"

"Because you're beautiful," he answered, as if it were the simplest explanation in the world. "And that is something you should share with people."

The sincerity in his voice took me by surprise. He hadn't complimented me to earn points; he believed what he said, and somehow, it seemed as if he wanted me to believe it too.

Yep, there was no way I was ever going to be able to walk away from this guy unscathed.

chapter seven

promises set in silver

THE SOUND OF AN opening door startled me awake. Sitting up, I turned to see Wren entering her apartment.

"Hey," I said, running a hand through my hair. "Sorry, we passed out while watching a movie."

"That's okay."

Glancing at the clock on my phone, I saw that it was just after four in the morning. "You're home early."

"Another tech showed up at two, so after we got caught up, they sent me home since I was in overtime."

"Oh."

Ryan stirred at my feet, finally waking to join our conversation. "Hey, how was work?" he asked.

Even from across the room, I noticed Wren's bottom lip quiver. She wouldn't cry though. I knew it for a fact. The girl wasn't one for waterworks. Even when we had watched the latest book-turned-movie from Nicholas Sparks, there had been no tears in sight. I could count on one hand the number of times I'd seen her cry, and one of those was on her birthday when she had discovered just how big of an asshole Liam was.

"Exhausting."

"You want to sit down?" I questioned.

"I want to sit and scream and eat and sleep." The heaviness lacing her voice was unmistakable.

"We can make some of those things happen," Ryan announced, jumping to his feet. "Why don't you go take a shower, and I'll make you something to eat."

"Okay." Wren dumped her stuff by the door and headed in the direction of the bathroom.

"Pancakes and bacon?"

As if by magic, her face lit up at Ryan's question. "That sounds like heaven."

While Ryan went to the kitchen to start cooking, I began straightening up the apartment once more. The decorative pillows I'd arranged on the bed were now scattered all over the floor from Ryan's attempt to construct himself a makeshift pallet in front of the television.

By the time I finished my task, and Ryan his, Wren emerged from the bathroom with damp hair and a fresh set of pajamas. Earlier in the evening, I'd decided to borrow a set for myself, so the two of us matched now. I was instantly reminded of all the sleepovers we'd had over the years.

"Thank you guys so much. The place looks amazing. And damn, Ryan, I didn't know you could cook!"

Ryan and I both smiled as Wren stared lovingly at the golden stack of pancakes in front of her. "I know my way around the kitchen."

"That's good to hear, because we don't let this one in there at all," she countered, nodding in my direction.

"Hey!"

"And why is it that we don't let Ter in the kitchen?"

"Because you'll wind up calling the fire department and your insurance claims adjuster."

Ryan's husky laugh sounded from every corner of the apartment.

"So what? Cooking isn't everything. That's why humanity evolved and invented restaurants."

Ryan inched closer so he could nudge my arm with his elbow. "Oh, is that so?"

"Yes, and I also have Wren to cook for me."

"And now Ryan. These pancakes are to die for, by the way," Wren added with a full mouth.

"I'm glad you like them."

"So, you're okay with all the decorations I picked out?" I questioned.

"Yeah. I love all of it. Thank you so much for going through all the trouble."

"It's nothing."

Wren dropped her dirty dishes in the sink before coming to wrap her arms around my waist. "Babe, you're the best."

I sighed, returning her hug. "So are you."

She pulled away from our embrace, covering her mouth as she yawned. "Bedtime?"

"Yeah." Wren and I buried ourselves beneath the covers of her bed. Out of the corner of my eye, I could see Ryan moving toward the tiny couch I'd passed out on earlier. "I know you're not one for crying, but if you need to, you know we won't judge."

She released a heavy sigh, and from that soft sound, I could tell there was still so much she was holding in. I'd usually pry whatever information I wanted from her, but not with something like this. Wren would have to open up on her own. "I won't shed another tear over him. The mess he's left me in . . . Sometimes, I think it's more than I can withstand. I feel lost and hurt and betrayed."

"What do you need me to do?" I asked in a soft voice.

"Just hold on to me."

"Okay." Sliding my arms around her shoulders, I held her body close to mine. A gleam of silver caught my attention—the bracelet I'd given Wren at our high school graduation fit snug around her wrist. The bent metal was so much more than a piece of jewelry. It was a promise that I would be there for her no matter what, like she was there for me when I lost Mom. Wren wasn't just my friend, she was family.

"You can lay down too, Ryan," Wren whispered.

"I don't want to make the two of you uncomfortable."

"You won't," I countered.

"Alright." Ryan stepped over to the opposite side of the bed before pulling back the comforter. Tossing a few pillows to the carpet, he paused. "Umm, do you care if I take my jeans off? These aren't the most comfortable things to sleep in."

"As long as you've got something on under those jeans," I stated.

"Boxers?"

"Come on, Ter, it's not like someone in this bed has never seen a penis before."

"Fine, boxer boy. Get your ass in the bed."

Ryan slid beneath the covers and shifted until he faced me. The two of us formed a cocoon around Wren, as if we sought to protect her from both sides. "I don't know the whole story, but I'm sorry about whatever your ex did to you," he breathed.

"Thanks."

"And if there is anything I can do, just let me know."

"I will."

Within minutes, Wren was fast asleep. All the hours she'd been clocking at her job had pushed her past the point of exhaustion. This entire situation had taken its toll on her. As my mind counted all the torturous things I'd love to do to Liam if given the chance, I noticed Ryan's gaze. That periwinkle blue called out to me in the darkness like a long-lost lover.

I was becoming *way* too familiar with those eyes.

"Thank you for being here," I whispered.

"Anytime."

Thanks to Wren's blackout curtains, the three of us didn't rouse until later that afternoon. I couldn't imagine working nights, but she'd always been a night owl and it accommodated her school schedule better.

I yawned and stretched my arms, watching as Wren brushed a few strands of hair out of her eyes.

"I think I slept like the dead," she stated.

"Same here," I countered. "What about you?"

"I slept in a bed with two women. How do you think it was for me?" Ryan asked with a grin.

I grabbed a pillow and flung it at him. "I swear you could turn anything into some kind of freaky ass sexual innuendo."

"Some of us are blessed," he countered stoically.

Wren's laughter distracted the two of us from the staring contest we'd been engaged in. "You guys are the best."

"I'm awesome, not so sure about the weirdo over there," I huffed.

"Don't let her fool you, Wren. She's infatuated with me. She just has a hard time expressing her emotions."

My cheeks burned from the inside out. I'll be damned if he didn't hit the metaphorical nail on the head. In the depths of my soul, I knew his statement about me was true, but *like hell* I'd ever tell him that. "Oh, whatever!" I grabbed another pillow and smacked it against Ryan's head, leaning over Wren in the process.

"Deny it all you want, but I know the truth," he teased, picking up a pillow and launching it in my direction.

"It's on now!" I stood on the bed and prepared myself to engage in a pillow fight of epic proportions, because I was nothing if not a child at heart.

"So you want a pillow fight? I'll be happy to give you exactly what you want, Ter."

His teasing tone was as irritating as someone chewing with their mouth wide open. "Come on, Wren, let's show him how it's done."

"I am not getting involved in this! Consider me Switzerland!"

"Betrayed at the last minute!" Ryan shouted.

"You are so dead!" Just as I was about to strike, Ryan flung another pillow at my face. Watching plenty of kung fu movies had apparently rubbed off on me, because I dodged the attack like a martial arts expert. Lunging forward, I hurled a pillow at his face.

I must've flung it harder than I had intended, because Ryan sat there for a moment in stunned silence. "This is a serious matter," he finally said, his voice devoid of humor.

The eyes I'd found myself admiring on more than one occasion filled with mischief. Whatever he was about to do, it was apparent I needed to put as much distance between the two of us as possible. Jumping to my feet, I hurled myself toward the far side of the apartment in search of refuge. Wren—now as neutral as Switzerland—sat on the bed, her body shaking from laughter. It'd been too long since I'd seen a genuine smile on her face, and if engaging in this ridiculous display kept it there, then I was more than happy to comply.

Ryan sprang from the bed, his entire countenance the epitome of seriousness.

"What's wrong?" I asked in a teasing tone. "Realizing you can't win this?"

"Hardly."

"You know, if you can't take the heat, you should get out of the kitchen."

At my reply, his lips split into a wide grin. "And here I was led to believe that you were the one banned from the kitchen."

"Oh, you've done it now!"

Before I could lunge for the numerous cushions on the couch, Ryan swept Wren off the bed and tossed her over his shoulder. "No standing on the sidelines, Switzerland. This is a war among all nations," he declared.

"Put me down!" she cried, her voice overflowing with laughter.

"Nope. You're a part of this now, and you and I are teaming up against Ter over there."

"I refuse!"

"I'll cook for you if you take my side," he offered.

Wren didn't hesitate for a moment before calling out the word "done!"

"Wren!" I shouted.

"What? You can't feed me, and he can make breakfast!"

"Years of friendship, and I'm betrayed for a meal?"

"I'm really hungry," she said softly.

Just as I was about to scream at the injustice of this world, Ryan's hands snagged my waist. Within seconds, my feet kicked air as he threw me over the opposite shoulder as Wren.

"Admit defeat, Ter."

"Go to hell!"

"Can't we just play nice?" he questioned.

I didn't think it would be possible for him to hold on to

both of us without any difficulty, but to my surprise, Ryan hopped around the apartment, spinning in circles like a joyous kid on Christmas morning. Wren's laughter seemed to drown out every other sound, and before long, I was joining in her amusement.

Part of being an artist meant I was able to observe people in a detailed manner. In order to depict someone, you must familiarize yourself with not only their features, but also their nature and personality. This is what makes the *Mona Lisa* so enrapturing. Da Vinci captured her enigmatic smile flawlessly, and when you study his work, you can see that he understood this woman's nature on an intimate level. In the last few days, I'd watched Ryan. I'd been studying him closely, even more so when I was drawing him. He had a good soul. I could sense that about him. And all his concern for Wren and I proved it.

There had always been two of us. It was always Wren and me, but now, I had a feeling there would be an addition to our duo. And as hesitant as I was at the prospect of being around someone who I was growing more and more fond of, part of me . . . a part I thought would never resurface . . . was elated.

As a woman, I'd been educated on the dangers lurking in this world. Don't get in the car with strangers. Don't go home with a guy you don't know. But the most dangerous experiences are the ones which can rock the foundations of your being. It's the situations which can totally change us that we should fear more than any others.

Because those are the ones that leave the most damage in their wake.

chapter eight

a sea of purple

WHEN OUR PILLOW FIGHT ended and Ryan and I called a truce, the three of us feasted on a delicious breakfast—cooked by Ryan, of course. Wren hadn't been lying when she said the man was skilled in the kitchen. Every time we hung out, I would find another thing to like about him. Seriously, the guy seemed damn near perfect. He must have a flaw, right? I enjoyed spending time with him, and I knew Wren did too, but that nagging voice in the back of my mind demanded I proceed with caution.

Wren flung a giant blanket over my legs and snuggled next to me. I was now smack dab in the middle of her and Ryan as we watched a movie together. Three bodies nestled under a purple comforter meant I was up close and personal with the blue eyes I couldn't seem to stop staring at. And I needed to do something, anything, to keep my hormones distracted.

"This movie reminds me that we need to discuss something very important," I announced as the opening credits for *Pet Sematary* began to roll. Thank God Wren wasn't one of those people who was opposed to talking during a movie. She understood it was damn near impossible for me to keep myself from shouting out spoilers or discussing my favorite nail polish, and like a true bestie, she rolled with it. I was also glad to discover Ryan was the same way. When he wasn't shouting at the television in my dorm room, we talked about anything and everything.

"What might that be?"

"Halloween," Wren said, answering Ryan's question. "Ter is a fiend about the holiday, and I have no doubts she will want to take the reins on costume planning for the three of us."

"So, wait . . . Do you mean to tell me that I'm being roped into spending Halloween with the two of you?"

"As if you weren't secretly hoping for that."

"Just go with the flow, dude. Your life will be so much easier that way," Wren said, leveling him with a pointed look. "Trust me on this."

Ry's features practically radiated with amusement. "And what if I already have my own costume?"

"Do you want to ruin my life?" I questioned.

"You know how Jack Skellington is obsessed with Christmas to the point where it's almost nauseating?"

Ryan tore his eyes away from the television screen to face Wren. "Yeah."

"That's how Ter feels about Halloween. Also, she's an artist, so we always have killer costumes."

He considered her statement for a second before exhaling in a heavy sigh. "I'm smart enough to know when I'm outnumbered. Ter, feel free to dress us as you see fit."

I squealed with delight, much to their dismay.

"Jesus, woman, must you always express your happiness at that decibel?"

"Babe, you know I know no other way," I countered, nudging Wren with my shoulder.

"So, do I dare ask what the three of us will be dressing up as?"

I gasped ever so slightly as I felt Ryan's breath warm my ear. I silently cursed the existence of female hormones before answering. "Hugh Hefner and two Playboy Bunnies, of course."

"I've always wanted to dress up as a Playboy Bunny," Ryan mused.

"Wait . . . what?"

Beside me, Wren giggled. "Oh my God! That so needs to happen!"

"Let's face it, I belong in women's lingerie and bunny ears."

"You're supposed to be Hugh Hefner," I countered.

"How dare you force strict gender stereotypes on me!" Ryan feigned shock as he placed his hand over his heart in a dramatic display of defiance.

"I mean if you really want to dress up as that, you can—"

"I'll be Hef!" Wren shouted. As soon as the words left her mouth, Ryan gave her a high five over my head.

"See, she gets me. I don't understand why you can't jump on the bandwagon."

I shrugged in a nonchalant manner. "I guess we will both be in lingerie then."

Ryan's laughter dissipated at my reply. "I didn't consider that."

"Well, we can't have two people dressed up as Hef. That wouldn't make sense." Combing my fingers through my hair, I stared up at him through my lashes. "Unless you have a problem with seeing me in lingerie, that is."

"Nothing I haven't seen before." Ryan's grin widened as he gave me a once-over.

"Hold the fuck up for one second." Wren was on her

feet, ready to pounce. To be honest, I wasn't sure which one of us would be her first victim. "What the hell do you mean by nothing you haven't seen before?"

I groaned inwardly. With Wren's breakneck pace at the hospital the past couple of weeks, I hadn't had a chance to tell her about the plan Ryan and I hatched to deal with Brooklyn. "There is a reason for that."

"Are y'all going to start dating? Did the two of you sleep together?" The pure glee dripping from her voice was unmistakable.

"No!" I shouted. "What on earth would make you think that?"

"Ryan's comment about your damn lingerie. Also, the fact that the two of you have ridiculous chemistry."

"We do not!"

"Denial," Wren intoned.

Ugh. This conversation was sinking faster than Jack's body at the end of *Titanic*. Wren knew I was attracted to and intrigued by Ryan. And that was dangerous information in the hands of a feisty redhead. "You see, we made this plan to . . ." Now that I was on the verge of relaying our devious scheme, the entire thing almost sounded too unbelievable. Was there any chance she would actually believe me?

"Well, Ter, I'm all ears!"

"Do you want to explain?" I asked, glancing at Ryan over my shoulder.

"But you're doing such a wonderful job," he countered with a laugh.

I rolled my eyes. Well, at least one of us was having a good time. "Okay, you know how Brooklyn and Joe's humping sessions have been making my dorm life a living hell?"

"Yeah."

"Ryan came up with a plan to give Brooklyn a taste of her own medicine. We met up in my room, stripped down to our undies, and pretended like we were in the middle of a hook-up when Brooklyn came home from class."

I watched as Wren's face lit up like a freaking fireworks display. "Oh, that is simply masterful. Why didn't we think of that?"

"Well, it's not like you and I could have faked something like that."

"We could so pretend to be lovers!"

"Yeah, but then there wouldn't have been any evidence for Brooklyn to clean up," Ryan stated.

"What do you mean by evidence?"

"We may or may not have planted unused condoms filled with a little lotion and some water around the dorm for Brooklyn to find."

Wren howled with laughter at my explanation. "This is the best fucking thing I've ever heard in my entire life. I so wish I could've been there to see the expression on her face."

"It was priceless. Especially considering that she and Joe have zero shame when it comes to their sex lives. I've gotten enough free shows that I didn't even need to study the human anatomy for my art classes."

"Sounds like she got a little taste of her own medicine, and I hope it was bitter as hell. I mean, I've seen a lot of shit at the hospital, but at least I don't have to listen to people screwing all the time."

Jumping to my feet, I threw my arms around her. "And now that I have a key to your place, neither will I!"

"Yay!" Wren called out as she headed for the bathroom.

As soon as she was out of earshot, it was as if someone had cranked the thermostat up a few degrees.

"How do you think she is doing?"

I blew out a deep breath as I considered Ryan's question. He didn't know about everything that went down between Wren and Liam, but he could still sense something was off. "Honestly, this is the most I've heard her laugh in a really long time. Even before everything went to shit, she wasn't happy."

"Her ex cheated on her?"

"That's putting it mildly."

"What happened?"

"It's not my life we're discussing, so it isn't my place to say, but I don't think Wren would mind if I filled you in a little bit," I answered in a low voice. "She walked in on him while he was screwing his ex."

"Damn."

"She caught him on her birthday too."

The sound of knuckles cracking distracted me for a moment. When I glanced at Ryan's hands, his fists were balled so hard I thought he might break a finger. "Fucking piece of shit," he muttered.

"I won't argue with you there."

"What's his name?"

"Liam."

"I'll remember that."

There was an unfamiliar edge to his voice. Sure, I'd only known Ryan a few days, but I'd never heard him take that tone before. I wasn't stupid. I had no doubts that if we ever ran into Liam, Ryan would make him pay. It was the way he was raised—to always make sure a woman felt safe with him.

And part of me couldn't help but wonder if the sentiment would hold true for me as well.

chapter nine

blades of green

"YOUR FACE ALWAYS GETS a really serious look to it whenever you're painting."

I moistened my lips with my tongue as my focus shifted from the canvas in front of me to the voice speaking to me. Who the hell was I kidding? It wasn't just any voice.

It was *his* voice.

"Yeah, people tend to do that whenever they are engrossed in something," I countered, my gaze finally meeting Ryan's.

"So, where should I strip?"

Grabbing the spare rag hanging over my shoulder, I tossed it in his direction. "I draw you one time and you act like you're the freaking statue of David."

"You mean I'm not on that level?" he questioned, feigning shock. The tips of his fingers curled underneath the bottom hem of his shirt. Lifting the fabric just a tad, he glanced at his abs. "And here I thought all that time I've been spending in the gym was paying off."

"Stop being such a drama queen. We all know your abs are wonderful."

As soon as the words left my mouth, I silently cursed. I seemed to be on the losing side of our never ending battle of wits, and any day now, I'd be reduced to cannon fodder. It wasn't like the man needed any more ammunition.

"So you can be nice to me."

"I'm nice to you all the time."

"You say that, but you coupled your reply with an eye roll that most likely allowed you to see the inside of your skull. You can see why that makes you seem less believable."

"So . . . what are you doing in the art annex, anyway?"

"I came to see you, duh."

"Why?"

"Do I really need a reason to come stare at a beautiful woman?"

"In my experience, yes, you absolutely fucking do."

Ryan rounded my easel and moved close enough to lean over my shoulder. He now had a full view of the piece I was working on. As an artist, some creations were so close to my heart that the thought of sharing it with another soul was daunting. And that was exactly how I felt about this painting. It was a fragment of me, of my memories. We're never capable of realizing the void a loved one can leave behind until the gaping hole is staring us in the face. I'd had some amazing years with my mom, but I wanted more. I wanted to hear her voice as she sang her favorite song or smell her perfume wafting throughout the house. And if that made me selfish, then so be it. Call me selfish, call me any imaginable name under the sun, cover my flesh with wounds, and take every single possession I own. I didn't care as long as I had her.

The soft touch of a hand at the base of my neck disrupted the thoughts plaguing my mind.

"Take a deep breath," Ryan whispered in my ear.

"I'm okay."

"Are you?"

I nodded. "I think so."

"She's exquisite."

"Huh?" Between the touch of his flesh and my train of thought, I was at a complete loss of who he was talking about.

He smiled, his hand moving to point at the painting. "Your mother."

"How did you know who she was?"

"She looks just like you."

"You can barely see a side profile of her face."

"Yeah," he answered, his eyes staring into mine. "But I'd know your face anywhere."

My heart pounded inside my chest. Wren probably knew the medical term for the way my body was reacting, but all I knew was that it felt like my heart was moving at a million miles per minute. Just how intimately did he know my face? The question, while filling me with elation, was also daunting. Whenever things got serious with a guy, I bailed faster than a fighter pilot ejecting from a nosediving plane. It was the only way I knew how to live. And the strength needed to break that habit was more than my heart could withstand.

"Is that so?" I leaned toward him, my need to be closer suddenly overpowering every ounce of apprehension.

"Yes."

The space between our mouths seemed to lessen by the second.

"Ry," I breathed. "If I share something personal, will you?"

"What do you want to know?" He responded without a moment's hesitation. Did he want to learn my secrets as much as I wanted to learn his?

The question I'd been mulling over since the night we pranked Brooklyn couldn't be silenced any longer. "Why do you hate your dad so much?" There was every possibility that this question would infuriate him, but I needed to know if the pain resonating inside of me also resided within him.

He exhaled sharply, and for a minute, I wondered if it had been the right decision to ask the question at all. It was obvious he harbored a lot of contempt for his father, but I wanted to help. He'd done so much for Wren in the past few days, and if there was something I could do to repay him, I would see it done to the best of my ability.

The room around us was drowning in silence. Even though we were the only people in the art studio, pressure intensified all around me, making me feel as though I was suffocating. I knew the pain, the heartache, written all over his face.

"That question has a really long answer."

"I've been known to be a good listener," I teased, hoping to lighten the mood a bit. My fingertips lightly brushed his shirt. The gesture was so intimate, so unlike me, that I wasn't sure if I should continue or pull my hand away.

Ryan, it seemed, already had the answer to my internal debate. Placing his hand over mine, he held me in place. His heart drummed beneath my flesh, the pace quickening just a bit as his eyes met mine.

"I would rather be tortured than talk about that man," he admitted. "But at the same time, I want you to know."

"Which do you want more?" The question rolled off my tongue as little more than a whisper. "Safety or confession?"

"And what if I want both?"

I shook my head, not understanding what he meant. "You can't have that."

"I could if I trust the person I confess to."

"You hardly know me."

"Do you trust me?"

I sighed. He already knew that I did, but such a notion was insanity, right? "I don't really know you," I answered.

"We're both masters of hesitation."

"So it would seem."

"Well, I'll cut you a deal. Whenever you're ready to tell me about her, I'll tell you about my father." His hand released mine, and as soon as the connection was severed, I longed for its return. Ryan turned toward my painting, moving close enough for the tip of his nose to be but a breath from the canvas. "Was your childhood home near an open field like that?" he asked.

"Nope."

"Then what made you decide to draw her sitting in a bed of grass?"

"It's my dream."

Lines formed across his forehead, scrunching together as he forced his attention away from the picture of my mother. "Come again?"

"My dream is to find my mother lying in a field, gazing up at the sky as she waits for me to join her. Once I'm there, I'd lie down next to her and tell her about my day or confess all of my deepest secrets. I'd describe my latest art project, including every single color I painted with." My fingers combed through my hair as I willed myself to continue. "It's hard to explain it, but I simply want a reminder of what our lives were like before she was taken away."

"I get it. You want to halt time and preserve that image of her forever."

"Yeah."

Shaking his head, Ryan's lips stretched into a smirk. "I really like that about you."

Settling on a nearby stool, I reached for my palette and brush. "What are you talking about?" I dabbed the brush into a mixture of yellow and green, blending the colors together until I had the perfect shade to highlight the blades of grass.

"It's easy to judge a book by its cover. I mean, I did that with you," he explained, combing his fingers through his hair. "Most people look at you, see that face, and never realize all this depth exists just beneath the surface."

His words touched something deep inside me. Wren had said similar words to me on more than one occasion, but I always ignored her. I didn't care what people thought about me, but I realized Ry was different. His opinion mattered.

Well, *shit*.

Even if I was totally screwed, there was nothing I could do about it now. The blond-haired, blue-eyed hottie from my statistics class was working his way underneath my skin. And if I was being honest with myself, I didn't hate it.

However, this acceptance of my fate was quick to be replaced with an overwhelming sense of panic. I prided myself on knowing, on obeying, the caution signs. But at the moment, I began to realize all my preparation was for nothing. Because if my heart wanted to fall for the man standing close enough to catch a whiff of my perfume, then there wasn't a damn thing I could do to stop it.

"You need to get out of there," Ry said, tapping his finger against my forehead. "You always seem to be so deep inside your head."

"What's wrong with that?"

"Usually nothing. But when I can tell you're thinking

about something upsetting, I feel like it's my duty to draw you out of the rabbit hole."

"Does that mean I'm Alice and you're the Mad Hatter?"

"Only if you want it to," he answered with a wink.

"So is there a potion lying around that will shrink you down to size? Because I'm a tad busy, in case you haven't noticed."

"You're the one who wanted to meet with Wren and me to discuss the idea you had for your next art assignment. I'm simply being a good friend."

I considered his reply for a minute. He was right. I had asked Wren and Ry to meet me tonight so I could explain my concept of using color on mediums other than paper or canvas. Not to toot my own horn, but I thought it was innovative to use our bodies as the canvas. My idea was to fill giant water guns with tons of food coloring and water. Then, while wearing solid white clothes, we would have a water gun fight to end all water gun fights. I've dubbed it the Crayola War, and I was hoping the results would be reminiscent of Monet. His impressionistic style—coupled with Seurat's pointillist technique—was the inspiration behind my idea.

Not to mention, soaking Ry with a water gun sounded pretty damn fun. He'd only known me for a matter of days, but he had the ability to annoy the hell out of me unlike anyone I'd ever known before. Wren would no doubt say that was a wonderful thing, but then again, Ry was sweet as pie whenever he was around her. And I appreciated that—the girl needed to be treated like a queen every single day for the rest of her life for all the shit she'd been put through.

"Is being a nuisance slang for being a good friend?"

"This is how you treat me after I helped you understand the Kirkwood approximation and offered to tutor you in statistics?"

"Well, maybe you should make good on your offer to teach me."

"It'll cost you."

"Alright, what's your rate?"

Breath caught in my throat as Ryan bent toward me. "Depends on the currency," he whispered with a wink.

"What did you have in mind?"

"Oh, I think you know."

I stepped backward, desperate to create a little space between us. "I should've known that your mind would go straight to the gutter."

"You say that as if it has ever left the gutter."

I groaned, my eyes making their regular upward arc. "Do you even want to be liked by people?"

"People? Fuck no," he answered. "But you? That's another story entirely."

I chewed on the end of one of my paintbrushes. I wasn't the nervous type, but Ryan had the ability to drive my sense of composure straight into the damn pavement. I needed to shift the direction of this conversation before I flung myself headfirst into the danger zone again. "What days do you have to work this week?"

"Thursday and Friday."

"Does that mean you're available Wednesday for my art project?"

"Yeah."

"Okay, good. And where is it you said you work again? I know you told me the other day, but I couldn't remember the name of it."

"Right now, I'm working at Halstead Accounting. I mostly prepare or read over reports and collect data, but I'll be able to do more once I graduate."

I nodded, my attention never turning from his face. "Does that mean you're going to stay here after you graduate?"

"Actually, I want to move to a bigger city. Being an investment banker would be awesome because it's interesting work, and would be a huge pay bump. Not to mention, it's impressive."

"And are you trying to impress your father?" I don't know what possessed me to question him further about his father, but the relationship between Ryan and his father had to be strained in more ways than one. Ryan was intelligent and ambitious by nature. However, there were reasons behind his motivations. He had something he wanted to prove.

He remained silent for a long moment. The majority of the population tended to be easy to read. You could tell what most people were thinking just by reading the lines of their face, but that wasn't the case with Ryan. Most of the time, his emotions were kept on a need-to-know basis. Unless you could catch him off guard like I did with the imaginary string in his hair at Wren's apartment the other night, you were shit out of luck. "Are you ever going to tell me what this project entails? Or are Wren and I going to be kept in the dark?" he finally asked in a clear attempt to steer our conversation in a different direction.

"I'm going to explain everything as soon as she gets here."

As if my reply conjured the very topic of our conversation, Wren burst into the art studio, still wearing her nursing school scrubs. "Hey! I'm not late, am I?"

"Not at all," Ryan answered, stepping in her direction. He slid her messenger bag off her shoulder before ushering her further into the room. "I got here early because I wanted to see Ter."

"Thanks, and of course you did." Her tone was the epitome of amusement. At least one of us was getting something out of this new friendship.

"I mean, can you really blame me?"

She elbowed him in the arm, a smile cutting across her face. "You know I wouldn't do that."

If I hadn't known that they'd met only a couple days ago, I would've thought Ryan and Wren were old friends. People just click sometimes—there's no rhyme or reason to it.

"Did the two of you have some secret *Baby-Sitters Club* meeting without me?" I asked in a teasing tone.

"Nope," Wren replied, sliding her arm around my waist. "This is just the kind of compassion I show people who feed me. You know how I am about food."

"You're basically a pint-sized version of the Hulk when you haven't had anything to eat."

"Truth."

"Rule number one of this friendship is that you don't let the redhead go hungry. Civilizations have crumbled into dust for far less."

"Yes, ma'am," Ryan answered, giving Wren and me a mock salute. "Are there any other rules? You know, 'cause that first one sounded like a reference to *Fight Club*."

Wren shrugged as she turned toward me. "He's got a point there."

"Yeah, the only other rule is that we hate the giant no-name douchebag, and if we meet him out in public, he must face a reckoning!"

"Ter—"

"I'm not budging on this one, babe. If I see that piece of shit, my foot will be introduced to his balls and then his teeth . . . in that exact order."

"I can help. I may not look like the boxing type, but I'm rather scrappy."

"I don't know about that. Ter seems to think you're pretty built."

That *mouth*. I shouldn't have been so surprised. Sass had been pouring out of her mouth from the moment she took her first breath in this world. The wide grin covering Ryan's face was second only to the one on Wren's. She was right. Ryan had a great body, and the fact I couldn't seem to stop myself from drawing parts of it was hard evidence. *Proof is in the pudding* is the phrase my grandma always liked to throw around, but with me, the proof was on every page of my newest sketch book.

When Ry's gaze shifted in my direction, I took the mature path and pretended to be engrossed in my painting. Acting like the entire conversation had never happened was allowed just this once, right? I mean, the guy really didn't need any more ammunition where I was concerned, so why the hell was Wren acting as his own personal armory supply line?

"I think many guys have pretty built bodies. He's no different than the nude model who posed for my class last semester." Sure, my retort was a bold-faced lie, but it wasn't like they needed to be privy to that little morsel of information. Truth be told, Ry's body was completely different than that of the male model we studied in class. For one thing, I found myself attracted to him at every turn. That isn't to say the model wasn't the stuff of every woman's fantasy—he definitely was. It was as if the cover of a romance novel had been ripped from its spine and made into flesh. But the model in question didn't appeal to me.

Ryan did.

"Is that right?" Wren asked. Her tone sounded bored,

but I knew that the topic was far from being dropped. If nursing hadn't have been her goal, the girl would have made one heck of a detective with the way she refused to let some shit go. I knew beyond the shadow of a doubt we'd be discussing this matter later.

"It's what I said, isn't it?"

"Sure thing, babe."

Ryan stood to the side, scratching his head. "I feel like a whole conversation just transpired and I have no idea what the two of you said."

"You're actually kind of spot on with that assumption," Wren confirmed.

"I figured as much."

I expected Ry to press further, because that seemed to be true to his character, but the entire subject was forgotten as Wren rounded the easel to study my latest creation.

"Oh, Ter, it looks just like her."

"I think I'm going to give it to Dad."

"He'll love it. I have no doubts."

"Thanks."

"So, what's the big art project you texted me about?"

Tucking a stray strand of hair behind my ear, I pulled a deep breath into my lungs. "My teacher wants the entire class to figure out how to make art in alternative ways. He thinks limiting ourselves to paper or canvas will only stunt our growth as artists. He is encouraging us to think outside the box and create art on alternative surfaces or objects . . . whatever we want."

"That sounds pretty cool," Ryan replied.

"My idea is to have the three of us dress in all white clothes and then fill three Super Soaker water guns with colored water."

"And then have a kickass water gun fight?" Wren asked.

"Exactly. After we're done, I want to take pictures of the three of us and see what our clothes look like. I'm hoping the end result will be similar to an impressionist painting, but there is no way to know for sure until we try it."

"Let me get this straight," Ry began. "You want me to have a water gun fight with two girls in wet white clothes?"

Wren's head whipped to look at me. "Didn't consider that, did you?"

Oh, *damn.* I understood exactly what he was getting at.

"Nope, not really," I admitted, feeling like a complete idiot.

"I give my full consent to be a part of this project."

"Of course you do," I spat.

"I mean, if we wear dark sports bras, it shouldn't be a problem."

I considered Wren's suggestion. She had a point. As long as we were covered, there should be no harm done. In all my excitement, I hadn't thought about the fact we would practically be engaging in a glorified wet T-shirt contest. "You're sure?"

"You know I don't care! I'll do whatever it takes to get you an A. I'm your ride-or-die."

"Thanks!" I squealed. I just knew this project was going to impress my teacher. Sure, it was a simple concept, but how many other people were going to think up an idea like mine? Points had to be given for taking a risk. This could simply turn out to be nothing more than a water gun fight, but I had a feeling our clothes would make for a beautiful work of art. If not, it wouldn't be the first time I had to scramble around at the last minute to finish an assignment. "Are you free Wednesday? Ryan and I both have that afternoon available, and I wasn't sure if you'd be working that night."

"I'm actually off work!"

"Yay!"

"I'll be sure to wear my best white outfit."

"Same here," Ryan added, wearing a devious smile.

"Now that we've gotten all the details of your art project figured out, can we please go get some food?" Wren questioned, her voice practically a whine.

"Yeah, I just have to clean this up really quick."

"Here, I'll help."

Ry helped me rinse out all the paintbrushes and clean up the area around my easel. I had always been a messy painter. There were some people who could paint an entire mural without getting dirty. But not me. Whenever I worked on a project, it seemed like getting tarred and feathered would be a cleaner alternative. Needless to say, paint has been discovered in some pretty odd places before.

"Thanks."

"I guess we should feed her before she has a hulk-out, right?"

"That's a good idea."

"She seems happier today," he whispered in my ear as he dried his hands on a towel.

Stealing a glance at Wren, I nodded. "Yeah, she does."

"It makes me happy. I know she's been put through hell."

"And that's sugar coating it."

Ryan flung his arm around my shoulder. "Then let's go make it better for her."

As much as I hated to admit it, Ry was quickly becoming one of my favorite people.

And in the very depths of my heart, I knew the only way this friendship could come to an end was up in smoke.

chapter ten

solid white

A FEW DAYS AFTER our meeting in the art annex, Wren, Ryan, and I were prepared for a battle to the death—Super Soaker style. Was my project the most childish idea of my entire class? Most likely. But at the same time, I couldn't imagine my teacher hating the concept. I'd gone the extra mile by testing the ratio of food coloring to water to ensure maximum concentration and mapping out the best location on campus to conduct my experiment. I even went as far as to buy pasties for Wren and I to wear underneath our sports bras. The last thing I wanted in my pictures was an accidental nip slip. Sure, Wren wouldn't have minded, but that also wasn't the point. I wanted to showcase the ingenuity of using a child's pastime to display the beauty residing in the innocence of childhood. We all remembered the days of riding our bikes through the neighborhood and searching for adventure just within our grasp, and those kinds of sentiments are what I wanted people to feel whenever they looked at my project.

The point was to create art on unconventional surfaces, but it was also about evoking emotions. That is the duty of an artist. We call out to recessed memories and forgotten feelings in order to seduce our audience. Good art elicits emotions, but great art changes you. And I sought to be a great artist. Mediocrity wouldn't serve me well in my dreams to be a full-time painter. Was it probable that I would be a starving artist most of my adult life? Of course. I was an artist, not stupid. But the thought wasn't enough to deter me from chasing my dreams.

Spreading out on top of Wren's bed, I waited not so patiently for Ryan to show us the outfit he'd selected to wear in the Crayola War. Was I hoping he'd be sporting less clothing and more skin?

Of course. I mean, I'm only human.

"How is this?" Ryan asked as he emerged from the bathroom, sporting a white button-up and a pair of linen shorts.

If I were being honest, I'd say he looked as if he'd just stepped off a yacht. And not in an annoyingly preppy sort of way, but in a way that made you wish he would whisk you away on his boat to some far-off location.

"You look great. Right, Ter?" Wren's voice thrust me from the daydream my mind was all too eager to concoct. So what if I'd been envisioning Ryan and myself coasting around the Mediterranean? It was a free country, and a girl was allowed to have her fantasies.

"Yeah," I agreed. "I mean, your clothes may be a bit too nice to soak with food coloring. Are you sure you want to wear them?"

Ryan crossed his arms and leaned against the bathroom doorframe. The fabric of his shirt stretched across his chest, highlighting every single muscle for my viewing pleasure. Thinking of a slew of curse words that was all too appropriate for the situation, I closed my eyes. I really didn't need more fodder for the fantasies plaguing my dreams every night.

"These clothes are really old, so I don't mind if they get ruined. Besides, it's all in the name of making your project the best, right? Personally, I can't think of a better use for these."

It was impossible not to smile at his comment. Creating art had always been a somewhat solitary experience for me, but knowing I had the full support of my friends was indescribable. I had people who believed in me, people who were rooting for me to succeed, and that was everything. "Thank you." I prayed my gratitude was apparent. Ry had done so much for Wren and me over the past week, and I wanted to make sure he understood how much I appreciated him. "I owe you one."

He shook his head, combing his fingers through the blond locks. "No, you don't. That smile just now was payment enough."

Out of the corner of my eye, I could just make out Wren staring at the two of us. A satisfied grin tugged at the edges of her lips. I knew what that girl was thinking. In fact, I'd gotten more than an earful of it over the past few days. She had made it abundantly clear she wanted Ryan and me to get together. She even threatened me under pain of death if I didn't muster up the courage to ask him out within the next week.

It was amazing that after everything she had been through, she still believed in the existence of love and wanted that kind of happiness for me. She understood that the prospect of caring for someone on such a level made me restless. Serious entanglements weren't my thing. The idea of someone possessing so much power over me was frightening. I'd forge my own path through life, even if I had to weather all the peaks and valleys alone.

"There she goes again," Ryan muttered as he bent in front of me. Warmth surged through my flesh as his gaze met mine. At some point while I was lost inside my own head, Ry had left the bathroom and made his way over to the bed. "She is always so inside her own head."

"Ter has been that way since we were kids," Wren replied. "It's funny how you seem to be one of the few people who notice that about her."

"I suppose most get distracted by that face of hers."

"Always teasing me," I stated.

"See, that's where you're wrong. I'm not teasing you at all. I mean every compliment I give."

The sincerity of his words stunned me. "Oh." It was officially the most lame reply in the history of lame replies, but it also happened to be the one word my brain was capable of forming. It wasn't like this was the first or only time Ry had ever complimented me. In fact, he had made similar comments several times before. So why did his words seem to have more weight than ever?

I suppose that's what happened when a person began to weave themselves into the fabric of your life. Little by little, each stroke of the paintbrush combines with the others in order to create one singular piece of art. The same held true for relationships. Each laugh, kind word, and hug built upon one another. The roles people assumed in our lives were diverse and multifaceted. My parents and Wren were proof of such a sentiment. Not to mention Wren's parents. Her mother had helped me shop for the perfect prom dress and taught me how to apply red lip liner. And hadn't Ry filled another void in my life? He was a comedian, an expert cook, and my partner in crime when it came to devising elaborate schemes against my horny roommate.

"Terayn Andrews, ladies and gentleman, expert painter and conversationalist," Ryan announced with a wink.

"Smartass," I mumbled. "Honestly, I don't know who has more sass, you or her."

Wren stood, snagging the clothes she'd selected for the Crayola War from her bed. "That would be me. Duh."

I sighed in a dramatic fashion, my eyes rolling upward. Those things seemed to have a mind of their own. It was like a bodily response that I had no control over. Fight or flight?

Not here. It was more like curse or eyeroll.

Once Wren and I were secluded within the privacy of her bathroom, she rounded on me. "Ter, he is completely taken with you!"

"Ugh. Not this shit again," I groaned, handing her a pair of pasties. I was becoming tired of having this conversation all the time. "We barely know one another, and I have issues with serious entanglements. I'm like a guy in that regard, babe. You know this about me."

"Why do you have to be so difficult? I mean, can't you just do what I want you to do?"

"Pretty sure that would put us into a sub and dom type of relationship."

Wren chewed on her bottom lip as she considered my words. "You've got a point there."

I shrugged, pulling the white long-sleeve shirt I had selected over my sports bra. "I know."

Now it was Wren's turn to roll her eyes. "All I'm trying to say is that Ryan is a nice guy and he likes you. Those two things are probably something you shouldn't pass up."

"I hear you loud and clear, but I like my life just the way it is."

"Alright."

The two of us finished dressing in silence. I knew Wren

far too well to ever think this conversation had been dropped. However, for the time being, she seemed content to let it go.

While Wren dressed in a white button-up and matching jeans, I opted for leggings to go with the long-sleeved T-shirt I'd selected. The three of us had to have resembled live versions of a Mr. Clean advertisement as we walked into campus with our pristine ensembles and water guns. But it didn't matter. We were simply ready for the fun to begin.

And begin it did.

Ushering for Wren and Ryan to join me, I made sure the three of us were all facing one another before commencing with my rule speech. Because, with a Super Soaker fight between friends, rules of engagement were a necessity. "I am hereby announcing the rules for the first ever Crayola War," I said, staring at them seriously. "Rule number one is to keep this game clean. This means no face or eye shots. The last thing we need is to be making a trip to the emergency room on Wren's night off. The second rule is that we have to stay on campus. We can't be running through the streets like a bunch of damn idiots. Am I understood?"

"Yes," Wren and Ry answered in unison.

"And the final rule is to take no prisoners!"

Wren and I broke away from Ryan as we hit him square in the chest with simultaneous streams of green and pink. To say our dual attack stunned him would have been an understatement. The look of surprise in those baby blue eyes was unmistakable. Apparently, he expected the two of us to play fair. Little did he know that was only the tip of the damn iceberg.

"Oh, you're asking for it now!" he shouted, chasing after us.

Our laughter rang out as we sprinted toward a couple of nearby trees, seeking cover. Wren, Sean, and I had spent more than one summer drenched to the bone. One time, the three of us even resorted to spraying one another with the hose after we had grown tired of refilling our water guns every few minutes. Needless to say, Wren and I were a formidable team in this kind of situation, and poor Ryan didn't even stand a chance.

"Bring it on, surfer boy!" I called out, spinning around the trunk of a tree and sprinting toward him. Ryan leapt over a small bush as he rushed in my direction. Dodging the stream of orange he shot at me, I fired back a shot of my own. The sight of my pink water soaking his preppy shorts filled my heart with glee. "No offense, but you kind of suck at this game."

"I'm just getting started," he taunted back.

"You're full of it!" Wren shouted. She peeled away from the tree she'd been hiding behind and sprinted to join me. Firing off her water gun, bright green mixed with the pink water already staining Ryan's clothes.

"Nice shot!" Wren made her way over to me and slapped my outstretched hand.

"What happened to being on my side?" Ry asked Wren.

She flung her copper ponytail over her shoulder as she stared at him. "I watched to see who was more skilled at this game—you or Ter—and clearly, you lost. Besides, we ascribe to the chicks-before-dicks philosophy."

"Pretty soon you'll be eating those words!" Ryan's feet dug into the grass as he sprinted for us. Orange streaks seemed to litter the air around us. In an act of pure desperation, Ry began firing his water gun relentlessly, in the hope he would be able to hit one of us.

And yet, all of his efforts were in vain. Wren and I were

able to avoid his attacks with ease. For someone in such great shape, Ry sure didn't have a handle on this game.

"Are you trying to be this shitty at water gun fights, or are you really just this shitty at them?"

Ryan stopped mid-attack to consider my question. As he stood there, his clothes dripping with green and pink water, he was too distracted to notice Wren sneaking up behind him. When she fired off her shot, it was as if the stream of water was moving in slow motion. Bright green catapulted through the air, only to make contact with Ry's pristine derriere.

"Double points for an ass shot!" she yelled.

"Is there no part of my body that is safe?"

"Only that pretty face!" I added, dousing each of his thighs.

"I have to look ridiculous right now."

In every direction, other students skirted around our game, their eyes fixated on us with looks of amusement. I could only imagine the kind of spectacle we were creating for them.

"Not going to disagree with you there, Ry," I stated in the sweetest tone imaginable.

"Was it your plan all along to gang up on me?" he questioned.

Wren and I nodded in unison. "Yeah, pretty much."

Ry dramatically clutched his heart, dropping to his knees. "Is this the betrayal Caesar felt in his final moments?"

"Sorry, but I had to do something to make up for the pillow fight the other day. I sided with you because you promised to cook for me, and this beauty over here will never let me forget it."

Flipping my hair over my shoulder, I couldn't fight the grin spreading across my face. "You better believe it, babe.

We will be in the nursing home together one day and I'll be reminding you of it."

"Can I be in the home with you guys too?" Ryan asked hopefully.

"If you want," I answered.

"Awesome." Before I could even comprehend what was happening, Ry dropped his water gun and lunged for us. Even though Wren was just a tiny little thing, she slipped away at a speed that would've made an Olympic sprinter proud. However, I had the strange suspicion I was the intended target all along as Ry crashed into me, his arms fastening around my waist. A single scream escaped my lips as we began to plummet toward the ground. My fingers dug into his back as I braced for impact.

But when I finally opened my eyes, Ry lay beneath me, his back flush against the grass.

"I may not have been able to land a hit on you, but I think I prefer this." His clothes pressed against mine, dampening the dry fabric. I shivered as the tips of his fingers brushed my waist. "If you're cold, I'd be more than happy to warm you up."

"Is that a promise?"

"Absolutely." A light breeze blew by and I shivered once more in response. "You really are cold," he whispered, tightening his arms around me. Our chests pressed further into one another with each breath we took. This wasn't the first time I'd found myself in Ry's arms, and I prayed to heaven above that it wouldn't be the last.

My thumb traced the line of his jaw as I continued to stare at him. I was aware that the world all around us kept spinning. Light radiated from the sun, illuminating everything in sight. Our fellow students bustled across campus in groups as they headed to their next class of the day. But as far as I was concerned, we were completely alone.

"I should get up."

"Don't," he begged. "Stay here with me."

"And why should I do that?" The words leaving my mouth may have been posed as a question, but it was actually a plea. Even if staying in his arms was dangerous, I needed Ry to give me a reason to stay. I wasn't brave enough to navigate these waters on my own. There were a million things I could do alone, but this wasn't one of them.

To build up the courage to leap, I would first have to know someone will be there to catch me.

"Because I'm not ready to stop holding on to you."

"Good, because I'm not ready for you to stop either."

I watched as the expression in his eyes brightened at my reply. Pure, unadulterated joy lit up my skin like a fireworks display on the Fourth of July as Ry brushed his nose against mine. The playful gesture elicited a smile from both of us. After a few seconds, the smiles faded as the space between our mouths began to vanish. In another breath, my lips would join with his.

And for the life of me, I couldn't think of *anything* I wanted more.

My body had been craving his touch since the night we fooled Brooklyn into thinking she had stumbled upon us mid-hookup. I thought denying myself this kind of satisfaction was the smart thing to do, but the more time passed, the more I wanted him.

"Umm, guys." The sound of Wren's voice was like a swift kick in the gut. "I know y'all are having a very intense moment and everything, but a lot of people have gathered around to stare at you."

I glanced upward only to see two dozen bodies hovering around us. Those students who were booking it to class a few minutes ago had stopped dead in their tracks to watch Ryan and me. Whistles and cheers sounded out. They were rooting for us to kiss, but what they didn't realize was the moment had already passed.

Ryan helped me to my feet before putting some distance between us. The gathering crowd slowly began to dissipate once they realized the show was over.

"Wow," Wren breathed.

"Can we pretend like that never happened?" I asked in a hushed voice.

"Not a snowball's chance in hell."

I groaned. "Of course not."

"Hey, you're the one recreating scenes from a steamy soap opera in public, babe. Not me."

"You always have to add insult to injury, don't you?"

She slid her arm around my waist, pulling me into her. "You know I love you."

"Yeah, yeah."

My spine stiffened as I noticed Ryan making his way over to us. "Are you still wanting to take pictures of our clothes?" he questioned. "Other than a single spot on Wren's shirt and a few splotches on yours, you guys pretty much look spotless."

I stared at my shirt. Even though I hadn't sustained a direct hit from Ry's water gun, some of the stains on his clothes had transferred to mine when I'd been laying on top of him. "Pristine outfits kind of defeat the purpose of my project."

"I figured as much."

Wren and I accepted the Super Soakers he handed off to us, knowing we wouldn't be able to gang up on him again. And much to Ry's elation, our trio was joined by two bystanders. Now, the Crayola War was a free-for-all match of epic proportions. A shower of red, blue, orange, pink, and green littered the air in a colorful display. It reminded me of the little fight between two of the good fairies in *Sleeping Beauty* and their incessant dissent over whether pink or blue should reign supreme.

We battled to our heart's content until our stores of water had been depleted. Watching my friends, I realized this project was more than a simple visual representation of color. My teacher wanted his students to push past the limits of conventional thinking. Had I turned our bodies into living canvases and created something eye-catching?

Yes.

Yet, this project broke through those boundaries. The smile on Wren and Ryan's faces said it all. The real art being created today were the memories we would share for a lifetime.

chapter eleven

a total blackout

"EVERYONE SETTLE DOWN AND pull out your completed assignments," Jonas stated. Even though he was our teacher, calling him Mr. Elam just didn't feel right.

I filtered past a few of my classmates to my assigned table and proceeded to pull out the dried clothes and pictures I'd taken following the Crayola War. To be honest, the clothes turned out better than I was expecting. I was hoping for something similar to one of Monet's paintings, and that goal had been achieved.

Taking a quick survey of the room, I studied all the projects people had been working on. It seemed creativity knew no bounds. Some people had painted elaborate pots while others constructed ornate jewelry. One girl even painted classic fairytale scenes on a shawl.

"So far, I'm pleased with what I see. I wanted to push you to think outside the box and it looks like most of you ran with that idea." Jonas approached the front row, bending to get a better look at Ben's project. "I am going to talk to each of you about your projects and the inspiration behind them. Then I'm going to select my five favorites pieces. If your piece is chosen, you will be able to exhibit your work on an entire wall in the art show next month."

Hushed whispers sounded throughout the room at his announcement. The art show was a huge deal, and most students were lucky to get a single painting or drawing included. But an entire wall to ourselves? Shit . . . That was like the equivalent of giving a historian the Holy Grail.

I nervously chewed on my fingernails while waiting for Jonas to make his rounds. Walking into class, I had been so confident in the work I'd done, but after seeing a bit of everyone else's projects, that confidence faded. Who was I kidding?

Everyone else had spent their time working their fingers to the bone to create something beautiful while I basically played water tag with my friends.

Ugh.

Why in the actual fuck did my brain have to think of this now?

Whipping out my phone, I sent a quick text to Ry, hoping he could convince me I wasn't a complete and utter failure.

Me: *I feel like the biggest failure of all time. I mean, why did I even think my project was anything special? Compared to everyone else in my class, I'm a freaking amateur. I'll never be taken seriously as an artist.*

Almost immediately, my phone vibrated in my hand, and a sense of relief filled my bones as I realized he had already texted me back.

Ryan: *What are you talking about? Your project is great! Did someone say something to you about it?*

Me: *No. But I'm sitting here in class, and as I look at the projects everyone else has come up with, I can't help but feel that mine is subpar. I mean, we played with Super Soakers, for God's sake.*

Ryan: *Ter, you're the most creative person I've ever met in my life. Not only was your project extremely imaginative, it was a fucking blast too. And if anyone tells you anything different, I'll beat their ass.*

Me: *Promise?*

Ryan: *Of course. When do you get done with class?*

Me: *I still have two hours left.*

Ryan: *I won't be done with my internship until 5:00. Come over to my place at 5:30 and I'll spend all night convincing you of what an amazing artist you are.*

Unable to help myself, I chuckled at his text. It didn't matter what kinds of thoughts or negativity were swimming about my head, Ry always knew how to make me smile. Not to mention, there were so many sexual innuendos lurking in that message that it was impossible to keep a straight face.

Me: *You didn't think about how dirty that message sounded before you sent it, did you?*

Ryan: *Nope.*

Me: *LOL I suspected as much.*

Ryan: *I made you laugh though, didn't I?*

Me: *Yep.*

Ryan: *Mission accomplished. I'll see you later.*

Despite having a few momentary confidence issues, my smile never faded. No matter what Jonas thought about my project, I was going to hang out with Ry later. And that was reason enough to be happy.

Those positive vibes lasted until Jonas arrived at my table. "So, tell me what we have here," he said, reaching for one of the colored shirts I brought.

Tucking a loose strand of hair behind my ear, I explained my entire thought process behind the Crayola War. "Well, I was originally inspired by the impressionistic painting styles of Monet, but as I delved deeper into the assignment, I also realized that I'd drawn a lot of inspiration from my childhood. My friends and I used to spend our summers soaking one another with water guns, and I thought the nostalgia from those memories would also be interesting to incorporate."

"I can see that," Jonas murmured as he looked through all the pictures Wren, Ryan, and I had taken. "And it looks like the three of you had a lot of fun as well."

I laughed, my mind recalling the way Wren and I had stood victorious against Ry. "Not going to lie, it was a freaking blast."

"So, what is the true art you created here?"

I smiled, already knowing the answer to his question. "The memories."

"Care to elaborate on that?"

"When I started this project, I thought the clothes would be my medium, and then I changed my mind and decided the pictures would be the true art because they would capture all of our expressions. But then, after everything was said and done, I realized the true art was the laughter and fun I had with my friends. My memories of that experience will stay with me for a very long time."

Jonas nodded his head before breaking into a wide grin. "I love it."

"Really?"

"Yes. I pushed you to think outside the box and you delivered—not only with your actual concept, but with the art you created as well. Art is meant to touch our souls, and yours has clearly been touched."

He patted me on the shoulder before moving on to the next person. At that moment, I was riding on the highest of highs. Maybe my dreams of being an artist weren't as farfetched as I thought.

Jonas spent the remainder of the class analyzing each project. He spent a considerable amount of time not only studying the items we'd created but talking to us as well. After what felt like an eternity and a couple new sketches in my pad, he returned to the front of the classroom. "I want to commend each and every one of you for a job well done! You all took a difficult assignment and made it your own," he announced. "Thank you for making my decision a very hard one. However, my favorite projects were created by the following students: Ben, Amara, Janine, Zachary, and Terayn."

An invigorating mixture of surprise and elation surged through my body. Holy shit! Jonas liked my project enough to not only let me be in the art show but have an entire wall to myself as well. If I pinched myself, I would surely discover this was all some wild dream. So, just to be sure, I squeezed a bit of skin between my thumb and index finger. After a few seconds passed, I released my fingers and opened my eyes. But nothing had changed, and I most definitely wasn't dreaming.

"Hey! Nice job," Ben said, walking over to give me a high five.

"I should be saying the same thing to you!"

"Feels pretty good, doesn't it?"

"I think *incredible* is the word you're looking for," I answered.

"You're right. Well, I have another class after this, but I just wanted to come over and say congrats."

"Thanks, and same to you! I can't wait to see your wall in the show."

"Same here," he called out, backing up toward the door.

With a final wave, I slid the sketch pad and pens I'd been drawing with into my messenger bag.

"I don't see what is so great about her project. I mean, she just made tie-dye shirts," a voice stated loudly from behind me. "I'm sorry, but I thought we were supposed to create an actual work of art."

My vision went black. I spun around to see who the owner of the voice was. McKenzie stood before me with her arms crossed over her chest defiantly. Although her comment was directed at me, her friends flanked her on either side. So, she was unhappy with Jonas's selection but wasn't brave enough to speak up about it in class? "I spent hours on the necklace I made, and you got to have a water gun fight. How is that an accurate representation of all the work we put into this assignment?"

There was only so much insult I could withstand before opening my damn mouth. I mean, did she expect me to sit there and say nothing? I'm all for constructive criticism, but her bitchy tone was far from it.

"Believe what you want, but I put a lot of thought and effort into my project. Not to mention, Jonas likes it, so if you have an issue with the projects he selected, then you should take it up with him."

"I just think the quality of our projects should be taken into account."

"I'm sure he factored it into his deliberation. I'm sorry your project wasn't chosen, but I didn't make that decision. In fact, you're nothing more than a sore loser, so if you'll excuse me, I have somewhere to be." I flung my messenger bag over my shoulder dramatically and waltzed out of the classroom like her words had zero effect on me. Even if the venom spewing from her lips had infiltrated my brain.

McKenzie had taken the word *rude* to a whole 'nother level. I'd been floating on cloud nine ever since Jonas uttered my name, but that mood had been pretty much obliterated by McKenzie's comments.

With a heavy sigh, I headed toward my car and began the drive to Ryan's apartment. The pit stop I made for milkshakes was a necessity. There was no way I could face these feelings of inadequacy without massive amounts of sugar.

Walking up the steps leading to Ryan's apartment, I rang the doorbell and waited patiently for him to answer.

The moment the door opened, I barged inside. "Here," I said, handing off a strawberry milkshake.

"What is this for?" Ry asked.

"A bitch in my art class was super sucky and made me feel like a fraud so I decided to ease my pain with a couple of milkshakes."

"A couple?"

"I drank half of yours in the car. Sorry, I couldn't decide between chocolate and strawberry."

"That's okay," he replied with a slight laugh. "So, why don't you tell me what happened?"

Dropping my bag on the floor, I crossed the living room of Ry's apartment and collapsed on the couch. "Well, Jonas, my art teacher, selected my project as one of his five favorites out of the entire class."

"Ter, that's amazing! I mean, the top five in the class is a good thing, right?"

"Yeah," I sighed.

His brow furrowed in confusion. "Then tell me what's wrong." The couch cushions sank beneath his weight. I'd only been to Ry's apartment one other time. Everything was decorated in neutral tones, and he was clearly a neat freak, because not a speck of dust seemed to exist inside this space. Wanting to move closer, Ry lifted my feet and laid them in his lap, causing my heart to quicken its pace.

"The top five students are also going to be featured in the big art show next month. As a matter of fact, we each get an entire wall to ourselves to display our work."

"I knew your project would be a hit! Everyone is finally going to be able to see how talented you are."

"Well, not everyone. Because after class was over, McKenzie reduced my project to tie-dyed shirts and a water gun fight," I explained. "I mean, I know that my project was essentially a water gun fight, but she didn't have to shit all over it in front of me. At least do the decent thing and talk about it behind my back like a true Southern lady."

"I'm sorry," he breathed. "That was a very childish reaction on her part. I'm guessing her project wasn't one of the top five?"

"Nope." I sniffled. "I don't know why I'm being so emotional. I mean, usually, I'd let a comment like that roll off my back."

"Because you're proud of the project you created, and you have every right to be. That's why her jealous remarks sting so much."

"I'm sorry I drank most of your milkshake."

Setting down our cups on the coffee table just in front of us, Ry reached for me. "Come here." His arms encompassed me, acting as a source of protection from the outside world. "I don't know who this McKenzie is, but she sounds like a jealous bitch. You shouldn't buy into any comments made by someone who can't handle the fact their project wasn't one of the best."

"Yeah."

"I know there is more running around inside your head than that. Sure, maybe I haven't known you for very long, but I have a small idea as to how your brain works. That mind of yours is always ticking away at something. You know what it means to be hurt, to feel pain on a level deep enough to scar your soul. So, talk to me."

Releasing a breath, I leaned against him even more.

This was the type of thing I was trying so desperately to avoid. Opening up to someone other than Wren about all of my fears and doubts was impossible for me because I couldn't allow someone to gaze into that portion of my soul.

"For the most part, I don't let other people dictate anything about me or about the way I live my life," I began.

"Ter, I knew that about you the first time I heard you speak in statistics class."

The tips of my fingers tugged on the fabric of his shirt. I wasn't sure if it was possible to increase my hold on him, and yet, I still needed him closer. "You may also have picked up on the fact I don't talk about my family very much."

"I have."

"There are several reasons for that. For one, my mother is gone, and the void she left behind will never be filled. I was a teenager when she passed, and because I was so young, some of my other family members assumed my father needed their input in raising me," I confessed. "Art allowed me to cope with the death of my mother. It was a solace for me. I'd always enjoyed drawing and painting, but my need to create developed into a way for me to heal. And after that, I knew it was a path I wanted pursue both personally and professionally," I said. "My aunt disagreed. She didn't want me to study art in college. She thought it was impractical and that I wouldn't be able to find a job, and maybe she was right. I don't think she meant to hurt me, but even still, the words she uttered are out in the universe and they can never be unsaid."

"What did she say to you?"

"That being an artist wasn't a real job and that I needed to think of more practical ways to support myself.

She thought it was a beautiful dream, and it should stay simply . . . a dream."

"What did your dad think about it?"

"He disagreed, of course. He encouraged me to follow my passions, but there was always that lingering voice in the back of my mind wondering if I would ever be able to make it as an artist. Would I struggle to feed myself on a daily basis? Would I have to wait tables for the rest of my life in order to make ends meet? Would I ever be good enough?"

"A lot of people struggle with those exact same questions. My mother did. She worked two jobs for several years just to support us. And after she went back to school and finished her degree, she managed to get a better job and didn't have to run herself into the ground anymore," he replied in a soft voice.

The continuous circular patterns his thumbs traced on my back were the most soothing form of comfort I'd known other than my mother's voice. Surely, the embrace of someone I'd been friends with for a week shouldn't hold so much power over me. Ry and I never discussed the fact we almost kissed during the Crayola War. But the moment we'd shared—gazes locked, lips a breath apart—had been burned into the recesses of my mind, never to be forgotten.

"Your mom sounds like an amazing woman."

"She is, but then again, so are you," he agreed. "And I think if your mother were still here, she would want you to be happy above everything else. Even if pursuing your passion is a risky choice, it's one I'm fairly certain she would want you to make. You are talented enough to make a career out of selling your work, and whatever lasting insecurities you possess about that fact, you need to let go of them."

"I know, but that's easier said than done."

"Then just take it one step at a time."

"How?"

"Create some paintings that will blow everyone away at the art show next month. Show them your ingenuity, your talent, and your drive."

"You really think I can do that?"

"I know you can."

Smiling against his chest, I savored all the confidence he had in me. By listening to me, by comforting me, he eased the insecurities and self-doubt that had been eating away at me. If he believed in me so fiercely, then shouldn't I believe in myself as well? "Okay. I'll do it."

"Good."

His arms released me, and reluctantly, I pulled away. Moving to opposite ends of the couch, we each picked up our milkshake.

"Thank you for everything."

"You're welcome."

For the first time since I'd arrived at his apartment, I took a second to glance around the room I was sitting in. Ry's place was small, but it still had more space than Wren's. A combined living room and kitchen led to a short hallway that was connected to his bedroom. I hadn't been back there yet, and the thought piqued my curiosity. You could learn a lot about a person by looking at their bedroom.

"Will you show me your room?" I questioned.

A smile that could give the Cheshire Cat a run for his money spread across Ry's face. I should've caught the implications lurking in the question I had asked, but it wasn't until his eyebrow arched that I realized I was in trouble. "And what do you want to do in my room?"

His question earned him a swift punch.

"Ow!" he cried out, massaging his arm. "What was that for?"

"Having your mind in the gutter."

"Alright, you got me there."

"No shit," I answered, jumping to my feet. "Well, lead the way."

To my surprise, Ry rolled his eyes at me. "Fine."

"You just rolled your eyes at me!"

"I've seen you do it enough times, I feel like I could be an expert at it."

I huffed loudly to demonstrate my annoyance. "Smartass," I muttered under my breath.

"Alright, here you go."

I scanned every part of his room. Just like the living areas, this room was also immaculate. The sheets and comforter covering his bed were navy blue and matched the curtains. His bedframe and dresser had been made out of a dark wood. A row of running shoes was perfectly positioned at the foot of his bed. The entire space exuded masculinity, except for a single picture hanging above his bed.

I nearly stopped breathing as I recognized the drawing I had given Ryan for helping me prank Brooklyn.

"You framed the sketch I gave you?"

"Of course."

"Why?" I questioned, unable to tear my eyes from the black frame encasing the orchid I'd drawn.

"Because who doesn't want to wake up and see something beautiful every single day?"

His question may have been in reference to my sketch, but a tiny voice in the deep crevices of my consciousness almost wished he was talking about me.

And it was a voice I wouldn't be able to ignore for much longer.

chapter twelve

singing nothing but the blues

WHAT I CONSIDERED TO be my normal routine had changed completely in the weeks following the Crayola War. Before, whenever Wren was at work, I would hang out in the common room of my dorm. But after meeting Ryan, I started spending most of my time with him. It was a nice change of pace from always being alone. And whenever Wren was actually off work, the three of us were inseparable.

When Ry first approached me in statistics class, I may have thought he was just a hottie with the best blue eyes I'd ever seen, but his sincerity and kindness never ceased to amaze me. Separate and together, Wren and I were nothing short of a handful, but Ry had no trouble keeping up with us. If anything, he was the one we had to keep in line at times.

"Thanks," I said, accepting the gummy bears Wren dropped in my hand.

"Do you guys always watch the same movies every year?"

"Sometimes," Wren answered, handing off the bag of

gummy bears to Ryan. "As far as Halloween movies go, we watch *Hocus Pocus*, *Nightmare on Elm Street*, and *The Crow* every year. Other than that, we mix it up."

"Are there any scary movies you don't care for?" he questioned.

"We don't watch anything with clowns in it," I answered. "Wren hates clowns."

Wren grimaced at the word, a visible shiver coursing down her spine. "They're Satan's minions."

"Not really going to disagree with you there," Ryan added with a laugh.

"I mean, whoever thought they were an appropriate source of amusement and laughter for children should have their head examined. Everything about those fuckers is so creepy! I really don't get it."

Sliding my arm around her, I moved to rest my head on her shoulder. "I agree one hundred percent, babe."

"You're the best."

"Anything you're afraid of?" Ry asked, turning his attention to me.

Committed romantic relationships was the first reply to pop inside my head. It had occurred to me on more than one occasion that watching the suffering and heartbreak my father had endured in the aftermath of Mom's death had damaged me beyond repair. I feared neither death nor solitude. Both were outcomes I could accept without hesitation. I was strong and had withstood my fair share of pain. But loving someone so deeply that their soul merged with mine—only to lose them later in life—was something I couldn't bear. It was a fate from which there was no return.

"Spiders," I answered after a long pause.

"Spiders?"

"That's what I said."

The intensity of his blue gaze startled me. He knew I wasn't being completely honest and that I had been lost in my thoughts again, and I could only wonder if he would call me out on my fib. "If you say so."

"I do."

Per usual, Wren watched our exchange with a look of utter fascination. Her incessant prodding about the budding relationship between Ry and me was starting to piss me off. She believed that after enough nagging, I'd raise my white flag. However, I could only hope she was fond of disappointment, because her two friends were experts at avoidance.

"Well then, what are you afraid of?" I posed my question with an overabundance of sass, hoping I'd be able to turn the tables on him.

"Being cheated on."

His blatant honesty stunned Wren and I into silence. Not only was his confession something we'd never heard him talk about before, but Wren could comprehend his fear better than anyone. For the most part, Ry was private about his dating life. He never divulged any details about past entanglements or current prospects, so this revelation was a complete shock.

The heaviness lacing his voice made my heart ache. A betrayal of that kind changed a person. In a relationship, trust must be earned. But when that faith is destroyed, it can seldom be repaired. When he finally met my gaze, an eternity of pain swam in the depths of those blue irises. Slowly, I moved to sit on the other side of him. I may not have known the source of his sadness, but I wanted to do everything within my power to make it dissipate.

"I'm sorry," I breathed, laying my head on his shoulder.

On his right, Wren mirrored me. "You're one of the

best guys I've ever met, and you know we're glad to have you as our friend," she whispered.

"What she said."

Ryan shifted to slide his arms around our waists. In an instant, I was reminded of the night the three of us slept in Wren's bed. Even though she didn't cry, her despair was almost palpable. She was in pieces, so Ry and I held on to her in the hopes we could keep her from breaking even more. And now, Wren and I surrounded Ryan, holding on to him in the hope we would be able to instill even a small amount of comfort into his soul.

"Did someone betray your trust?" Wren questioned.

"Yes."

"When I caught Liam with his ex, I was so stunned that it took a couple days for the weight of his betrayal to sink in. And when it did, I felt so used, so disposable. It's damaged my ability to trust. I doubt I'll ever be able to have a relationship where I don't suspect every sweet word is a lie." Her voice was hoarse, a flurry of sentiments dampening the usual light tone. "I can say that talking about what happened has definitely helped me. I know it's hard to open up, but if you ever want to talk about it, we're more than willing to listen."

"As much as you've been there for us in the past few weeks, we are here for you," I added. "And if there is something we can do to help, please let us know."

"Thank you," he croaked.

Sometimes, words failed to accurately capture our emotions. We were only human, and our shortcomings were plenty. But hopefully, Ry understood that we were here for him, that he could count on us.

"Whenever you're ready, we'll be here."

"I appreciate it."

The thought of someone cheating on Ry seemed

unfathomable. He had it all, and he was one of the most considerate human beings I'd ever met. Who could throw away someone like that?

For one thing, she'd have to be insane.

With a heavy sigh, Ry leaned forward to grab his beer. After draining the rest of the bottle, he stood. "I'm getting another. Do you guys want one?"

"Sure."

"I'll take one too," Wren added.

"Alright. I'll be right back."

I watched to make sure he was out of earshot before leaning in toward Wren.

"I feel so bad," I said in the softest voice I could manage.

"I know. He nearly broke my heart."

"He's the sweetest guy I've ever met."

"Yes, Ter, I'm well aware of the fact."

"No one likes a smartass."

"Glass or bottle?" Ry shouted his question from the kitchen.

"Bottle is fine for both of us," Wren answered, loud enough for him to hear.

"Do we need more popcorn?"

"Yes! That would be great," she called back to him.

The familiar sounds of a microwave roared to life.

Dropping my voice even further, I slid closer to ask, "I mean, what kind of girl would be stupid enough to pass him up?"

She leveled me with a glare that was strong enough to topple a building. "Yes, what kind of girl, indeed?"

"I have my reasons, and so does he."

A smirk altered her features. "So you admit there is something between the two of you?"

"It's not like that."

Que eyeroll. "But isn't it, though?"

"No!"

"All I'm saying is that you have a hard time letting yourself connect with another person in that way, and from the sound of it, so does he. A guy who can understand the pain you've been through and your reservations about being in a relationship is someone you don't throw away. Trust me on this one, babe."

"Putting it like that makes it all sound so easy, and it's not."

"I know. One step at a time."

I smiled at her choice of words. "He told me that a few weeks ago."

"It's good advice."

I nodded. "I'm working on it. Believe me, part of me wants to be brave."

"Sometimes, the hope that things can change and be different is all you need."

A heavy combination of sadness, hope, regret, and fear spun together, like paint mixed on a palette. It always seemed to be so contradictory how a multitude of emotions could all exist at the same time. I mean, is there a person who has only felt a single emotion at any given moment in time? Personally, I found the prospect to be unimaginable. The feelings locked within the human mind were as vast as the sea.

Or at least, that's how I was. And I had the strange suspicion Ry was the same way.

"Have the two of you talked about what almost happened at the Crayola War?"

I knew the fact she hadn't interrogated me at length about the almost kiss Ry and I shared was because she was waiting until the perfect time. There was no way she would forget about it; I wasn't that lucky. But if I was being honest with myself, I would be the exact same. If our roles were reversed and there was an amazing guy who was interested in Wren, I would pester the fuck out of her about it until she admitted defeat. Sure, mothers knew best, but sometimes even they didn't have the ability to call you out on your shit like a best friend could.

"Nope. We've been avoiding it like the plague."

"Funny."

Shrugging, I gave her a sly smile. "I thought so."

"Joke around all you want, but the longer you wait, the deeper in you'll be."

Her statement had an eerie ring to it, as if the statement she made was more a promise than anything else.

The sound of Ry approaching brought our conversation to a screeching halt. "Here are the beers," he said, handing one to each of us. "I'll be right back with the popcorn." Less than a minute later, the three of us were seated in front of the television, ready to watch *The Crow*. A sea of popcorn, candy, and beer bottles littered the floor around us. We were gearing up for a scary movie marathon that would last until morning. Nights like this were a blast. Wren and I had been like sisters for so long, and it wasn't until we met Ry that we realized something was missing . . . him.

As much as I denied it, and as much as I wanted to ignore it, something was happening between the two of us. And if I didn't figure out what to do about it, the dynamic of our trio would suffer the consequences.

"Sorry if I dampened the mood with my confession earlier," Ry said as he started the movie.

"Don't be. Dealing with stuff is hard."

"Yeah," Wren agreed. "It's why B.B. King, Buddy Guy, and Muddy Waters sang the blues. Because how else were they supposed to deal with all their shit?"

"You've got a point there."

"So after this movie marathon, are we going to sing the blues together?" I questioned.

Ry gave me a rue smile for the first time tonight. "I've got Buddy Guy on my iPod."

chapter thirteen

black satin

A COUPLE OF DAYS after our movie marathon, the three of us were dressing in our costumes and preparing to dance the night away. I'd opted for the iconic black satin uniform, bowtie, and bunny ears. With my hair curled to perfection and my body clad in a revealing costume, I felt every bit a Playboy Bunny. As I was dabbing on a fresh layer of red lipstick, Ry joined me in his living room.

"So, how do I look?" he asked, waltzing into the room like a contestant in the Miss America pageant. The sight of Ryan wearing a bustier almost identical to mine and high heels was one of the best things I'd ever seen in my entire life. Part of me had believed he wouldn't have the balls to dress like a woman, but I'd be damned if he didn't prove me wrong.

"Tim Curry wore it better."

"Is it because I'm missing the pearls?"

"Oh my God!" Wren screamed, running up to Ryan. "You actually fucking did it! Ter, do you see this right now?"

"No. I missed the giant man wearing women's hosiery,"

I deadpanned.

"Someone needs an alcoholic beverage . . . or maybe five."

I stuck my tongue out at her. "I mean, he's pretty much impossible to miss."

I watched as she tied the ends of the smoking jacket she wore. From head to toe, she was dressed like Hugh Hefner. Girl even had the pipe and matching slippers to boot. "This is going to be the best Halloween ever!"

"Alright, tell me I did a good job." Ry slid next to Wren and flung his arm around her shoulders. "I mean, come on, we look fucking amazing."

Tapping my finger against my chin, I pretended to be contemplating his assertion. "I don't know. I feel like something is missing."

As I glanced between the two of them, Wren and Ry regarded me with confusion.

"Me! Duh." Jumping to my feet, I sauntered over in my too tall heels and positioned myself on Wren's left.

Across from me, Ry gave me a once-over. My skin burned as if I'd been slapped on a spit roast and held over an open flame. That look was one I knew all too well. I'd seen it before, on the night we stripped down to our underwear and pretended to be lovers.

And oh, what a night that had been. My hands running through his hair while his cradled my body was a memory I never wanted to forget.

"You look incredible," he said, his voice slightly catching.

I winked at him. Usually, I loved our relentless back and forth banter, but for the rest of the night, I wanted us to be honest with one another. "I think you look incredible too."

"Do I need to get my ears checked, or did she just

compliment me?" he asked, directing his question to Wren.

"No, I heard it too! And she's checking you out too."

"I am," I admitted. "You look hot in women's lingerie. Sue me."

"Hell yes!" he shouted. "This officially just became the best damn night of my life, and you know what that means!"

"Shots!" Wren cried, spinning in a circle.

"All the shots!" I added.

After three shots of tequila for each of us, we were ready to call a cab to take us out. One of the clubs downtown was hosting a costume contest, and I could feel it in my bones that the three of us were destined to win it. By the time we reached Club NV, we had passed the giddy drunk phase and had landed in the "trust me, you can dance like a god" phase. Music pounded in our eardrums, the beat infusing itself into our bloodstream. A sea of bodies swayed in time with the beat. It seemed we weren't the only ones set on having a killer Halloween.

Wren's hand closed around my wrist as she pulled me out to the dance floor. The girl had insane moves, and whenever a good song was playing, it was impossible for her to keep still.

"You don't want to get a drink first?" I asked.

"Hell no! I want to dance, bitch!"

Our laughter was lost in the crowd as we made our way to the center of the dance floor. Alcohol surged through my veins as my body submitted to its will. Cheers rang out as Ry joined us, his costume earning him a multitude of high fives.

"Alright, which one of us gets to be in the middle of this ass shaking train?" he asked with a devious grin.

"You pick."

Ry's hand fastened around my waist at my reply.

Pulling me into him, my breath faltered as his chest met with my back. "How is this?" he asked, whispering into my ear.

We were in a club that was packed to the brim, but the second his warm breath hit my ear, we might as well have been alone for all I cared. "Feels nice."

Liquor did precisely two things to my body. It made me shake my ass like a Laker Girl, and it made me honest. A combination that was especially dangerous while in close proximity with Ry. But for one night, screw danger. Standing on the sidelines never made anyone happy. If some unseen force was pulling Ry and I together for the past month, who was I to put up a fight?

"Is that so?"

"Yes, more than you could ever know."

My comment was the equivalent of showing caution the middle finger and jumping off the ledge.

"I'll be honest," he began so only I could hear him. "That is music to my ears." The tips of his fingers traveled leisurely from my waist to the tops of my thighs. Sighing, I reveled in the way his skin felt against mine. The two of us sharing the same space, the same air, was absolute bliss.

"You must be feeling bold tonight."

"How can I not when your grinding your ass against me?"

"I take it you don't want me to stop?"

"Not at all." His lips brushed against the back of my neck, making me wish we were alone in his room.

Giggling, I spun around to face him. "I like it when you're drunk," I confessed.

"Am I reminding you of our dorm room scheme?"

"Maybe." Shoving my chest into his, I increased my hold on him. "Could we recreate our scheme, but for real?" I gasped upon realizing what I was truly asking him.

Being cautious only forced me to suppress my desires. And now that my body was imbued with liquid courage, my brain wasn't telling me to hold my tongue.

"There is nothing I want more. But not like this, not wasted."

I bit my lip, a smile drawing the edges of my mouth upward. "Agreed."

Just as he set his forehead against mine, Wren began screaming. "Fucking finally!"

Our arms wrapped around one another like vines, sealing our intimate embrace. At first, I wasn't sure what Wren was screaming about, but after another high-pitched squeal, I realized we were the cause of her excitement.

Grinning from ear to ear, Ry stared down at me. "We probably shouldn't disappoint her then." His mouth dropped to the side of my neck, gently kissing my flesh.

"Probably not." I wasn't sure if he'd heard the words I'd uttered. Hell, I wasn't sure I'd spoken them in the first place. And I was too distracted to even care.

"Is everyone having a good time out there?" The sound of the DJ's voice boomed all around us and every soul inside the club screamed in answer. "We're just about to kick off the costume contest, so if you think you've got what it takes to win, line up at my booth in the next five minutes and we'll get started. The winners will receive a one-hundred-dollar prize and free drinks."

More cheers and applause broke out among the crowd.

"Oh! We are so entering that shit!" Wren called out, grabbing Ry and I by our wrists.

It was the second time we had almost kissed, and I wasn't sure my body could handle a third. The waiting, the thundering of my heart inside my chest, was enough to incapacitate me. I was ready to discover the way his lips felt against mine.

We flocked with a dozen others to join the line for the costume contest. Ours might not have been as original as some of the others, but we did have a hot guy wearing women's lingerie in our group, and I was feeling especially confident about that fact.

"Okay, first up in our costume contest, we have Bonnie and Clyde!"

A couple dressed in Depression era clothing made their way onto the small stage by the DJ booth. They pretended to tango, much to the excitement of their onlookers.

"Up next we have Julius Caesar and Cleopatra!"

Again, the couple danced a bit and really played up the characters they were portraying. It was obvious the competition in this contest was going to be especially stiff.

The three of us waited patiently as the DJ called out each of the contestants who were in line before us. With each entry, the cheers seemed to grow louder. It was going to be a tough decision because everyone was dressed to the nines for the holiday. When it was finally our turn, excitement churned in the pit of my stomach.

"And last but certainly not least, we have Hugh Hefner and his Playboy Bunnies!"

Ry and I looped our arms through Wren's and allowed her to escort us on stage. A mixture of applause and screaming filled our ears as we modeled our costumes. Wanting to add to the fun, Wren slapped Ry and I on our asses, causing the audience to cheer even louder. Then, to top off our entire charade, Ry sauntered to the edge of the stage and dropped it like it was fucking hot.

The screams of all the women in the room drowned out the music playing overhead. If I thought we had a good chance at winning the contest before, that move just sealed the deal.

Holy hell. Ry could dance too? The revelation was

almost too much for my tequila-addled brain to handle. Seriously, drunk me knew he was the perfect guy, so what was the hold up for my sober alter ego?

Laughing, the DJ grabbed a microphone and joined us onstage. "That was one hell of a costume contest, wasn't it?" he asked, smiling as the crowd roared. "When I point to each contestant or group, I want you to scream as loud as you can for who you think should win. Whoever gets the loudest response will be the winner."

One by one, he went through everyone before finally reaching the three of us. "And let's hear it for Hef and his Bunnies!"

The crowd's response was overwhelming. Whistles and screams flooded the room with noise, marking us as the clear winners.

"And it seems like the winners are Hef and his Bunnies! Show them some love!"

Unable to temper their excitement, Ry and Wren bombarded me with hugs.

"I can't believe we just fucking won that!" Wren screamed. "Oh my God. That was so much fun!"

"Shout out to the MVP who secured us this win!"

Wren and I surprised Ry by kissing him on each cheek. "I want to celebrate this victory by taking some shots with my girls!"

I cheered loudly at his suggestion. "Hell yes!"

Ry accepted the gift card from the DJ before the three of us jumped off the stage. Weaving through the crowd, we left the dance floor behind and headed for the bar to claim our free round of drinks.

"Six shots of Jack Daniels," Ry called out to the bartender.

Like magic, six shot glasses filled with amber liquid appeared before us.

I held my shot glass up in the air to make a toast. "To black satin bustiers and high heels."

Clinking our glasses together, Ryan added, "Fuck yes."

Wren downed her shot like a damn pro. The girl never had any trouble holding her whiskey. "This has been the best night!"

After another hour of dancing and drinking to our hearts' content, I couldn't have agreed more with Wren's statement. The night had surpassed being amazing and had hurtled into epic territory.

But I'd spoken too soon. Suddenly, Wren froze beside me, her body halting despite the upbeat tune playing. Following her gaze, I cursed as I laid eyes on Liam.

"What the hell is he doing here?" I asked, my voice the epitome of hatred.

"To destroy my night."

"That's him?" Ry asked her.

Wren nodded in response, her giddy expression from moments ago completely obliterated. "Yeah."

The three of us watched as Liam ground his crotch against some random chick's ass. It infuriated me that he was out living his fucking life to the fullest with no regard for the pain, suffering, and embarrassment he'd put my friend through. The fucking nerve of that asshole.

"That fucking piece of shit," I spat. Pure hatred infiltrated my mind, causing me to see red.

"I couldn't agree with you more." Ry moved to stand next to Wren, his glare never breaking from Liam.

"This isn't fucking fair!" she screamed. "I'm over here feeling every bit the broken, used, discarded mess he tossed to the side, and he's out there rubbing his dick on anything with tits and a pulse."

"I'm sorry, babe. Tell me what I can do to make it better."

"One night of fun is all I wanted. Is that too much to ask for? Am I undeserving or something?"

"Of course not," Ry added in a soothing tone.

Turning to him, she buried her face in his chest, her body shaking. "I can't take it anymore. This pit, this endless hole he left me in, is too much for me to bear."

All around us, people continued writhing their bodies in time to the music. They were none the wiser about the despair creeping into my best friend's heart.

"Have we tipped the bartender yet?" Ry asked.

Wren's brow furrowed as she looked up at him. "Yeah. Why?"

"Because this will probably get us kicked out of here." He released her and stormed for the far side of the dance floor.

"Wait!" I called out to him, trying to keep his pace. Even with heels on, the guy could still book it. "What are you going to do?"

"Settle the fucking score!"

There was only one thing he could mean. Wren and I stared at him in shock for a brief moment. The look of seething, unadulterated rage masking his blue eyes was something I'd never seen from him before. Animosity seemed to radiate from every part of his flesh. Whatever fate he had in mind for Liam was sure to include his fists.

And my heart leapt with joy at the thought.

Ry approached Liam with his fists balled. One word was all it was going to take for him to snap.

"Hey, man, is your name Liam?"

"Yeah. What of it?" Liam asked, shouting his question as he broke away from the girl he was dancing with.

His cocky attitude was the equivalent of nails on a chalkboard. I couldn't stand it.

"It seems you used to know my friend here."

Liam's gaze shifted past Ry, focusing on Wren. The fucker even had the nerve to smirk at her. "So you've picked up my leftovers?"

A fire lit behind my eyes. I lunged forward, but Ry caught me before I could land my hands around Liam's throat. "I'll rip your fucking throat out, you piece of shit!"

"Ter, calm down and let me handle this," Ry ordered with complete authority. "I'm going to ask that you apologize to Wren."

Liam laughed at the suggestion. "Yeah, right."

Wrath welled inside me, so much that I had to keep myself in check as Ry released me.

Nodding, Ry smirked. "In a few minutes, you'll be regretting that decision." Then he turned to Wren and kissed her forehead. "Just so you know, this is for you."

She glanced up at him hopefully, water swimming in her brown eyes. In this moment, if Ry could help ease her pain, I would be forever grateful.

Without warning, Ry stomped toward Liam and cocked his fist. The prick didn't even know what was coming until the sound of his laughter was silenced. Ry's fist collided with Liam's jaw hard enough to make me wince. If the music hadn't been so loud, I was positive the sound of breaking bones would have been heard throughout the room.

"I dare you to laugh at her again, you fucking asshole!" Ry shouted as he dragged Liam to his feet. Over and over again, he punched Liam until a shower of blood sprayed from his mouth. The spectacle had drawn the attention of those nearby, and a circle formed around us, making escape impossible for Liam. Although, I seriously doubted he was still capable of coherent thoughts with the way Ry was laying into him. "How about now? Are you fucking sorry yet?" Ry's voice boomed, silencing everyone. "I asked you a question. Are you fucking sorry yet?"

Liam held up his hands in defeat. Blood dripped from his palms as he pleaded with Ry to stop. "I'm sorry, I'm sorry! Please, no more."

"Say it again."

"I'm sorry!"

"To her, not me, you fucking idiot." Ry had a death grip on Liam's collar. The only way this was going to end was with more blood.

Liam's eyes filled with fear as he looked at Wren. "I'm sorry."

"For what?" Ry asked, shouting his question.

"For fucking you over," he cried out.

"That's what I thought." Ry dropped him like a sack of bricks, and I'd be lying if I said I didn't savor the way his body smacked against the cement floor. Leaving Liam a bloody mess on the floor, Ry draped his arm over Wren's shoulders, leading her away from the dance floor.

I was a person of faith. The concept of right and wrong had been instilled into me from a young age. But at the same time, Wren was my ride-or-die, and I would never forgive myself if I didn't get my own chance to stick up for her.

Sauntering up to Liam, I stared down at him like he was nothing more than a speck of dirt on my black pumps. "Where you are right now is where you belong, you fucking worthless piece of shit." I smiled at his pain and reeled my foot back. "You never deserved Wren in the first place. Remember that." With my final word, I kicked Liam as hard as I could in his crotch. His howls of pain were music to my ears.

"Oh my God, Ter!" Wren yelled.

"Just try to cheat on another girl with that mangled

thing!"

Ry beamed at me with pride. Offering up his hand for a high five. "Nice job!"

"Nobody fucks with our girl!"

"The three of you, out! Now!" A menacing bouncer appeared before us just as we stepped off the dance floor.

"Sorry, man. We're already on our way," Ry promised. "We won't cause any more trouble."

The bouncer focused his attention on Wren and I. We smiled sweetly because getting arrested was not on our to-do list for the evening. "He make a pass at one of your girls?"

"That's putting it mildly."

Nodding, the bouncer moved out of the way. "I've got a younger sister, so I understand completely."

"Thank you," I said as we passed him.

The bouncer grunted in reply, disappearing into the crowd.

I breathed a sigh of relief as we exited the club. A cool breeze blew by, prompting the three of us to huddle together.

"I don't know what to say, you guys." Wren's voice shook as she spoke. "I mean, the way y'all stuck up for me . . . I'll never forget it."

"You deserve way more than an asshole like that, and never forget it."

"I'm with him. Don't let one prick make you question your own worth. You're priceless, babe," I added with a smile.

"I know I said this before, but this is still the best night ever. I love you guys."

Flinging my arms around her, I held on tight to her. "We love you too."

"How's your fist?" she asked Ry.

Red coated his knuckles. "Couldn't be better."

"Should we keep the party going?" I questioned.

"Hell yes!" she shouted. "I'm not ready for this night to end just yet."

"Same here. Let me call us a cab," Ry offered.

He stepped away from the group as he whipped out his cell phone. I wasn't exactly sure where he'd stashed it, but if I had to guess, I was going to say the breast area of his bustier.

Sidling up next to me, Wren threw her arm around me in an attempt to fight off the cold. "I really want to make this a night to remember!"

She stared at me in confusion for half a second. "Right, because winning a costume contest, watching Liam get his ass kicked, and seeing Ryan wear women's lingerie aren't memorable enough," she replied sarcastically.

I rolled my eyes. So much sass shouldn't be able to fit in such a tiny frame. "This night has to be one to remember."

"What do you have in mind?"

"Streaking."

"Us?"

I beamed at her, my expression a combination of excitement and mischief. "Him. Think he would do it?"

She chuckled, shaking her head. "You won't let yourself realize it yet, but there isn't much that boy wouldn't do for you."

"I think I'm beginning to realize it."

"Well then, you're in deep shit."

"You're not telling me anything I don't already know."

"It's okay to let yourself fall for him." She squeezed me even tighter. "That's something you don't know."

Damn, even drunk off liquor and on cloud nine after seeing her ex beaten to a pulp, the girl still had a point.

And I was still the one who needed a wake-up call.

chapter fourteen

fields of yellow flowers

HALLOWEEN WAS A NIGHT I was going to remember until the end of time. Karma was a bitch, and apparently, said bitch was code for Ry beating Liam into the ground. Call it petty, call it whatever you want, but the sight had brought my girl some semblance of peace—and I would relish in that fact forever. She should be treated like a queen, and as her friend, it was my duty to remind her of it.

Pushing open the door, I exited the art building and made my way across campus. I'd just gotten out of my meeting with Jonas. He had asked me to relay my ideas for my wall in the art show. So far, the only complete painting I'd done was the piece of my mother. It was a beautiful depiction of her, but I knew Jonas would want me to delve deeper for the show. *Dive into the deep recesses of your soul and pick out something that frightens you. You're great at evoking emotions with your work, but I know you can push yourself further. Give us something to remember.*

Jonas's advice rang inside my mind.

Hadn't Wren been pushing me to do the same thing?

There was only one thing I was afraid of, and that was suffering the same fate as my dad had.

No sooner than I had the thought, my phone began to vibrate. Staring at the screen, I saw the object of my thoughts was the person calling me.

"Hey, Daddy."

"Hey, angel. How was Halloween?" he asked. "I know you said you were going out with Wren and your new friend, Ryan."

"We had a great time! We even managed to win a costume contest at the club we went to."

"Sounds like it was a fun night then."

"Yeah. I really enjoy spending time with Ry. He's a good guy."

"Any young man who can keep Wren and you in line has my vote of approval."

"Dad!"

His laughter vibrated through the phone. "You know I'm only joking. He better be good to you girls," Dad replied in a slightly sterner tone of voice.

"I should've known idle threats were coming."

"What? Am I not allowed to be concerned about my favorite daughter?"

Huffing as loud as I could, I hoped he could sense my annoyance. "I'm your only daughter."

"And that's what makes the joke so funny."

It had only been a couple days since the last time we had talked, but in the past few weeks, his voice didn't seem quite so heavy.

"Whatever."

"So, this guy, Ryan. Are you interested in him as more than a friend?"

Unlike most girls my age, I was comfortable talking about guys with my dad. That isn't to say we discussed my sex life . . . because that would be awkward as hell, but Dad always liked to know if there was a guy I was interested in. As a single parent, he had to fulfill both roles in my life, which meant acting as a mother and a father.

"Yeah, I think I might be."

"You know what your mom would say."

I sighed heavily, my eyes closing as I imagined the advice she would've given me if she were still alive. "I know, but that's easier said than done." Stopping at the bottom of the steps leading to my dorm, I glanced up at the sky. In the depths of my being, I believed Mom was in a better place, that she was in heaven. She was one of those people who lived unapologetically. Her spirit was wild, her heart bursting with kindness, and she was as brave as they come.

But not me. Compared to her, I was nothing more than a coward.

"Life doesn't have to be perfect. Most of the time, it's messy and the majority of us have no idea what the hell we're doing. But there is one thing which makes it all worthwhile."

"And what is that?"

"Finding someone to share your time with."

His statement stilled the breath in my lungs. "What do I do if there isn't anyone for me?"

"There is."

"Right."

"You have to be brave enough to give them a chance."

Dad was the only person besides Wren who had the ability to call me out on my shit. I continued to stand on the concrete steps as I nervously twisted a strand of my hair. "What if I'm not?"

"You are."

"You always have so much confidence in me."

"That's because you take after your mother."

"You make it sound so simple."

He chuckled, his typical reaction whenever I whined about something. "I said you needed to be brave, not that the task would be simple."

"Do you enjoy lecturing me?"

"As a matter of fact, yes. It's one of the perks of being a father."

"Alright, so I need to be brave. Is there any other advice you would like to give me?"

He was silent for a moment before replying. "Yeah, get the oil changed in your car and study."

"Richard Andrews, ladies and gentlemen . . . Father of the Year," I teased.

"Well, I'm sure you're busy brainstorming ideas for the big art show, so I won't keep you any longer."

"Okay."

"Just promise me that you'll take a risk on something."

He said the word *something*, but deep down, we both knew he meant someone. A chill crept up the back of my neck as I realized the advice my dad was giving me was the same thing Jonas had told me in our meeting. Both wanted me to be brave, to face my fears, and I only hoped to God I wouldn't let either of them down.

"I promise," I whispered.

"Call me if you need anything, and I'll talk to you in a few days."

"I will. I love you, Daddy."

"I love you too."

I sucked in a deep breath to settle my nerves. The tips of my fingers wiped away the lone tear trailing down my cheek.

All right, universe, duly *fucking* noted. I was all in favor of searching for signs or listening to the world around me, but honestly, it didn't feel so amazing when I was the one being smacked in the face.

What was I afraid of?

Love . . . loss . . . or some amalgamation of the two? I didn't believe an existence teeming with regret could still be considered living. Sure, the body would continue to function. The heart would beat, the tongue would taste, and the lungs would breathe, but does an empty shell equate to true life?

No, it doesn't.

I was afraid of that hospital bed and all the machines hooked up to her frail body. For months, I lived moment to moment, wondering when it would be the last time I heard her voice. At the end, she felt no pain. She simply closed her eyes and never woke up. My mother left this world with as much grace as she entered it.

But even drawing my last breath was not my greatest fear. The thing I feared most in this world was sharing the same fate as my parents. My father held my mother's hand as cancer riddled her body—he was there the last time she opened her eyes, and he stood in the rain, watching as his wife's casket was lowered into the earth.

My father had been fortunate enough to find the person who completed his soul. Yet, his good fortune came to an end. He lost his other half, and he would never be whole again.

A lump appeared in the back of my throat. Scrambling up the steps to my dorm, I had to get inside before I lost my nerve. My hands seemed to move of their own volition as I swiped my key card and pushed through the door. I scaled more steps, or at least I think I did. My mind was in such a daze that it was impossible to do more than breathe in and out.

When I finally reached my room, I was relieved to find

it empty. Tubes of paint, brushes, and paper were strewn across my bed. In an instant, I gathered up everything I could lay my hands on and shoved it in my duffel bag until the seams were ready to burst. Tears dripped from my chin as I stormed back into the hallway. There was somewhere I needed to be.

I pulled out my phone and clicked on Ry's number, my heart picking up speed with each ring. An eternity passed as I waited for him to answer.

"Damnit, Ry. Answer the freaking phone."

"Hey, what's up?" The sound of his voice was the equivalent of angels singing a beautiful melody.

"Where are you?"

"I just left Halstead. I had to complete a few hours for my internship today."

"Oh, that's right. I forgot about that."

"Your voice sounds off. What's wrong?"

Sniffling, I tried my best to sound composed. "I-I just . . . need to come over."

I heard him unlock his Jeep. "I can be at my apartment in ten minutes. Is that okay? Or do you need me to come pick you up?"

"I can drive."

"Are you sure?" he asked.

"Yeah. I'll see you soon."

"Okay."

The drive to Ry's apartment passed in a blur. My body went through the motions, but it was as if no one was home. So many thoughts bombarded my consciousness. Anxiety, turmoil, and despair bubbled in the pit of my stomach. As I climbed up the steps to his place, part of me wanted to run away and never look back. If I didn't confess the source of my trepidation, then I could pretend like it didn't exist at all.

Readjusting the strap of my duffel bag so it wouldn't cut into my shoulder, I slammed my left fist against his door. After a minute, the flesh covering my hand began to sting, and I had to stop. Had I made it here before him?

No sooner than I had the thought, I heard my name from somewhere behind me.

"Ter, what's going on?" Concern laced Ry's words, and he quickly made his way up the steps toward me.

I didn't even give him a chance to open his door before I leapt at him. My arms curled around his neck as I cemented our embrace. And the moment his hands touched my waist, tears surged from my eyes with a vengeance.

"I'm sorry, but I had to see you."

"Stop apologizing," he said, unlocking his door. Somehow, Ry managed to carry my belongings and me into his apartment.

Relief washed over me like a stream of running water. His presence, his touch, held so much sway with me. I had to relay my fears to him. Not because of the guidance I'd received from Jonas and my dad, but because Ry was the one person who I wanted to open up to so that he could truly understand me.

"Did something happen?" he asked. "You're crying."

"No. Well, yes."

"What is it?"

Burying my face in his chest, I breathed in the scent of his cologne. "I need to tell you about my mom."

His fingers combed through the long strands of my hair, and with every repeated touch, the tension coiling around my heart began to loosen. "You know you can tell me anything, right?"

"I know."

"Ter, look at me." At his command, my gaze lifted.

Concern stared back at me from the depths of those light blue irises. "What do you want to tell me?"

I'd been acting on instinct when I rushed over here, but now that I stood here in his arms, part of my brain was pleading with me to make an escape.

"This isn't easy for me. I want you to know that."

Upon hearing my words, his expression turned somber. "The things we avoid talking about will never be easy to discuss. But I'll tell you why I don't let myself get too involved with anyone if you tell me why you don't," he stated.

I nodded. Admitting that my heart had been invariably closed off to the prospect of love wasn't an easy thing to confess. But if by some miracle, Ry possessed the same trepidations as I did, then he wouldn't mind the constant broken state I was in. "Did someone hurt you?" I questioned softly.

"Yeah."

"Who?"

"My father." His resounding sigh was so heavy I could feel the weight of the burdens Ry carried on his shoulders. Guiding me toward the couch, he helped me settle in across from him. "If we're going to talk about this shit, then we need to be comfortable." After removing his tie, he deftly unfastened the top three buttons of his shirt.

"Should we have a drink?"

Ry shook his head. "No, we can't keep avoiding this."

"Okay."

"It's been over a year since I last talked to my father," he said. "You see, the two of us don't get along. He is an extremely selfish person and I would rather have nothing to do with him than pretend like he didn't rip our family apart."

"What did he do?" I asked, taking Ry's hand in mine.

"I was eleven years old when I found out my parents were getting a divorce. The perfect, happy existence I believed would last forever was shattered beyond repair. Turns out that my father was having an affair with another woman and he was leaving my mom to be with her."

"Oh, Ry." My fingertips traced the creases covering his palm. His greatest fear was being cheated on—a fate his mother had experienced—while mine was losing the person I loved the most—a fate my dad had endured. Drawing his hand to my lips, I kissed his flesh. "I'm so sorry."

"Believe it or not, the story actually gets better," he joked, his voice breaking on the last word. "He didn't simply have an affair with this woman; they had children together too."

Gasping at the gravity of this information, I moved closer. Even if we were nothing more than broken souls, at least we could share in our pain together. "So, you have a brother or sister out there?"

His attention shifted to the far side of the room, and for the first time since the day we'd met, he refused to meet my gaze. "Technically, I have two half-brothers. We share blood, but I can count on one hand the number of times I've seen them. We're not close, and why would we be?" Anger seeped into his tone. "The person who I thought was my father, the man who I thought loved me and enjoyed taking me to baseball games every weekend, tossed me aside to pursue a life with his new family. He left my mom in debt, and she nearly worked herself to death just so we could scrape by. She went back to school and graduated to get a better job and to have the ability to provide us with nice things. And that jackass was nowhere to be found."

The pain and hatred Ry displayed as he explained the

estranged relationship he had with his father was all consuming. He had been abandoned by someone he thought would love him forever. How could a person ever learn to trust after something like that? Death was the only thing capable of tearing my mother away, but for Ry, his father had chosen to leave. He cared more for his other children than he did for his first son.

So much space seemed to exist between us. In this moment, Ry believed himself to be alone, but I needed him to know he wasn't. I wanted him to realize he could count on me just like all the times I've had to count on him. "Ry," I began softly, "you are twice the man your father could ever hope to be. You are so kind, strong, and thoughtful—it's enough to take my breath away. Your father is the one I feel sorry for, not you. Because he discarded one of the best souls he'll ever have the fortune of meeting." I inched closer to him, only stopping when I was fully seated in his lap. His strong arms cradled me as I touched my lips to his forehead. "It's his loss. Never forget that."

"I'll try."

I sighed, knowing his confession needed to be repaid in kind.

"The worst part about Mom getting sick was watching the effect it had on my dad," I confessed with more confidence than I felt. "At the end, her body was so frail that I was sometimes afraid to touch her, because it looked as if she might break." My voice wavered slightly, and I knew more tears wouldn't be far behind. Thinking of those last few months, of the hope my father had continued to carry in his heart, was the worst pain I'd ever known. "But he was so strong through it all. He was there for her when we were told she had cancer, he was there for all the chemo treatments that made her sick for days on end, and he was there when her hair began to fall out." My hold on him increased and I exhaled with relief as his hands began to rub my back. "My mom was strong and beautiful. She lived her life without regrets, and when she learned that she only had a few months left on this earth, she accepted her fate without a shred of fear. The love my parents had for one another is unlike anything I've ever seen before. They were soulmates, and when Mom was gone, part of my dad was missing too." Swallowing hard, I willed myself to keep speaking. "And he was never the same again."

"I don't know what to say. I'm so sorry."

"I'm afraid of going down the same path he did. I'm terrified that one day I'll care for someone so much that I'll never recover if they get taken away from me. I don't want my happiness to be solely dependent on another human being. I would rather be alone than wander the earth, missing the other half of my soul."

My heart thrashed against my ribcage. The secret fear that had been weighing me down had been released into the world. Confession could be as cathartic as it was terrifying. And I could only pray Ry wouldn't judge me too harshly.

"Both of our biggest fears stem from fates our parents shared," he whispered, his mouth brushing the side of my neck.

The gesture was barely anything at all, but I didn't want him to stop. Why was it the things that frightened us the most were also the things we wanted more than anything else? Was it some sort of subconscious reverse psychology? Or maybe even a common trick of nature?

Every living creature on this earth had wants and desires, but their minds were also awakened to the concept of fear. It was as if the universe continually sought to make mankind walk a tightrope, teetering between temptation and reluctance.

"I had the exact same thought when you were telling me about your dad."

"Whoever would've guessed that?" His question was meant to help lighten the mood, but a small part of me still felt burdened.

"Ry . . ."

"What?"

"There is one more thing I want you to know."

"Okay."

Closing my eyes, I inhaled. "I'm not as brave as I've led you to believe, especially not about things that matter."

"Then I guess we can be cowards together, because neither am I."

"Don't make light of the situation. This is difficult for me."

"What are you trying to say exactly?"

I continued holding on to him out of fear that he would be pulled from my grasp at any second. "I don't—"

"Ter," he whispered. "You don't have to confess every secret you have in a single night."

"Are you sure?"

Again, his lips met with my flesh. "Does it look like I'm going anywhere?"

.

Sometime during the course of our conversation, my legs had wrapped around his waist. "It's not as if I'm really giving you a choice."

"Believe me, I'd rather die than leave."

My nails dug into the fabric of his shirt as I attempted to pull him closer. "Please don't say something like that to me."

"Shit," he muttered. "I'm an ass, I wasn't thinking—"

"It's fine, but just let me stay here tonight."

"Whatever you want."

I couldn't help but find a small amount of humor in his reply. If he knew what I truly wanted from him, would he even give it to me? Sleeping at his place without Wren present was dangerous. There were clear lines establishing the boundaries of our friendship, but those restrictions became more blurred by the day.

On Halloween, we had both hinted at wanting something more than friendship, but was that just the alcohol and excitement of the environment talking? Clothes were limited, our thinking hindered, and we had rubbed up against one another. In the heat of the moment, it had been allowable to let the situation get out of hand. But what about now? There were no lapses in our judgment this time, so if we truly wanted to broaden the spectrum of our platonic relationship, then why weren't we doing so?

After talking for what felt like hours on end, we decided to lie down in his bed. There was only so much emotional strife the mind could take before raising a white flag

"Hey, Ter?" he asked.

I rolled over to face him. Even in the dim light, I was still able to make out every single line of his face. That was one of the drawbacks of being an artist. Whenever someone got under your skin, you had to recreate them in a variety of mediums. But I had my doubts that paint, charcoal, pencil, or ink could do him the true justice of capturing every emotion locked within his expression.

"Yeah?"

"How was your appointment with Jonas? Did he like the concept you came up with for the show?"

"Well, he didn't tell me to change my concept as much as he encouraged me to confront my deepest fears. He told me that I was great at evoking emotion with my work, but he wants me to delve deeper and deliver something everyone is sure to remember."

Absorbing my words, Ry nodded. "He's right, you know."

"Gee, thanks for the vote of confidence."

"You are great at evoking emotion with your work, but you do always play it safe."

My lips pursed together as I glared at him. "I'm going to be honest, you're not one of my favorite people at the moment."

"You know what I mean."

I rolled my eyes at him, knowing he wasn't completely wrong. "He did like my idea to use human bodies as canvas for the show."

"I didn't know you were planning on doing that."

"Didn't I tell you about it?" I asked, infusing my voice with excessive amounts of sweetness.

"No."

"Alright, you kind of got me there. I was struck with the idea while I was in Jonas's office and it slipped out. Fortunately, he loved it."

"I take it you're planning on using Wren and I as your guinea pigs then?"

My eyebrow arched as I leaned toward him. "You mean to tell me that you're opposed to letting me cover your entire body with paint?"

His gaze narrowed slightly as he regarded me. "Never said that, but I am wondering what I get out of helping you with this art show."

"My hands touching every single part of your body."

"I'm in."

"That didn't take much."

Feigning shock, he gasped. "Should you really be insulting the help like that?"

"Oh, shut up!" When I tried to smack his chest, Ry's hands caught my wrist. "Ry," I warned.

"You should use your new drawing as your inspiration for the show."

"What new drawing?" I asked.

"The one where you're standing with your dad in a meadow of yellow flowers."

My heart fluttered like the wings of a butterfly. How had he even seen that drawing?

"How?"

"You thought I was asleep, but I was actually watching you."

He tried to move next to me, but I pulled away. "That's a huge invasion of privacy!"

"You were just sitting on the couch. How was I supposed to know you didn't want me to see it?"

"Because."

"The figure standing between you and your dad, it's the spirit of your mother, right?"

I nodded, my mouth suddenly incapable of speech.

"I think it's beautiful and it'd be a crime if you didn't share it with everyone."

"You do?" His hands continued to hold my wrists, and I cherished the sensation of his skin on mine.

He stared at me intently, his eyes studying every single curve of my face. "I think it's the second most beautiful thing I've ever seen in my life."

This was one of those moments where I needed to bridge the gap between us, where I needed to show him that I was willing to meet him halfway. But despite my desire to do so, my body wouldn't move.

He pulled me closer until the tips of our noses touched. "Should I come to you then?" he questioned in a whisper. All I had to do was lean in and press my mouth to his. An inch of air separated us. How could such little space feel like miles?

My heart was dragging me to the edge of a cliff. If I took one more step, I'd be free-falling through the air. But what would happen when I hit the ground? A fall from that height would change me in ways I couldn't yet comprehend.

"Stop going places where I can't follow."

His request was enough to break the daze I'd been wrapped up in. "What do you mean?"

"I can only imagine how beautiful it is inside here." His lips lingered against my flesh as he kissed my forehead. "But since I can't join you there, won't you stay out here with me?"

It was impossible not to smile at his question. He may not have known it, but I would've gone anywhere he asked. "If that's what you want."

"What I want is to show you something."

"Then show me."

He shook his head, a smile barely discernable on the edges of his lips. "You're not ready to see it just yet."

chapter fifteen

lies made of gold

I AWOKE THE NEXT morning to the feel of Ry's arms wrapped around my waist. I think we'd fallen asleep sometime after midnight, but I wasn't sure. When I tried to slip from his grasp, his hands tugged me closer to him.

Heat from his flesh seeped through the thin T-shirt I wore, warming me from the outside in. "Ry," I whispered, "I need to get up."

"Not yet," he mumbled sleepily.

"Well, it seems like my bladder is happy to disagree with you."

"Five more minutes."

"Ry . . ."

When I tried to move, he held me in place. Then, without warning, his hand slipped beneath the fabric of my shirt, migrating past my belly button and up to my chest. Shock rippled through my body in a series of waves.

This kind of touch was definitely outside the confines of our friendship.

"Jesus Christ!" I called out. "Ryan!"

"What?" His voice indicated irritation.

Well, join the *fucking* club, dude. Touching me like that was a tease in the worst possible way, so if he had no intentions of finishing what he was starting, then he needed to leave me the hell alone.

"If you don't remove your hands from my tits in the next five seconds, I'm going to sucker punch you in the throat."

My threat, it seemed, was enough to startle him awake. He bolted upright, his hands ripping away from me. "Fuck, I wasn't trying to—"

"Cop a feel?"

"I promise I was asleep. If I'd been awake, I wouldn't have been touching you like that."

"Am I that repulsive?"

"You don't get to play both sides like that," he countered. "You can't be pissed I felt you up and then ticked off when I say I wouldn't do something like that while awake."

"Then—"

"I wouldn't consciously do something like that without your consent." Leaping out of bed, Ry picked up a shirt from the floor and pulled it on. "And now, I'm going to cook breakfast because you're always nicer to me after you've eaten."

He slipped into the hallway, but I managed to catch up with him. Weaving my arms around his waist, I rested my cheek against his back as I held on to him. "Thank you for listening to me and talking with me last night."

"You did the same for me."

"I know, but you've done so much for Wren and me. We're lucky to have you."

"You've got that wrong, because I'm the lucky one."

I gave him a final squeeze before releasing him. "Will you make me an omelet?"

"Of course. Anything else you want?"

"Coffee, please."

Heading for the kitchen, he said, "I can make that happen."

"Thank you! You're the breast!"

"Just couldn't resist slipping that one in there, could you?"

I laughed, thoroughly sensing his discomfort. "You mean like you slipped your hand up my shirt just a bit ago?"

He groaned loudly. "I'm never going to live that down, am I?"

"I'll forget about it once I can't think of any more titillating replies." Doubling over, I laughed until I was gasping for air.

"Yeah, that just doesn't sit well with me." By the time I realized he was charging for me, it was already too late. Ry scooped me up in his arms, rushing toward his room. Together, we crashed on top of his bed.

"Ry!"

"Admit defeat right now, and I'll let go."

"I'll admit defeat when hell freezes over!"

"Always so stubborn."

I tried to escape, but Ry had me pinned to the bed. "I'm going to give you one more chance, and then I'm going to tickle you, starting with your feet."

"You wouldn't dare."

"Oh, I think I would," he replied with a wily grin.

"I'll never admit defeat."

"Then this is your fault." His fingers trailed down the length of my legs, halting as he reached my feet.

I squirmed beneath him, my desperation to slip away increasing with every passing second. "Ryan," I seethed. "Don't you dare do it."

"Nope, still not the response I was looking for."

Squealing, I thrashed back and forth as he tickled the soles of my feet. "Please, Ry." Laughter filled the air around us, echoing off the walls of his room. "Please, stop."

"Not possible, babe."

The term of endearment brought our lighthearted encounter to an abrupt halt.

My chest heaved as I tried to catch my breath. "Am I your babe now?"

"Would you like to be?"

Words were only simple groupings of letters, but some possessed enough power to decimate an entire city. And his question was no different.

"Did you mean what you said on Halloween?" I asked.

"I drank a lot of alcohol and ran stark naked through the yard of every house on Greek Row on Halloween, so I'm going to need you to be a bit more specific."

"When we were dancing at the club . . ."

"That doesn't really narrow it down, so I'm going to need you to spell it out for me."

I was officially an idiot for bringing up the conversation at all. Things said under the influence of liquor weren't always truthful.

Ry wasn't the one hitting on me—tequila was.

"It was just a stupid joke we made," I lied, praying he wouldn't press the subject any further.

"A joke?"

"Yeah, between two drunk people. Really, I don't even remember all of it."

The look of disbelief altering his features informed me that he didn't believe a single word I was saying. "Okay. Well, I better get started on breakfast."

"Okay."

My heart sank as I watched him walk away. This is what I deserved for not being honest with myself or with him.

Part of my mind believed owning up to my fears would change the way I behaved in situations like this. Self-preservation wasn't an issue for those who had nerves of steel. I wanted to be brave, to stare down my own apprehension in the face. But when push came to shove, I was all too willing to deflect toward my usual comfort zone.

The sad part was that I yearned to become this unattainable, idolized version of myself. Yet, I wasn't made of gold, and eventually, there would come a day when Ry would grow tired of hanging around me. If I was incapable of being honest, then he deserved something better than I could offer.

I was a fool for even dreaming he would stick around forever. Everything in life was temporary. That was a universal truth known far and wide. Last night, Ry told me I was the most beautiful thing he'd ever seen. More than anything, I wanted to be the person he saw whenever he looked at me. But unfortunately, such a reality would never come to pass. It was only a matter of time before my luster faded in his eyes, and when that day came, I'd have no choice but to watch him walk away.

Terror pumped through my heart like blood. In the short time Ry and I had known each other, I'd come to need him. Yesterday, when it had felt as though I was suffocating from all the thoughts weighing me down, I ran to him as fast as my feet could carry me.

And if I allowed him to slip through my fingers, it would be a regret I'd carry with me until the end of my days.

chapter sixteen

sheets as white as snow

RY AND I ATE breakfast in silence, and for the rest of the day, we mostly kept to ourselves. While he worked on a paper for his Economic Analysis class, I brainstormed a central theme for the art show. I'd been running from my fears for far too long. Everything Ry and I had discussed yesterday was a step in the right direction, but there was so much more I needed to do.

I was applying the advice I had received from him just last night. He thought the sketch I'd done to commemorate our last set of family photos should be my sole source of inspiration for the show.

If everyone wanted me to create art that would evoke emotion from my audience, then I was going to deliver. Lord knows I had enough feelings surging through my body to get the job done.

After our earlier conversation in his room, the proper thing to do would've been to keep my distance. Yet, here I was. Ry hadn't asked me to leave, and truthfully, I wanted to stay. Even if there was tension hovering in the air around us, I couldn't resist the temptation to be near him. Spreading out on the floor of his living room, I laid out a couple different sketches. The theme I was going to portray was lost love. My plan was to specifically focus on Mom's battle with cancer. I would paint different depictions from her life—like her diagnosis, chemotherapy, and hospice care. She would be rendered in various images, times of happiness and times of sorrow. The point was to show people the harsh reality of a terminal illness and how it could impact the loved ones who weren't sick. Because eventually, those loved ones would be left behind. Using Wren and Ry as part of the show would make the entire thing even more meaningful. It would shroud the entire display in shades of truth.

Dragging the tip of a charcoal pencil in a downward arc, I began to outline my mother's jaw. I could draw her straight from memory. In all actuality, I could probably draw her with my eyes closed. She was the one who had given me my first sketchpad and set of charcoal pencils. Her continued gifts of paints and canvases were meant to be a distraction. Something to keep me from noticing how pale and thin she was or how nauseated the chemo made her. But at the end of the day, it had worked.

I sketched until my skin was smudged with black and my fingers went numb. Creating was my release. It was a way for me to purge all the stress my body seemed to soak up like a sponge. Not to mention, it had made mom happy. She used to love watching me delve into my own realm of creativity. Her dream had been for me to pursue art.

However, above all else, she had simply wanted me to be happy.

And that was the reason I wished I could talk to her right now. I was at a crossroads in my life—I knew that beyond the shadow of a doubt. But everything happening between Ry and me—the things we were brave enough to say and the things we weren't—only added to my confusion about the entire matter. Mom would know exactly what advice to give. The comfort her voice had provided was ingrained into my consciousness from the time I was in diapers. I'd give anything to be able to share my newest adventures with her. No matter what, she had always been there with a hug and a kiss. Even though Dad and I had a special connection of our own, Mom had been the glue holding everything together, and her absence would always be felt.

My hand flitted across the paper. Her eyes stared up at me as I continued to recreate her face. To my left, I could sense Ry hovering just a foot away. He didn't speak but, instead, moved in so close that his knee brushed my thigh as he sat next to me.

"Did you finish your paper?"

"Yeah."

"That didn't take too long."

"It only has to be six pages. So, it was a rather short assignment."

I giggled at the vast differences in our school coursework.

"What's so amusing?" he questioned.

"Your major requires you to write papers about economics and finance, and mine requires that I spend my afternoon covering myself in charcoal and paint."

He smiled, playfully knocking his shoulder into mine. "Are you trying to insinuate that your major is more fun than mine?"

"I didn't think there was anything to insinuate. It's rather obvious."

"Economics can be just as exciting as painting."

My eyes rolled upward and most likely slipped into an

alternate dimension for a few seconds. Did he even believe the *BS* spewing from his mouth? "That's the biggest crock of shit I've ever heard in my entire life. Even economists would disagree with you."

He reached for the pencil I'd tucked away in my bun and removed it, causing my hair to tumble around my face. "Well, we can't all have lives that are as exciting as yours."

"Sure you can. All you have to do is not pick a major that's a fucking bore."

"Why do I put up with you, again?"

"Because you can't live without me."

His fingers intertwined with the long strands of my hair. "Thought Wren and I were the only ones who knew that," he said with a grin.

My heart, which had been racing, suddenly halted. "What?"

"You always have that same expression in your eyes."

I was in a daze. Was he just going to gloss over a revelation of that magnitude like it was nothing?

Or, perhaps, he was just joking. That seemed like a more plausible explanation.

"What?" I asked my question a second time, because I was apparently the clueless one between the two of us.

"Pretty sure I was loud enough for you to hear."

Pursing my lips together, I set down my charcoal pencil and turned to face him. "Is there something you'd like to say to me?"

He continued combing his fingers through my hair as he fixed me with an intense gaze. "There are a lot of things I'd like to say to you. Doesn't mean you're ready to hear them, though."

Not content with his reply, I pulled my hair out of his grasp and piled it into another bun on top of my head. "Well, if you're going to keep speaking to me in puzzles, then you might as well at least let me practice painting on you."

"Fine," he replied, sighing heavily. "What do you need me to do?"

I set aside the half-completed drawing of Mom and began pulling out all the tubes of paint I'd brought. "I'm going to be painting all over your skin, so just strip down to a pair of boxers. Preferably ones you don't mind getting dirty."

"Right."

"Which reminds me," I added, laying a couple brushes and my palette next to the paint, "do you have an older shirt I can wear? I don't want to get paint on this sweater."

"Yeah, I'll bring it to you."

While Ry was in his room, I headed to the kitchen and grabbed a couple of unused trash bags. Cutting down each of the seams, I opened up the bags and spread them out as a makeshift drop cloth. I'd just finished taping everything to the carpet when he returned.

"Here."

"Thanks." I accepted the white button-up and tugged my cream sweater over my head. Sliding my arms through the sleeves of his shirt, I shifted my attention to Ry.

He stood before me, dressed in nothing but a tight pair of black boxers. My eyes followed every single hardened line of his body. The fact I was going to be painting his flesh in an attempt to transform him into a part of my show was almost laughable.

The guy was already a work of art.

"Do you just want me to stand over there?"

I tied the ends of his shirt together so the garment wouldn't hang off my body. "Yeah, that would be great."

Ry moved to stand in the center of his living room while I assembled an assortment of paints on my palette.

Mixing a bit of white, black, and brown together, I blended the colors until I had the perfect shade of gray. My idea included painting chains all over Ry's body. I wanted to depict how grounded his body and soul were to the physical world, just as my father was.

Starting at his feet, I painted for what felt like hours. Chains climbed up his legs and waist, all the way to his shoulders. I'd never painted on skin before, but my goal was to attain realism. I needed it to really appear as if Ry's entire body was bound in chains.

Dabbing a bit of white paint on my brush, I leaned toward him. A tiny highlight on the metal link would give it more dimension. Carefully, I dragged the bristles across his flesh. Having a steady hand was imperative for this type of work. Usually, I never faltered. But Ry's shirt was enormous on me. Every time I tried to move, the sleeves slid over my wrists. In a huff of anger, I stepped away from my canvas and ripped off his shirt.

"Is everything okay?" he asked.

I threw the button-up on the floor and stared at him, my brow furrowing in confusion. "Yeah. Why?"

"Well, you just seem a bit irritated."

"The sleeves kept sliding down my arms and it was making it impossible to paint anything."

"Oh."

As idiotic as it sounds, it took me a second to realize that I now stood before Ry in nothing but a pair of jeans and a black bra. Not that he hadn't seen me in my underwear before, but the tension existing between us had more than tripled in the time since we first met. "I'm painting on a three-dimensional medium. If I can't reach every part of your body, there will be patches of unpainted skin breaking up the continuity of my concept," I explained in exasperation.

Resuming my seat on the floor, I continued high-lighting the metal links covering Ry's thigh. Silence beckoned to us from every corner of the apartment. Most of the time, we couldn't go more than a few minutes without teasing one another, but tonight, it seemed we were both content not to speak. I wasn't sure how long we had been silent. Hours? Minutes? Either way, the lack of sound had almost become deafening.

More than once, I opened my mouth to speak, but no sound came from it. Even if I did find the nerve to break the silence, would he even want to hear my thoughts?

"I lied to you earlier," Ry finally whispered after an eternity of quiet.

"About what?" Focusing on my palette once more, I mixed a touch of blue into the gray paint I was using.

"I remember every single word I said to you on Halloween."

Breath caught in my throat as I gazed up at him. "You do?" He nodded, his eyes never turning away from mine. "Then why did you—"

"I want you to answer me one thing," he began, interrupting me. "Do you believe in love?"

"I do."

"You just don't believe it's possible for you to experience it?"

"I can't hand myself over to someone completely enough to allow myself to feel it."

"I see."

Shame overpowered every other emotion swirling inside my brain. I wished I was brave enough to lay my soul bare before him. My view of love had been forever tainted, but did he even realize how badly I desired redemption? If he alone held the key to my salvation, then running away would be an unforgiveable sin.

"But part of me does believe I could hand myself over to you."

One sentence was all it took for me to throw caution to the wind. Blood rushed through my veins at the speed of a raging river. My revelation had the ability to change everything between us. Safety was an attractive alternative when the things you feared the most could bring the entire world crumbling around you.

Kneeling in front of me, Ry eased the paintbrush and palette from my hands. "I know for a fact I could hand myself over to you."

Those blue irises, which had seen me at my best and my most vulnerable, seemed to bore right through me.

Could he really hand himself over to me? No sooner than I had the thought, his lips caressed mine so softly that I feared everything that had just transpired was all an elaborate hallucination created by my mind.

"And whenever you're ready, I'll be here," he promised.

When he stood, I realized there was nothing I wouldn't give to live in that moment until the universe ended and time ceased to exist.

My mouth parched as I tried to think of the right thing to say. He was waiting for me to be bold enough to take a chance on something we both wanted, and I didn't want to let him down.

Sixty seconds later, it was as if nothing had happened. Ry resumed his stoic pose, allowing me to finish my work.

I blinked and missed my opportunity to say all the words hanging on the tip of my tongue. My hands reached for the palette, but I stopped myself. I'd been safe for far too long. Jumping to my feet, I stepped so close to him, nothing seeming to exist between us.

"I'm tired of being scared," I breathed. "I want to hand myself over to you."

"Are you sure?"

"I've never been more sure of anything in my entire life." His responding smile was the only encouragement I needed to release the ledge I'd been clutching . . . and fall. His hands found the small of my back as my fingers slid up the length of his arms, smearing the paint that covered his flesh. Excitement lit up my skin like electricity, and when the anticipation of kissing him became too overwhelming, my lips united with his.

The kiss we shared set off a chain reaction inside our bodies. Desire exploded between us as our mouths moved in a decadent harmony, stealing the very breath from my lungs. But just kissing wasn't going to be enough—it wasn't even going to be close.

Everywhere he touched me, he left trails of color in his wake. I gasped with delight as his tongue traveled along the side of my neck. Control over my body was no longer a possible notion. The only thing I was now capable of doing was responding to each movement Ry made. Tangling my fingers in his hair, I jerked his face toward mine. His lips consumed mine completely, and I never wanted him to stop. Opening my mouth, I reveled in the way he tasted.

Strong hands grasped the curve of my hips and lifted me into the air. I wrapped my legs around Ry's waist as he began carrying me toward the hallway. In a few steps, my back met with the wall. As I touched my toes to the ground and sighed, his hips rolled into me, pinning me in place.

My lip caught between my teeth as I considered the pleasure those hips could create.

"Ry."

"What?"

"Take me to bed."

The grin covering his face informed me there was

nothing else he'd rather do. "I'm going to do a hell of a lot more than that."

In the next breath, he scooped me up in his arms and sprinted toward his room. I squealed as we landed on his bed, our bodies entwined. Dipping my head so I could kiss him again, I decided his lips were the best thing I'd ever tasted. For so long, I had wondered what it would feel like to be with him like this. I yearned for him to discover every dip and curve of my flesh. And now that it was happening, I wanted more.

So much more.

Laying on my back, I watched as Ry bent before me. This time, when his tongue slid down my abdomen, the desire lacing his gaze wasn't a ruse. This time, every lick and touch were real. My heart pounded with a newfound anticipation as he slowly removed my jeans. His mouth left a path of kisses up my legs. Unable to help myself, I squirmed beneath the pressure of his hands, craving more.

"Please don't stop," I begged.

"I've wanted you from the first time I heard you speak, so believe me when I say that I don't plan on stopping anytime soon." His devious expression disappeared as his face settled between my legs. The warmth of his breath on my skin elicited a rush of excitement to overtake every conscious thought I had. My back arched off the bed as his lips kissed the lace covering my most tender flesh. Then, in one fluid movement, Ry slipped his fingers underneath the edges of my panties and removed the garment before tossing it to the side. "Now, there's nothing to keep me from tasting you."

I moaned with delight the moment his tongue delivered on his promise. "Oh my God."

His tongue moved in slow, deliberate strokes, and when that sensation became too overwhelming, he pulled back.

Drawing ragged breaths into my lungs, I stared up at him.

"May I?" he asked, his fingertips tugging at my bra.

Returning his smile, I nodded. "Yes."

When all my clothes had been removed and my body was no longer hidden from him, Ry hovered over me, his eyes studying every curve.

"I want to be completely honest with you," he whispered, pressing his lips to mine. "I've thought about seeing you like this, dreamed about it even. But touching you and tasting you is even better than anything I've imagined."

"I was just thinking the same thing."

"Do you even realize how beautiful you are?"

"You could always tell me again," I teased, sitting up.

"I know I've told you before, but you truly are the most beautiful thing I've ever laid eyes on."

"So are you." Winding my fingers into his hair, I pulled Ry closer. My lips brushed against the tip of his ear as I whispered, "And now, it's my turn to look at you without any clothes on."

No sooner than the words left my mouth, he slithered out of my grasp and removed his boxers. Scanning him from head to toe, I made sure to admire every muscle.

He ripped back the covers, revealing crisp sheets. A streak of gray covered the skin between my breasts. I waited while Ry ripped open a foil packet and sat on the bed. Tracing the tip of my finger through the smudges blanketing his flesh, I crawled onto his lap. Slowly, I lowered myself on top of him. He inhaled at the sudden contact, and my head rolled back as I relished the way he felt inside me. His hands guided my hips in a steady rhythm as we moved together.

"God, you feel good," he panted.

"So do you."

I rocked back and forth as a wonderful sensation pumped through my being—from the ends of my hair to the tips of my fingers. Somewhere in the haze of desire we had been swept up in, his lips reclaimed mine, and I moaned into his mouth. The sensation of pleasure was all-consuming. Just as the feeling was about to be too over-whelming, his fingers curled into my thighs. Holding on to me tight, he flipped me on my back and pushed into me in a smooth, single movement. My nails dug into his flesh as I begged for him to keep going.

More paint from his body smeared over my skin and marred his sheets that were as white as freshly fallen snow. His bedsheet served as a blank canvas, and with each movement, each stroke we made together, we left our story behind.

Over and over, he rocked into me until we could hardly breathe. Sweat beaded across his chest before dripping onto my skin. Every one of my senses had been exponentially heightened. Weaving my hands around his waist, I pulled him deeper into me.

"Fuck, yes," I moaned.

"I take it I must be doing something right then?"

"You're doing everything right."

His lips nipped at my ear. "Glad to hear it."

After a couple more thrusts of his hips, I was a breath away from coming undone.

Explosions ignited behind my eyelids, swarming my senses with an array of colors. Every hue imaginable played through my consciousness and elevated the pleasure humming through my body to the next level. The connection we had was exactly what I'd come to crave every time Ry and I were in the same room together. And in the back of my mind, I knew nothing else would ever be able to compare to this. I was experiencing the pinnacle of ecstasy as his body took me higher and higher. As I rode a wave of euphoria, Ry's body trembled above me. Muttering a string of curse words, he finally stilled.

When I noticed his attention was focused on me once more, I chewed on my bottom lip. "I don't know about you, but I'm glad we did that."

"Me too." Bending forward, he kissed me. "Sorry I ruined your painting."

"Strangely, I'm fine with it. And besides, it's not like I didn't help."

"True." He chuckled lightly and brushed his nose against mine. "Why don't we take a shower and then I can make us something to eat?"

I smiled at him, my thumb tracing the line of his jaw. "Well, it's apparent you know the way to my heart."

"That was my goal all along."

chapter seventeen

beautiful blue eyes

THE TIPS OF HIS fingers massaged the length of my back. "Mmm. You keep that up and I may never leave."

"Is that a promise?" he asked.

"Only one way to find out."

Ry stepped closer, his hands leisurely traveling past my waist to my hips. A caress like this should never be rushed. Shared warmth is something that should be savored with every fiber of your being. Drops of water rolled off our skin as we stood beneath the showerhead. I laughed as he trailed a line of kisses along the curve of my jaw.

"Thank you," he mumbled against my flesh.

"For what?"

"Staying with me."

"Whoever said I was staying again tonight?"

Without so much as a warning, his hand smacked my ass hard enough to make me yelp. "You're staying."

"You didn't even ask me——"

I barely had time to say anything before his mouth consumed mine, kissing and sucking until we were both left breathless and wanting more. In all honesty, I couldn't remember the last time I felt this happy. The emotion was practically radiating from all my pores, and my mind had been on a high since he first kissed me.

"Ter, would you stay with me tonight? I'd love nothing more than to spend an evening staring into your beautiful blue eyes."

"You're so over the top," I replied with a laugh.

"I'm sorry, but are you actually complaining?"

"Not really, but you know I'm going to stay."

"Are you being nice to me because I made you very happy a little while ago?"

"Maybe I just like you. Ever think of that?"

He pinned me to the wall of his shower as he pressed his hips against mine. "I like you too."

My body's natural reflex was to keep him as close to me as possible. Hooking my leg around his thigh, I intensified our hold on one another.

"Do you think we ruined your sheets and comforter?"

"Does it look like I fucking care?" he questioned, nipping at the curve of my shoulder.

"Honestly, you seem much more interested in me."

He left kiss after kiss across my chest. "Wow, that only took you, like, a month to figure out."

"Shut up."

"I can do that . . . or we could get out of here and do something else."

Running my hands through his hair, I pressed my mouth to his. "I like that idea."

Turning off the shower, we raced from the bathroom without even bothering to dry off. I crashed on the stained sheets with him on top of me. His bed was a beautiful sight. Each smear of paint was a memory of how our bodies had merged and moved as a singular being. Everything we'd been through had built up to this

—the realization that we meant more to one another than just a friend.

His palms caressed my skin in a slow, decadent manner. He traced every inch of my body as if he were afraid I would disappear from sight.

"You trying to memorize the layout of my body?" I questioned playfully.

He stopped kissing the curve of my breast as he glanced up at me. "I'm trying to commit everything about you to memory."

"That's a nice thought."

He gave me a sinful grin. "I think so too."

I'd been with other guys before, but none of them had made me feel the way Ry did. His presence was captivating. And whenever he touched or kissed me, the sensation was overpowering. He was like the most addictive drug, and a voice in the back of my mind warned me that I would never be able to get enough.

But the look in his eyes informed me that he was equally hooked on me.

Lips locked, arms intertwined, Ry and I devoured one another with a sense of urgency that couldn't be satiated.

Was this what it was like to be so wrapped up in another human being that nothing else mattered? The world could be ripped in half and I wouldn't care. This singular moment was it for me. That and the man hovering over me.

After every curve of my figure had been properly worshipped, Ry spread my knees apart and slid inside me. The anticipation of experiencing our bodies fully connected to one another again was almost excruciating.

"Oh," I moaned, savoring the feel of him.

His teeth nipped the base of my neck, and I tilted my head out of the way so he wouldn't have to stop. Deliberately, his hips rolled into me, the pace as steady and incessant as the tide. Heat blossomed in my chest, shooting through my fingertips with each thrust. I sucked in a deep breath, my lungs desperate for air.

My consciousness was only aware of two things—the endless pleasure running through my veins and the fact Ry was its source. Part of me ached for him to increase our pace, but the other part loved his leisurely movements.

And there was no reason to hasten something that felt so good.

I dug my nails into the flesh covering his back as he pressed deeper inside me. My senses were already at their limits, yet I still craved so much more.

Love frightened me. I feared the way it would make me so dependent on another that my own happiness would be a direct result of theirs. My soul was a creative one. I thrived on art, light, and beauty. But I never realized how incomplete I was until now. For decades, I could have wandered the earth in search of redemption; however, such a fate would be impossible without him.

The one outcome I'd been trying to evade since the day we'd lost mom had found me nonetheless.

Gradually, he rolled his hips again, prompting my back to arch away from the mattress. We were already breathing the very same air, but every part of me yearned to be closer. It was as if his body were calling out to mine, like the whispered name of a long lost lover on the wind.

"Is that okay?" he asked, sliding his tongue past my lips to taste me.

"Uh huh." My reply was half moan, half whisper. Too many wonderful feelings were bombarding my consciousness and it was hard to focus on anything but him. "More than okay."

"Good."

He grabbed my thighs and pressed them against the mattress to open my body even more. The new angle allowed him to push even deeper. I wasn't sure if my body could handle anything better, but he was constantly bending and breaking my own limits. The feeling was indescribable. It was akin to viewing a masterpiece, such as *The Last Supper* or *The Mona Lisa*, for the first time. Something within me was being changed irrevocably, and nothing would ever be able to surpass this.

His steady cadence only intensified my arousal with each fleeting second. But I didn't want to be a passive player in this encounter. Ry needed to know that I wanted to return the favor. So, when he rolled his hips again, I thrust mine forward to meet him.

"Fuck," he murmured in my ear. "That felt—"

I planted my mouth on the side of his neck, running my tongue down his flesh. "I want to make you feel as good as you're making me feel."

"It's definitely working."

"If you're close, just go, baby."

As if my words were crucial to conjuring his release, Ry's body trembled above me.

Not to be outdone, he slipped his fingers between us. Fireworks lit behind my eyelids as he began massaging my most sensitive part. His touch forced me closer to the edge, and when a groan sounded from his lips, the remaining vestiges of my composure shattered. I unraveled with him, because of him, and when I finished shaking from the swells of ecstasy that overwhelmed me, we collapsed on the bed as a singular being.

Smiling, I kissed his cheeks, forehead, and even the tip of his nose.

"You seem happy," he stated, burying his face in the curve of my neck.

"That's because I am."

"Good." Before I even had a chance to catch my breath, Ry lifted me into his arms and headed in the direction of the bathroom. "I know I promised to cook for you after we finished showering earlier, but I really mean it this time."

"I'm not exactly complaining here."

"I realize that, but I also want to be meeting all your needs."

I couldn't help but laugh. "You met my needs and then fucking surpassed them."

This time when Ry and I showered together, we managed to keep our hands somewhat to ourselves. But the task proved to be more difficult than what should have been possible. Although, there was no reason for me to be surprised. We'd had ridiculous chemistry surging between us since we chugged vodka and stripped down to our underwear in my dorm room.

By the time we ate and finished cleaning up his apartment, it was well after midnight. Lying on his couch, I rested my head on his chest as we watched a movie together. I was dressed in another one of his button-up shirts, and the fabric was like a second skin. I'd only worn his clothing a handful of times up to this point, but whenever I was surrounded by his scent, it felt like home.

"Is there anything I can do to help you with the show?" Ry asked halfway through the second installment of the *Lord of the Rings* trilogy. Last week, on a whim, we'd decided to watch the entire franchise together. We'd already seen all of them, but it was way more fun to watch one of your favorite series with one of your favorite people.

"Just let me use you as one of my living canvases."

"Sounds like a plan to me," he replied. "I think what you finished of the chains looked incredible."

"I have to say that I was pretty happy with them too. I've never painted on anyone's skin, but it turned out better than I expected."

"Will Wren be painted to represent your mother?"

Lifting my head, I met his gaze head-on. "How is it that you always seem to know what I'm planning?"

"Because I'm fascinated with the way your mind works, and I want to not only understand your art, but also the inspiration behind it."

"You're amazing. You know that, right?"

"Am I?"

I nodded, unable to stare at anything but him. "More than you could ever realize."

"I know you spend a lot of time at Wren's apartment and that you sleep there most nights, but you can stay here too if you want."

"Are you low-key offering me a drawer?"

He laughed, the deep sound floating into my ears like a perfect melody. "A drawer, a dresser . . . Hell, you can even have my room if you want it."

I shifted over him until my legs were straddling his waist. He peered up at me with enough intensity reflecting in his eyes to catch my skin on fire. "And what if all I wanted was you?"

"Then you're in luck, because you've already got me."

"Ry." His name was nothing more than a plea rolling off the tip of my tongue.

"What is it?"

"I need you to do something for me." My teeth chewed on my bottom lip as I anxiously pondered whether or not I was bold enough to voice my request.

His thumb rubbed the edge of my lip gently. "Okay. What do you need me to do?"

Inhaling, I ignored all the doubts creeping into my mind. "Kiss me like you never plan to let me go."

Tugging my chin forward, his mouth claimed mine with so much need that I could feel his desire for me radiating from his body into mine. Sometimes, kissing could be even more intimate than lying skin to skin with nothing but drops of sweat between. That's exactly what this was like. I'd been stripped down to my most basic form and made anew.

Our lips stayed locked for a while, neither of us eager to separate. I asked Ry to kiss me like he never planned on letting me go, and he exceeded all of my expectations. The way his arms cradled me made me feel as though I was his most coveted possession. Wren had been right. I was in way too deep. Ignoring the chemistry Ry and I had only put me in more of a bind. I thought avoidance was the right path, but it just made it harder to stay away.

And now that I'd gotten my first taste, I was hungry for more.

Honestly, it seemed like a miracle that there was a guy who not only knew of all the pain I harbored in my soul, but who also understood it. Mom would've been proud that I was putting myself out there and taking a risk on something worthwhile.

Dad too.

When Ry and I finally got our fill, we separated from one another.

Tightening his hold on my shoulders, he made sure to keep me just within kissing distance. "Why did you ask me for that?"

Heat flooded my cheeks as he continued to stare at me. "Why did you give it to me without hesitation?"

The sly smile spreading across his face was one I knew all too well. "Because there's nothing I wouldn't do for you," he replied as if his sentiment were the most simple explanation in the entire world. "Which should've been apparent when I ran around campus stark naked because you asked me to."

Giggling, I chewed on my lip to stifle the sound. "Sorry to burst your bubble, but that just makes you sound kind of crazy."

"You're the one who concocted that plan! Shouldn't you be the crazy one?"

"I mean, you are entitled to your own opinion, even if you happen to be wrong."

"You do know what the word opinion means, though, right?"

"I know what right and wrong mean, and you, sir, are wrong."

His brow furrowed as he shook his head. "I should probably just give in now."

"The path of least resistance is always the best route to take with me."

"That sounded strangely like a warning."

I winked and plastered on a smile to match his. "Oh, it is."

A strand of hair fell in front of my eyes, and before I had a chance to move, Ry brushed it away. "Can we talk about something serious for a minute?"

The rate of my breathing quickened. I wasn't one to engage in serious entanglements unless you happened to have red hair and freckles. Wren was the only person I ever confided in completely. But that hesitance also needed to change. I needed to grow up and find someone to rely on who hadn't known me since I had braces and a wavy perm.

"Okay."

"I know opening up to people isn't easy for you. Hell,

it's just as hard for me, but I'm glad you told me about your mom."

I nodded in reply while my fingers traced a small circle on his chest. "I'm glad you explained your past with your father. I know how difficult that was for you."

"I wanted you to know."

I leaned in to press my forehead against his. "I feel the same way."

"Good."

"So, what do you want to do when the movie is over?" I questioned.

"Who says we have to wait for the movie to be over?"

I squealed as Ry grabbed my waist and flung me over his shoulder. There was barely enough time for me to realize we'd left his couch behind when he began sprinting for the hallway. I didn't know what he was planning, but the tone of his voice left little to the imagination.

For now, we couldn't get enough of each other, and part of me hoped that dynamic would never change.

His fingers tangled in my hair as the weight of his chest fully pressed into mine. He kissed me as if we were the only two surviving souls in existence. His touch was hot, heavy, and every other wonderfully explicit adjective in between. I'd always believed abstaining from a connection like this was imperative to protecting myself from the dangers of the heart. But not handing myself over to another had only kept me from experiencing life to the fullest.

"Will you stay tomorrow too?" he asked, his lips brushing mine.

"Just how long do you want me to stay?"

I trailed my hands along the length of his back. The sensation of his skin flush with mine was by far one of my favorite things. It was almost as if we'd been made to touch one another.

"A while."

"Only a while? From the way you're talking, it sounds like you want me to stay for a hell of a lot longer than that."

He snickered at my comment. "Figured if I were truthful, you'd classify me as a creepy weirdo who belonged in an episode of *Criminal Minds*."

"Oh, I most definitely would."

"What will it take to win you over?"

I peppered kisses across his cheeks and mouth. "Who says you haven't already?"

"That so?"

Shyness crept into my mind, making it difficult to answer him. Instead of speaking, I smiled and nodded my head. I may not have been capable of expressing my thoughts with words, but I did know another means of communication.

Reluctantly, I separated from him and climbed out of bed. Ry stared at me quizzically from where he still lay. Without explanation, I raced for the living room to retrieve my sketch pad and set of charcoal pencils. No more than a minute had passed by the time I returned, and upon entering his room again, I found Ry stretched out on the mattress, hands folded underneath his head. There was no doubt that the guy was handsome. From his blond hair and blue eyes to the toned muscles in his legs, he was utter perfection.

It wasn't as if I hadn't drawn him before. I had more sketches of Ry than I would ever admit, but there was a subtle difference to his countenance that I wanted to capture. Even though I couldn't quite figure out what had changed, I needed to draw him all the same.

"What are you up to now?" he questioned in a playful tone.

"You're going to be my muse."

"Come again?"

"I don't know why you're so surprised. You've been offering to pose for me ever since we met."

"Yeah, and the majority of the time, you turned me down. That includes the times I offered to pose naked as well."

"That's because I didn't want to see you naked for the first time as part of a project for school," I spat in exasperation. "I wanted it to happen because we were together." I slapped a hand over my mouth, wishing I could swallow the words that had just slipped out. That particular part of my body seemed all too eager to spill my secrets.

And Ry already knew more than he should.

I tried to keep my distance, but Ry had other plans. He captured my wrists before I could slip away. "I wanted it to happen that way too, but if you'd have asked me to strip, I wouldn't have told you no." As he inched closer, I was hypnotized by the expression in his eyes. "I know you've been through a lot, but I'm handing myself over to you as well, so you don't have to keep me at arm's length any longer."

Ry was the only person who had the ability to render me speechless. I had a knack for witty responses, but he always knew what to say to tie my tongue in knots. After what felt like eons of silence, I was finally able to reply.

"I'm not."

His grin informed me that I was knee-deep in trouble. "You're just a conversation extraordinaire."

"I don't like you much."

"Yes, you do," he countered without hesitation. "You like me a lot, in fact, and I'll prove it."

I didn't even have time to blink before he lunged for me. Ry's arms caught me around my waist as he pinned me to the bed.

"Ry—"

The fact I had even able to utter his name was incredible, because his lips fastened to mine fast enough to steal my breath away. The embrace we shared may have only been a kiss, but the feelings it conjured had a much deeper meaning. Time slipped away as our mouths moved in unison, tasting and touching to our heart's content. When we eventually parted, my chest heaved, and once again, my lungs craved the air we had deprived them of.

Ry had awoken something buried within me, something I never dreamed would see the light of day.

Hope.

I hoped he would kiss me until my lips cracked and bled, I hoped he would hold me until his arms grew numb, and I hoped above all that I could stare into his blue eyes until no other colors seemed to exist.

After a long while, he released me. "Alright, I'm ready to be your muse now."

The electrically charged air hovering between us dissipated. The change left me reeling, as if I'd experienced whiplash. I was at a loss for what to say, so instead, I picked up my sketch pad and pencils.

Ry leisurely propped himself against a pillow. My hand worked in a frenzy to depict him. As I sketched his face, I noticed his eyes never left me. Emotions were etched into every single line I made. He'd always been a beguiling person, but the fact Ry could continually keep me on my toes set him apart from every other guy.

Smudging a line with the tip of my finger, I scrutinized the work I had done thus far. The edge of his jaw had been perfectly recreated, but I needed to focus my efforts on his brow. A plethora of emotions existed within the space between his eyes. Even if I studied him for an eternity, I'd still never be able to guess all his secrets. My heart soared as I continued to draw. The curve of his smile, the bulging muscle in his bicep . . . Every inch of him was represented on my sketch pad. The majority of the time, I would draw whatever piqued my interest. I loved creating flowers and landscapes as much as I did people. Only Mom's face had ever haunted my thoughts, but Ry was slowly overtaking my mind.

And whether that was a good or bad thing, I wasn't sure.

"Are you ever going to let me draw you?" he asked.

"Huh?"

"You're using me as a model right now, so I only feel like it's fair."

"Do you even draw or sketch?"

"I draw stick figures."

I snorted. "You want to draw me as a stick figure?"

"No, I just want to stare at you for long periods of time. I know that would make you nervous, though. So, I figured, if I was pretending to draw you, it wouldn't make you feel as uncomfortable."

"Oh," I answered. Chewing on the end of my pencil, I considered the best way to answer. "I could try to not fidget a lot."

"That so?"

"I'm not making any promises."

"Of course not."

I shrugged. "But I'll admit, it would be the fair thing to do."

His smile widened. "Yes, it would."

Sighing heavily, I finished shading in the majority of

his boxers before relinquishing the pad of paper. "Have at it."

"Thank you."

Over the course of the next few minutes, I watched as Ry tried his best to draw me. With his tongue poking out through his lips, he regarded me with a serious expression as his hand flitted across the paper. I didn't know what to expect, but watching Ry attempt to draw me was even more entertaining than the movie had been.

"You look so serious."

"In case you haven't noticed, I'm trying to draw a beautiful woman over here," he explained. "This is a very delicate matter and I want to be sure to do you justice."

"Are you even drawing anything, or just scribbling?"

"So many assumptions and accusations."

"Well, your brain is hardwired for business and economics. It's not like the assumptions I'm making are all that inconceivable."

"Hush."

"Can I at least see what the hell you're doing over there?"

After giving me an exasperated sigh, Ry consented. Handing over the sketch pad, I barely had time to curl my fingers around the edges before laughter bubbled up from my stomach. Art comes in a variety of forms. Music, paintings, graffiti, sewing, and literature are all fine examples, but Ry's creation couldn't even pass as a drawing.

"Alright, so it's not that great," he admitted, the apples of his cheeks tinged with red.

"Not that great?" I glanced several times between him and the picture I held. "This doesn't even look like a person! I mean, basically, it's scribbled nonsense."

"I was going for an abstract style."

"Picasso is an abstract artist, and at the end of the day, you can still discern what his subject matter is. This looks like you had a seizure while trying to draw an atomic particle."

He shot me a glare. "It's not that bad."

"It's not that great either." I studied the sketch again, still not quite sure what the hell I was even looking at. "I'm trying to figure out what you were drawing."

"We both know I was drawing you."

"But were you?" I questioned in disbelief. "Because if this is what I really look like, I'm jumping off a bridge."

"Always so dramatic," he replied, crawling over to me. Easing the sketch pad out of my hand, Ry hovered over me.

"A lot of people happen to like drama. Shakespeare made a career out of it."

"I suppose you have a point there."

"I have a lot of points."

"I know." His mouth nipped at the collar of my shirt. "And I like all of them."

chapter eighteen

a sky full of purple clouds

THREE DAYS PASSED IN the blink of an eye. Ry and I spent practically every waking moment with one another. I even went as far as skipping a few of my classes because I had no desire to leave his apartment. If it was an activity happening outside of the bed, it held no interest for me. Ry, on the other hand, only managed to skip one class. Believe me, I coaxed and coaxed, but the guy had goals. He was intent on graduating school with a double major, which only made me like him even more.

Actually, there wasn't one single thing about him that I didn't like. Even the walls I'd erected around my heart hadn't deterred him.

The touch of a hand on my back chased away the dregs of sleep. Scooting over, I pulled back the edge of the comforter. "Go ahead and get in."

"I can't."

"Just so you know, I'm not a fan of your answer."

"I promise to make it up to you."

"Promises, promises," I sighed. "I want you to get in bed with me right now."

Ry's laughter slid over my flesh like a warm blanket. "I wish I could, but I'm meeting Logan at the gym."

I pouted to demonstrate my utter dislike of this information. "But why?"

"Because I love working out and it relaxes me."

"I can help you relax."

"Like hell. Whenever I'm around you, relaxing is the furthest thing from my mind."

"Then I guess I know what we're doing when you get home."

Home. The word slid off my tongue so naturally that I almost didn't realize what I'd said. But the space within these walls did feel like home to me. And I wasn't talking about the couch or the cabinets in the kitchen. I was talking about the person who lived here, the one who made me smile whenever I was on the verge of tears. Wherever he was would always feel like home to me.

Dread spread throughout my body like wildfire. I'd gotten in too deep. I tried to be cautious, tried to deny the connection Ry and I shared, but all of my efforts had been in vain. I fell for him, despite knowing better. Entanglements of the heart only ended one way—with tears.

Love wasn't supposed to be a part of my destiny. It never had been and it never would be. I dated Blake knowing he wasn't the one for me. I stayed with him for months because it was safe. My heart would never allow me to get too involved. But that sentiment no longer held true. Ry had invaded my consciousness. He painted himself into the fabric of my life, and the fact I let him in left me feeling terrified.

"Sounds good to me, babe," he whispered, leaving a kiss on my temple.

I smiled. My face feigned happiness so he wouldn't be

aware of the turmoil surging inside of me. It took every ounce of willpower I possessed to keep myself from latching on to his arm and begging him to stay. Part of me believed he could fix whatever was wrong with me. The other part understood I couldn't be fixed, that I couldn't be saved. The right thing to do would be to let him go and never look back. He should be happy, not tied to someone who was incapable of allowing herself to feel anything remotely similar to the word *love*.

"Okay," I croaked. I prayed he would assume my trembling voice came from being half asleep, because he couldn't know what I was planning.

His eyes connected with mine and, for a second, a lopsided grin covered his face. The gaze we shared only lasted for a moment, but for me, an eternity passed. It physically pained me, but I made myself memorize every darker fleck of blue in his irises. I wanted to remember everything about him so that, when I was old and gray, my mind would recall his visage with perfect clarity. I had no doubts his face would be one to linger. Would I spend a hundred nights sketching the most minute details of his face? Or would it be a thousand?

That was the one quality about time people tended to overlook. Time persisted in spite of love, hate, fear . . . everything, really. When you've lost someone who is such an integral part of your soul, you stop thinking about the years you spent together and begin to dread the years you'll spend without them. The truth is that time is a shackle from which you can never escape. It will chase you to the ends of the earth and make you become its prisoner until your last breath. That is the only kind of promise life has to offer. You will love, you will lose, and you will die.

The *end*.

When I heard the door to the apartment close, I fought back tears. I didn't deserve to cry. I was the lowest of the low, a deplorable human being too far removed from the depths of compassion. Sometimes in life, the only choice was to bite the bullet. The pain I felt now would be indescribable, but in the long run, my wounds would heal and I would forget.

Eventually, I wouldn't be able to recall the exact scent of his body wash or the warmth of his hands on my skin. His laugh, his smile, every wonderful thing about him would fade from my memory. He'd cease to exist in my thoughts and in my soul.

This wasn't a simple fling or even a hookup. The connection we shared possessed a permanence my heart wasn't courageous enough to attempt. I was and always would be a coward. Any fears Ry had quelled in the last few days only gave birth to new ones. My trepidation was like a glowing ember. If you didn't extinguish the cinders, it was only a matter of time before it erupted in flames.

I had the ability to destroy both of us, and even though I was a piece of shit, there was something I could do to protect Ry. He would hate me now, but after some time passed, he would thank me. This was the right decision. Actually, it was the only one.

My warnings had been loud and clear. I expressed my hesitations to him on more than one occasion. But despite my efforts, the rules I established in order to protect myself had been obliterated. Now, retreat was my only alternative. I'd be able to accept his hate. Hell, it would be what I deserved. Because the real sin would be allowing him to love me when it was inevitable that I would let him down. The fact I would disappoint him was almost as inevitable as time. This wasn't make-believe. It was reality, and sometimes, things don't end the way we intend. Death, taxes, and Terayn Andrews being a royal fuckup were the only certainties life had to offer. I was fully aware of my place in this world, but after a few days with him, my perspective had shifted.

Unfortunately, it was the kind of shift that would never last.

A couple days couldn't undo years of conditioning . . . and that was a truth I needed to remember.

Hopping out of bed, I raced to grab some clean clothes. I slipped on a pair of jeans and sneakers faster than what should be humanly possible. After sliding on a sweatshirt, I focused my energy on gathering all my things. Art supplies, clothes, and makeup were tossed into my duffel bag at random. When I finished, the only indication I'd ever been here was the drawing Ry had framed above his bed. I'd given it to him out of appreciation and it wasn't my place to take it away.

I made his bed and fluffed the pillows while a timid voice in the back of my mind pleaded with me to stay. Maybe Ry was the solution to all my problems. Maybe I did need to take a chance on something worthwhile. But in the end, fear won out. Scribbling out a quick note, I left my apology on the kitchen counter and ran away as fast as my feet could carry me.

When Ry went to the gym, he was usually gone for at least an hour. I prayed the same held true today as well. Hopping into my car, I caught a glimpse of the morning sky. Storm clouds in shades of purple and gray littered the horizon. I dropped my belongings in the passenger seat and rounded the front of my car to slide behind the steering wheel. Everything about this felt wrong. A sensation of dread seeped all the way into my bones. This was the right decision—in fact, it was the only decision. I glanced at the clouds one more time. It was almost as if the universe was attuned to the tempest raging within me.

What would Mom think if she could see me now?

Brushing away the tears dripping from my eyes, I sucked in the deepest breath I could manage. Asphalt passed beneath the car in a blur as I drove. I wasn't sure where to go, but when I finally put the car in park, I realized I was at Wren's apartment. A quick scan of the parking lot informed me that she wasn't here. Whipping out my phone, I tapped her name and waited for her to answer. After the fourth ring, I began to panic. Luckily, her voice was the next sound to fill my ears.

"Hey, I'm somewhat busy at the moment."

"I'm in trouble."

"What? What do you mean?" she asked, anxiety lacing her voice.

"Where are you?"

"At clinical. I don't have much time to talk."

"Oh, I didn't even think about you having clinical today. Wait a second, how are you even answering the phone? Aren't you supposed to be helping take care of people in the hospital?"

"I'm peeing, if you must know! I felt my phone buzzing in my pocket and saw it was you, so I answered," she explained. "So, what's going on? Do I need to leave to come get you? Are you in jail?"

I sighed with exasperation. "I call you to say I need help and your first question is if I've been arrested?"

"Have you met you?"

"I just want you to know I resent that question."

"Ter, you could talk a Baptist pastor into drinking hard liquor, buying a motorcycle, and getting a 'Hell Raiser' tattoo on his neck."

"Alright, I'll concede. That's fairly accurate."

"Oh, I know it is."

"Why do I put up with you again?"

"Because you love me."

"At the moment, that's debatable."

"So, what do you need?" she asked again. "Do I need to go find a bail bondsman?"

God, was I the most selfish person on the planet? My best friend was taking care of sick people and I was bothering her while she was on a pee break. My personal crisis could wait a few hours. "No. It's just something stupid. I'll tell you about it later."

"You sure?"

"Yeah. I'm sorry I bothered you."

"You've got that tone."

"No, I don't."

"You do."

I scoffed at her insinuation. "Alright, and what tone might that be?"

"The something-is-really-fucking-wrong tone."

"It's nothing, I promise."

"Okay. Well, if you change your mind, just call me back."

"I will. Love you."

"Love you too."

I hung up feeling more confused and stressed than when I first called. I should've told her about all the thoughts having one hell of a rave party inside my head, but she had enough on her plate. There was no need for me to add to her burdens. This was something I needed to figure out for myself, even if she did have advice to offer. At the end of the day, it was my life. I was the artist holding the paintbrush, and I would have to be the one to decide what to create.

Doubt swelled in my throat. What was I doing? I

should drive back to his place and beg for forgiveness. Then again . . . I didn't know how to love someone without abandon. In the grand scheme of things, I had nothing to offer Ry. His heart was a selfless one. He would give and give and give until there was nothing left. There was no way I could force such a fate on him. An act of that magnitude would be unforgiveable.

If I put a stop to the connection we shared before it could grow any further, my pain and his would be so much less. He could find someone else, someone who could give him everything he wanted without fear or hesitation. That's what Ry truly deserved. After everything his dad had put him through, he should be loved unconditionally. And the woman who was able to do that wasn't me. She wasn't someone so frightened of experiencing love that she closed in on herself just when the hope of something more seemed possible. She would be the type of person who chased after what she wanted without a single shred of fear.

I *wished* I could be her. I *tried* to be her.

But I was pretending. This wasn't some fairytale that would have a happy ending. This was the real world, and sometimes in the real world, things don't work out like you expect or like you hope.

A flurry of emotions continued to rage inside me like a typhoon. I tried to take a quick minute for meditation, to silence the storm, but it still persisted. My body was being pulled in two different directions. I was near the breaking point. A few more pounds of pressure and I'd split, never to be whole again.

I understood pain and loss, felt it within every fiber of my being. But if I allowed this thing between us to progress, I'd never recover from losing Ry.

When life was unpredictable, the only certainty you

could count on was loss. Things, people, and lives could be ripped away in the blink of an eye. People always preached that it was better to have loved and lost than to never have loved at all. But was that alternative really preferable? The best artists were always inspired by their tumultuous lives. Desire, love, obsession, jealousy, and death—the lives of Da Vinci, Van Gogh, Picasso, Kahlo, and Degas were ruled by every emotion known to man.

Mom would want me to fall in love. She would want me to experience the happiness of surrendering your heart to another. But she never saw what happened to Dad after she was gone. She didn't hear him sobbing in his bedroom late at night after he had assumed I'd gone to sleep. The fragmented remnants of the man she'd married would never be whole again. I didn't want to spend the rest of my days as nothing more than a broken shell.

I'd rather be alone.

My knuckles blanched as I gripped the steering wheel. This was day one. Tomorrow would be easier.

No sooner than I had the thought, my phone began to ring. The sound jarred the silence of my car and I jumped in response. Whatever shred of positivity had entered my mind was destroyed. Ry's name covered the screen. Chewing on my bottom lip, my fingers trembled as I declined his call. Was he already back at his apartment? Had he found my note?

More tears fell as I declined his call three more times. However, persistence was Ry's strong suit.

Ry: *Ter, you know the note you left is bullshit, and so is running away. Talk to me. Whatever hesitations you have, we can work through them together.*

Ry: *I'm headed to Wren's. My gut tells me that's the first place you would go.*

If he was headed here, then I needed to leave as soon

as possible. I didn't have the nerve to face him yet. And when he realized I wasn't at Wren's apartment, I had no doubts that he would head for my dorm.

Throwing my car in reverse, I sped out of the parking lot and made a beeline for the interstate. There was only one place left for me to go.

chapter nineteen

golden flames

I STARED AT THE door to my childhood home. Perhaps I was being overly dramatic, but this was the only place I could think to escape. Ry wouldn't be able to follow me here. He had no idea where my dad's house was, and I could only pray Wren wouldn't tell him where to find me.

Walking through the red front door, I passed through the kitchen and carried everything up the stairs to my room. The sage-colored walls were a source of comfort for me, a reminder that I was in a safe place. Discarding my things on the bed, I made my way to the bathroom just down the hall. The large tub was calling my name. If I soaked for long enough, maybe my troubles would rise into the air and evaporate like steam. Turning the faucet, I added a dash of my favorite lavender-scented bubble bath and waited for the tub to fill.

Lowering myself into the scalding liquid, I breathed a sigh of relief. Everything about this house was reassuring. It may have only been a couple hours from campus, but it felt as if I had traveled to another world. For once, I did the wise thing and left my phone on my bed. No good would come from staring at Ry's text messages for hours on end. Did he understand how difficult it was for me to leave? I wondered if he could see the tearstains marring the note I'd left.

I'm sorry, but I was wrong. I can't hand myself over to someone after all.

My hand had trembled as I scrawled those sentences. Tears had poured from my eyes and dotted the ink in varying places. I was surprised the note was even legible. Even more surprising was that despite the fact I'd bailed, he still wanted to see me. Ry believed my hesitations could be fixed. But he was wrong.

We both were.

I stayed in the tub until the skin on my toes wrinkled and the water turned cold. I was officially the worst person on the face of the earth. But nevertheless, I had still chased after Ry. I'd flirted with him relentlessly, shook my ass on him when we went out for Halloween, and almost kissed him at least half a dozen times. The fault lies with me, and despite the fact I knew to keep my distance, I still gave in to temptation.

The slight relief the bath had provided was annihilated the moment I checked my phone. I had four missed calls. Two were from Wren and two from Ry. And that wasn't even including all the text messages.

I'd have to face the firing squad sooner or later, so I might as well get it over with.

Wren: *What the hell is going on? Ryan called me almost in a panic, and after your phone call this morning, I'm a bit worried. I know you've been preoccupied with this upcoming show, so I told him you've locked yourself away to paint for a few days. That is what's going on, right?*

Ry: *I know you're scared. Hell, I am too.*

Wren: *Answer your damn phone, bitch. Love you.*

Ry: *If we took things too fast, let me know. Whatever it is, just talk to me. I'm here for you. Always.*

Always.

That word was a promise. It's meaning carried more weight than other words, just like *lovely*, *yours*, and *forever* did. Was he even aware of the impact such a declaration had?

I only replied to Wren, because there was nothing to say to Ry. And the sooner he realized he didn't need me, the better. It wouldn't be long until he found someone worthy of him.

Pulling my robe tighter around me, I collapsed on my bed to read the remaining texts.

Wren: *See my previous text for instructions. Seriously, the two of you are going to give me an ulcer.*

Ry: *I stand by what I said in my last message, but you have to talk to me.*

The scent of lavender clung to my skin. Rolling over, I buried my face in the closest pillow I could find. But really, I was just delaying the inevitable. After a few minutes, I exhaled and pushed up to lean on my elbow. Tapping on Wren's name, I prepared myself for the sass that was sure to come hurtling through the phone. The girl was basically a walking, talking, breathing ball of sassiness—which actually sounded like a pretty good description of myself too.

"About fucking time," she hissed.

"I'm sorry."

"What the actual hell is going on, Ter?"

"I had a lot of shit swirling around inside my head and I figured it would be best to get out of town for a few days."

"Right."

"I still have a few paintings I need to finish before the

art show, and I guess the pressure was just getting to me. I want to make something worthy of Jonas's praise."

What was one more little white lie? It wasn't like my nose was going to start growing Pinocchio-style or anything. Not that having a tree branch for a nose could make this mess even worse.

"Do you even believe the things coming out of your mouth?"

"What do you want to know, babe?" I questioned in an exasperated tone. "Ry and I spent the past few days together and it made me realize that I was getting in over my head. You know I like him, but you also know my heart won't let me get too involved. I'm a coward, have been since Mom died."

Her heavy sigh was full of emotion. "You've been through a lot, and if you feel the need to protect yourself, then I can certainly understand that. Letting yourself care for someone on that kind of level is a risk. But Ryan is one of those guys you don't let slip away."

"You make it sound so easy," I replied, choking on my words.

"It's not, but I don't want you to wake up one day and realize you missed the chance to be with someone truly special."

"We aren't meant to be."

"And you know that how?"

A lone tear meandered down the surface of my cheek. "I just do."

"Right." A few seconds of silence elapsed between us. "Look, you know I'm here for you no matter what, but I would hate it if you passed up the chance to be happy. That's all I want for you, babe. I want you to live without regrets and hesitation. You're an artist and that means you see the world in a completely different way than me. You find beauty in things I wouldn't look at twice, but I don't want you to look back on your life one day and wish you would've taken a chance on Ryan."

"I know, but—"

"Letting him go is the kind of regret you don't outgrow or forget."

"Again, you make it sound so easy. Like I can simply undo the defense mechanisms that my brain put in place the moment I watched Mom's coffin lower into the ground. Believe me, I've tried to take risks. I want to change and open up my heart to someone, I just can't."

"I know how hard it is for you."

"Do you?"

"I won't pretend to understand the loss you've suffered. I mean, I still have my mom, but I do know that you stop yourself from opening up to people because you're afraid of getting hurt. But those of us who haven't lost anyone have those exact same fears. We're all in the same boat, and the only way you get out of it is if you take the plunge and risk safety for something even better."

"So you're saying there's something better than safety?"

"There are a lot of things that are better."

"You seem so certain."

"My parents have it and yours did too. The time they had together wasn't long, but it was still filled with love. They were happy."

"Not at the end."

"Babe, you're only remembering the bad things."

"And what's wrong with that?"

"The fact that suffering through those hard times was worth the love your parents shared."

I huffed loudly. Verbalizing something and actually

doing it were two very different things. "And you know this how?"

"Because your dad told my parents. They were all friends for years, remember?"

"Yeah."

"I won't tell you how to live your life. What you decide to do is up to you."

"Really?" I asked in a hushed voice. "Because I'm pretty sure I've told you how to live your life before."

"That's because you're a pain in the ass."

Her response lived up to its purpose and managed to make me laugh a little. "Thanks for listening to me."

"Any time you need to clear your head, you know I'm here."

"Thanks, babe."

"Call me tomorrow?"

"Yeah."

"Okay, love you."

"Love you too."

Dropping my phone on the bed beside me, I released a long breath. Everything she said was right. I understood the fault rested solely on me. Wren wasn't the only person in my life encouraging me to take risks. Dad and Jonas expressed the same sentiments, but just as I felt strong enough to weather the oncoming storm, I caved. Rolling over, I stared at the picture that had always decorated the table next to the bed. Mom's eyes were always the first feature to jump out at me. The bright blue was the exact same shade as mine. So much of her was reflected in my face. From the slope of my smile to the tip of my nose, I was practically a mirror image of her, except for the one thing I didn't inherit.

Her lust for life was second to none. Mom and Dad went on adventures together that I could only dream of.

Once, when they were still in college, they'd decided to jump in the car and drive all the way to California together. Even though they barely had any money, they managed to reach the west coast. That kind of spontaneity was awe-inspiring. They'd lived in the moment and for one another. There was some truth to Wren's statement. My mind did tend to focus on the rough times and the chemo treatments. The shadow cast in her absence blotted out all the years filled with joy and laughter.

I stared at her picture for hours, completely lost in thought. Across from me, the sky darkened outside the window. It seemed the gloomy clouds from Knoxville had followed me all the way here. Suddenly, a loud clap of thunder disrupted the silence of the house. Drops of rain pelted the glass. There was something so cathartic about listening to the rain. The simple monotony was soothing, and I needed something to combat my tumultuous thoughts . But for once, my brain admitted defeat. Wrapped in a fluffy robe and lulled into a state of tranquility by the growing storm, my eyes closed and I slept.

My room was drenched in darkness when I finally awoke. The sound of the front door slamming shut forced me to my feet.

"Hey, angel," Dad called out. "I didn't know you were coming in for a visit." I listened as his footsteps thudded up the steps. Within a matter of seconds, he appeared in my doorway.

"I decided to come get away for a few days."

"Classes getting to ya?"

I shrugged and dropped my gaze. "Something like that."

His head bobbed in understanding. "Well, I'm glad you came. I've missed you."

"I've missed you too." I walked into his outstretched

arms. There was something about the way he hugged me that made me feel like everything would be okay. That was the power of any father or mother. Their presence could quiet even the strongest storm. I held on to Dad like he was my only remaining lifeline.

"I see you brought your paints. Are you going to be working on projects for the art show all weekend or will you have a little bit of time to spend with your old man?"

I socked him on the chest. "I need to finish a few pieces, but you know I always have time for you. And you still look pretty good. I'd hardly classify you as old."

"That's why you'll always be my favorite daughter."

My eyes rolled in a perfect circle. "You always say that, and I always remind you that I'm your *only* daughter."

Laughter caused his chest to vibrate. "Are you hungry? I can start some dinner while you change."

"That sounds good."

"Is spaghetti okay?" he questioned.

"Absolutely!"

He turned to head for the door. "Alright, I'll see you downstairs."

"Thanks, Dad."

With a parting wink, he closed the door behind him. Walking over to my dresser, I threw on the first underwear set and pair of sweatpants I could lay my hands on. If Dad was making pasta for dinner, then I would need as much wiggle room as possible. He may not have been able to make as many different things as Mom once could, but the man knew how to make a delicious Italian dish. After throwing on a baggy T-shirt and running a brush through my long locks, I raced for the kitchen.

The smell of garlic flooded my senses the moment I stepped on the tile floor. Tomato sauce bubbled on top of the stove. Walking over, I grabbed a wooden spoon and began to stir. My infamy for being a terror in the kitchen was known far and wide, so this was the only way I was allowed to help. As I was stirring, Dad sprinkled a handful of fresh basil into the sauce.

"Would you rather have a salad or garlic bread?" he asked, checking on the boiling noodles.

I gave him a knowing look. Usually, I loved a good salad, but after the day I'd had, the more carbs, the better.

He chuckled at my response. "Okay, bread it is."

"And we're going to need some wine too."

"Of course." Dad tossed a loaf of garlic bread into the oven while the sauce simmered. When he finished draining the noodles, he turned to face me. "You know, I've raised you from the time you were in diapers and I can always tell when something is bothering you."

Pursing my lips together, I nodded. "Am I that obvious?"

"Only to me."

"And Wren and Ry apparently," I muttered under my breath.

"It's just as I suspected."

My head snapped upward fast enough to make my neck look like a damn rubber band. "What did you suspect?"

"That you liked him."

"I do not like him."

My enunciation of the word not only made Dad's smile widen. "Look at us, gabbing like a couple of teenage girls."

"Must you always act like this?"

"For your information, yes. It's my right as a parent. Also, you realize I'm the one who gives you money, right?"

Damn if he didn't have a point there. Mom always did say I inherited his knack for witty replies. "I mean, I suppose you do."

"Wouldn't you say that entitles me to express my opinion whenever I feel like it?"

I huffed to demonstrate my disapproval. "I wouldn't go that far . . ."

"Well, it does."

"I haven't had a chance to eat yet. Can't we at least wait until I have food and wine in my system?"

"I'll allow you that one comfort, but then we are discussing things."

I knew admitting defeat was the only plausible alternative in this scenario. Not that I was ever one to throw in the towel, but I was also smart enough to know when I was outgunned. "Okay."

Dad finished making dinner while I set the table. Cutlery was way safer in my hands than pots and pans. Most people burn things from time to time—it's unavoidable—but on the same note, most people aren't the sole cause behind the need for a kitchen remodel. I believe knowing one's strengths is important in life. Mine just happen to take place as far from a stove as humanly possible.

When we were both seated with piping plates of spaghetti and bread, Dad opened a bottle of red wine. As soon as he set a full glass in front of me, I reached for it. Draining half of the liquid, I mentally prepared myself for the conversation that would follow. Two lit candles sat in the center of the table. I watched as the golden flames flickered. Mom always believed dinner should be eaten by candlelight, and it was a tradition Dad and I always continued whenever we shared a meal together.

"Do you feel ready to talk now?" Dad asked.

"Yeah, I guess so." This was going to be the equivalent of ripping off a Band-Aid. Sure, there was going to be discomfort, but it was best to get it done and over with than to prolong the suffering.

"So, tell me a little more about Ryan."

Tucking a strand of hair behind my ear, I took another quick sip of wine before opening my mouth to speak. "He's really easy to talk to, and he's been through his fair share of tough times. His dad basically walked out on him, so he understands some of what I've been through."

When I glanced up at Dad, he softly smiled at me. "It's really nice he has the ability to understand you like that."

"But it's so, so much more than that. I mean, sometimes, it's almost as if he knows exactly what I'm thinking. Like he realizes how much I live inside my own head, and he doesn't try to force me out of my comfort zone," I confessed, sucking in a deep breath. "He also supports my dreams of being an artist. He believes in me and my abilities without fail. And he's been amazing with Wren. I mean, after everything she's been through, he's been there to help me cheer her up and take care of her whenever she has a really bad day."

"He sounds like a good guy."

"He is."

"Then why are you here, hanging out with your old man instead of him?"

I shrugged, shifting around some of the noodles on my plate. "I don't know."

"Yes, you do." Dad chuckled and picked up his glass of wine. "Did you try what we talked about on the phone the other day?"

"Yeah."

"And?"

"Some things are easier said than done."

"That's true. It can be a scary thing to go after what you most want in the world."

"That seems like the understatement of the century."

"So, does he feel the same way about you?"

"I never said I had feelings for him!" I shouted.

This time, it was Dad's turn to shrug nonchalantly. "You didn't have to, because it's written all over your face," he explained. "I know after everything we've been through, it's really hard for you to open up."

"I just—"

"You don't want to get hurt again, and that is understandable. Some days, I still miss your mother so much that it nearly kills me, but then I remember how much joy you bring into my life. I've loved watching you grow up, and I want nothing more than for you to be happy. Your mother and I had a wonderful life together, and I hope you will find the same kind of love."

I took a minute to absorb his words. "I want to be happy too. It's not like I don't want that for myself."

"I know," he replied in a soothing tone. "But you can't let yourself be vulnerable."

"Yeah."

"And you did try before with Blake . . . You dated him for several months . . . but in the end, it didn't work out."

I finished chewing a bite of food and washed it down with another large gulp of wine. "We were also very young, Dad. I mean, we were still in high school," I countered. "And why does everyone like to bring him up?"

"Because he was the only boy you've ever dated somewhat seriously."

"Alright, I'll give you that."

"You also broke his heart."

"Dad!"

"I mean, you did though." The two of us sat in silence for a few minutes. I watched as he finished off the rest of his dinner and wiped his mouth on a napkin. "So, what happened with Ryan?"

"I realized I wanted to be more than just friends, so we sat down and talked about some things and I found out he wanted the same thing. I really care about him and I know he feels the same way about me. I thought I was strong enough for us to try being together, but as soon as things began to get more serious, I panicked." The words were pouring from my mouth like a river, but my body wasn't ready to stop just yet. "It was like I leapt off the edge of a cliff and started free-falling through the air."

"I see."

"And then the moment I realized how badly I needed him, my brain switched to survival mode."

"So you ran away."

"I didn't know what else to do." I wiped both eyes with the backs of my hands and prayed I could keep it together for the rest of this conversation. "I know that sounds like such a lame excuse, and maybe it is. But I was scared that I'd lose him just like we lost Mom, and I'm not strong enough to make it through something like that again."

Sadness altered the features of his face as he looked at me. Had he always known how much of a coward I was? To some extent, I was certain he did, but at the same time, maybe he was hoping I would outgrow my fears. Normal adults didn't behave this way. Most people didn't allow loss to alter their lives so completely. Death was a natural part of life, but there was nothing natural about your loved one being ripped away from you so unexpectedly.

"I'm sorry, angel, I should've realized how much you were hurting."

"It's not your fault, and you were hurting just as much as I was."

"That's not an excuse."

"I don't know, I think it's a pretty good one," I joked.

Rising from the table, he moved to kneel beside my chair. "Terayn, whatever path you decide to take in life, I'll support you with every fiber of my being. You are my daughter, and the love I feel for you will never fade. As I sit here, I see how much you're hurting and it causes my own chest to tighten. All I want is for you to be happy, but I also want to be honest with you."

"Okay." My reply was more of a choked sob than an actual word, but I tried my best to quell the sadness surging through my heart.

"I realize I don't know every detail of your life, and that's fine. In fact, I prefer it that way, but from what you've told me and from what I've seen, I think what you feel for Ryan goes deeper than even you realize."

"I can't love someone like that."

Taking one of my hands in his, Dad squeezed it gently. "I feel like I'm to blame here. I had a hard time after I lost your mom, and instead of protecting you from that harsh reality, I let you watch me suffer."

"You didn't do anything wrong."

"Doesn't mean I did things right either."

I exhaled deeply. "Ugh. Why do things like this have to be so hard?"

"That's just the way life is."

"I'll be honest, I'm not a big fan of it at the moment."

His easy laughter was enough to lighten the heaviness surrounding us. "Sometimes, I'm not a big fan of it either." Sighing, I leaned into his open arms. The embrace was comforting, and the sense of protection I felt was unmistakable, as if I'd been dressed in a suit of armor. "You know what she'd tell you."

"To face my fears."

"She was the most courageous person I've ever known."

"I wish I could be like her."

"The two of you are more similar than you know."

"Really?" I asked, still holding back tears.

"You both have the same vivacious spirit."

"That isn't a lot."

"You didn't let me finish."

My hold on him tightened as I breathed in the familiar woodsy scent of his cologne. "I'm sorry."

"You have it in you to be as fierce, as fearless as your mother was. I've already seen that kind of determination in you in the last few years. Despite what things you've been told, you still decided to pursue art. You didn't allow the hesitations of others to alter your goals; if anything, that has forced you to try even harder."

"I never thought about it like that."

"You're just as strong as she was."

"Dad, what should I do?"

At my question, his arms released me. Pulling away, he stared at me for a moment. "The answer to that question is a lot more simple than you may think. You've already told me how important Ryan is to you and how you feel about him. On the other hand, you've also confessed your own fears are preventing you from having any kind of relationship with him. What you have to decide is if you can be satisfied with a life without him, or would you rather take the risk and have him in your life even though you may lose him?"

"Sure as hell doesn't sound all that easy."

"It is if you think about it."

"I'll be sure to give it some serious thought."

He walked back to his end of the table. "Good," he

replied, smiling. "And if you need to talk some more, you know I'm always here for you."

"Thanks, Dad."

"Anytime."

I finished the rest of my food while Dad nursed his glass of wine. Sometimes, no matter how crazy life gets, or how stressed I am, coming home and spending time with Dad is like the perfect recipe for peace of mind.

When I finished eating, I cleared the table and started washing the dishes. I never minded washing dishes because it allowed me time to think. Without fail, there were always five hundred different thoughts buzzing inside my brain at any given time. I'd been that way ever since I was a child. Keeping my hands busy with a menial task always gave my mind time to soar. Like me, Dad didn't sugar coat shit. He was more apt to tell people the truth, and that's the same philosophy I've always employed.

He was right. There was an important decision I needed to make. But more than that, he also believed my feelings for Ry were more serious than I was willing to admit. I was aware of what he was insinuating, but he wasn't the one who stated the obvious.

I was.

Before Dad had even had the opportunity to state his assumption, I'd confessed I couldn't love someone in that way. He didn't even state the word, I did. I was the one putting the sentiment out into the universe. No one forced that particular combination of letters from my lips—I offered it up freely.

Yet the real question remained. Did I bail because I didn't want to get in too deep or because I was already there?

"You want any help?" Dad asked beside me.

"You cooked dinner. The least I can do is clean everything up."

"Alright. Do you have work you need to do or are you up for a movie marathon?"

"You know I've always got time for you."

"You pick the movie and I'll get the popcorn."

"Deal."

A couple minutes later, we were sprawled across the couch, watching the opening credits for *Indiana Jones and the Temple of Doom*. Wrapped up in a blanket with a huge bowl of popcorn and my dad sitting next to me, the only thing that could have made this whole scenario even better was if Mom were here.

However, even as I had the thought, I realized something else was also missing.

Ry.

chapter twenty

red lids

I SPENT THREE DAYS practically locked within the walls of my childhood home. I painted, slept, cried, and hung out with Dad. It was a much-needed escape.

But you can only run for so long before everything you've been avoiding begins to catch up with you.

Answering Wren's call on the fourth ring, I held the phone to my ear. "So, you ever coming back?" she asked, getting right down to business.

"I'm thinking about it."

"Interesting, because your cryptic messages over the past few days have me thinking you're halfway to Key West or Canada by now."

"Seriously, babe. You know I'm at home."

"Are you?"

I groaned in an epic display of frustration. "Yes, and I feel like we've been through this a hundred times already."

"Then why is your ass in Elizabethton and not here chasing after a certain blond-haired, blue-eyed charmer we know?"

"Because it's complicated." I rolled over, burying my face in the pile of pillows resting on top of my bed.

"Seems to me like you're the only one making it complicated."

"You're really starting to sound like a broken record."

"Only because you still haven't filled me in on what's going on. Ryan picked me up and took me to breakfast yesterday. And believe me, I tried interrogating him like I was on an episode of *Forensic Files*, but he wasn't talking either. My best guess is that he took you on a date and you freaked the fuck out because, despite all the defense mechanisms you have in place, you couldn't help wanting more."

"No," I spat. "That's not what happened."

"Well, until you get back to Knox and explain everything in person, that's the story I'm going with."

I wasn't sure why I was so hesitant to confess my sins to Wren. I knew judgment wasn't even an issue between the two of us, but it was as if I couldn't get myself to utter the truth. I submitted to Ry in ways I never dreamed possible, but once I'd passed the point of no return, I allowed cowardice to devour my soul.

"I'm coming back tomorrow."

"Is there any way I can get that in writing?"

"I'll see what I can do." Drawing my lip between my teeth, I chewed on my flesh for a moment before summoning the courage to ask her about Ry. "Did he say anything?"

"Not one word," she answered with an air of finality. "But he looked as if he hadn't slept in a few days."

"Really?"

"His hair was unkempt, his eyelids were rimmed with red, and he was rocking the beginning of a lumberjack beard."

A sharp pain shot through my heart. I was the cause of his suffering. I was the reason sleep eluded him. "Oh."

"Yeah."

"What did you say?" I questioned, my voice teeming with heaviness.

"I told him to go home, take a damn shower, and get some sleep. Then I promised to meet up with him sometime tonight."

"Oh."

"For someone who usually has a hard time closing her mouth, you seem to be pretty tight-lipped today."

"I'm not tight-lipped."

"Whatever."

"Anyway, can't we talk about something else for a minute?"

I didn't have to see Wren to know she was rolling her eyes. She always did give as good as she got. "Why the hell not? It's not like this conversation is really going anywhere."

"Jesus, woman, if I wanted the third degree, I'd call up Mrs. Bleeker and ask to be lectured on the proper way to recognize symbolism in modern literature."

"Damn, I forgot how much she lived for that shit."

"How could you forget? I thought we'd never stop writing papers about it."

"True, but what she always failed to remember was that we were only ninth graders. While I can appreciate some of the concepts she was trying to teach us, the things she expected us to know were also a bit beyond our depth."

"That was the only time Dad confessed to disliking one of my teachers."

"Do you remember when she caught us reading the online summaries of *Ethan Frome*?"

"Remember?" I asked incredulously. "She assigned us

to early morning trash pickup for an entire week! I mean, it wasn't like we failed to do the assignment or something. We read the book . . . We just didn't understand a damn word of it."

"She was a holy terror. The school basically threw a party when she retired. Well, of course they threw her a retirement party, but us students also had a party of our own."

"It was pretty much the equivalent of all the munchkins celebrating the death of the Wicked Witch of the West."

"Too bad she didn't get crushed by a house."

"Wren!"

"What? I'm just saying."

"Anyway, how are you doing with work and school and everything?"

"Just so you know, I'm allowing you to shift the focus of this talk we're having."

I snickered at her admission. Honestly, we were two fucking sassy peas in a damn pod. "Wow, that's so kind of you."

"Whatever home we end up in together is going to have their damn hands full. That's all I have to say about the two of us," she replied. "I'm doing okay. Exhausted, but you know me. I'll make it through."

"I know you will."

"Thanks, babe. It also helps that the beautiful scene of Liam getting his ass beat into the ground has imprinted itself in my memory."

"And while the best part was Liam getting what was coming to his lying, cheating ass, it only made it even better that the guy fucking up his world was dressed in women's lingerie."

"Seriously, there's a special place in heaven for Ryan."

"Yeah, there really is."

A loud gasp distracted me from the blue eyes swimming through my mind. "I knew it!" she shouted. "You got in over your head."

"I didn't do anything."

"Not alone, you didn't."

Well . . . she actually had a point there. "Hey, Dad just started yelling at me, so I better let you go."

"Of course he did."

"Can we not right now?"

"We can do whatever you want. Ball's in your court, so to speak."

"I'll call you when I leave."

"Alright, love you, babe."

"Love you too."

I ended the call and tossed my phone on the floor. Ry stopped messaging me two days ago. After I failed to respond to his pleas to talk, he became silent. Not that I deserved a response from him, but my Jane Austen-infused brain was hoping he would track me down and confront me. Lord knew I wasn't bold enough to make any contact of that nature. However, deep down, I wished he'd be the one to save me from myself.

Because I certainly wasn't strong enough to do it on my own. Nuzzling beneath the comforter covering my bed, I willed my body and mind to rest. No sooner than I found some semblance of respite, Dad was knocking on the door to my room.

"May I come in?"

"Yeah, it's not locked."

He moved to sit on the edge of my bed. Even though there were a few wrinkles at the outer corners of his eyes and mouth, he still looked fairly young. "So, I take it Wren is doing okay?"

"She's been really busy with work and school, but you know her, there's nothing she can't handle."

"I'm glad to hear it."

"What's up?" I asked.

He scratched the area of his scalp directly above his right ear. It was the only patch of gray in his hair. "I know you're probably still stuffed from dinner, but I wanted to ask if there's anything I can get you."

"Thanks, Dad. But I'm okay."

He stood and stepped around the paints and canvases littering the floor. "I really like this one." The painting was an image he was more than familiar with. In the painting, Dad knelt at Mom's feet while his lips caressed her outstretched hand. Her white gown and bouquet of peonies were utter perfection in my opinion. My mom had been the most beautiful bride. When I was really little, I chased after the dream of wearing a dress just like hers one day. And I wasn't one of those girls who wanted the attention only a wedding could provide. If I ever got married, I wanted it to be because I'd found someone who completed my soul.

"It's one of the paintings I'll be featuring in the show."

"You captured her smile perfectly. I love it and I know she would too."

"When the show is over, I planned on giving you a couple of the pieces I created." Sitting up, my fingers began twisting a long section of my hair. "Each painting is of her. I hope that's okay."

"Why wouldn't it be?" he asked.

"I don't know, because it's also a reminder of what you lost."

He leaned forward to pat my arm. "I'm going to have to disagree with you there, because I see it as a reminder of everything I had."

"If you had the chance to do it all again, is there anything you would change?"

Would you still marry her knowing she'd die years ahead of you? We both understood the true question my heart longed to ask.

Dad answered without hesitation. "Not a damn thing." I knew he was informing me that the sadness he endured would never outweigh the happiness he'd felt.

"Thanks for listening to me these past few days."

"You mean thanks for letting you hide out?" he teased.

"Geez, you didn't sugar coat that at all, did you? Has Wren been texting you?"

"She may have sent me a message or two to ask about you."

"Bunch of traitors."

"She's your best friend. You know she has a right to be concerned about you."

"I suppose so——"

"Terayn," he countered in a stern tone.

"Alright, so you may have a point. I would be doing the exact same thing if our roles were reversed."

"How about we have another movie marathon to get your mind off things."

"Okay, but can we watch *Star Wars* this time?"

"Anything you want."

"Deal."

I crawled out of bed and retrieved my phone before following him down the steps. Our home was like many others—mostly neutral tones, a few dents and scratches here and there from years of being lived in, pictures along the walls of the stairwell. But unlike other homes, many drawings that I had created over the years were littered among the photographs.

Every inch of this house had been filled with love and

laughter, and although Mom was no longer with us, Dad wanted to make sure I knew he wouldn't trade the years they'd spent together for anything.

Rounding the bottom banister, I entered the kitchen and poured us each a glass of water. Dad was already throwing a bag of popcorn into the microwave. "Just so you know, there are two pints of mint chocolate chip ice cream in the freezer."

"Really?" I asked, my voice the epitome of glee. "You know how I feel about mint chocolate chip."

"Yes, I remember. I'm the one who was covered in green puke, after all."

"So I'm not the best with portion control."

Dad's laughter rang throughout the kitchen. "No, you're not the best with listening."

"That's debatable."

"I told you not to keep eating the ice cream because it was going to give you a stomachache, and what did you do? You continued eating it in secret until you puked."

Heading in the direction of the refrigerator, I cringed at the memory. "In my defense, mint chocolate chip is delicious."

"While that may be true, it doesn't mean I want to be covered in its regurgitated form."

I joined in his laughter, removing both containers of ice cream. Needless to say, I was lucky he could even love me again after enduring something so disgusting. But then again, that's what parents do. They love us in spite of our faults. They love us no matter what.

And yet, that wasn't the case with Ry's dad. His father didn't care at all.

It was impossible for me to fathom what that must have felt like for him. Someone he'd believed hung the moon bailed without hesitation. Was his father even aware of the man he had become? Ry possessed a level of compassion some of us can only dream of. He didn't allow his father's mistakes to keep him from being a decent human being. Somehow, despite everything he'd suffered, Ry still found the courage to trust me. He cared for me so deeply, so completely, and how did I repay him?

By bailing, just like his father did.

A lump formed in the back of my throat, making it almost impossible to breathe. The revelation of what I had done hit me like a sack of bricks. My hands opened, and I watched as the ice cream plummeted toward the tile floor. Running away was supposed to be my way of protecting both of us. If Ry realized how terrible I was, then he would be free to fall for someone who deserved to be loved.

At least, that was the piss-poor reasoning I'd used to justify my actions. In hindsight, I could finally see how big of an idiot I was. I wasn't protecting Ry.

All I did was make him relive one of his worst memories.

All I did was reaffirm the buried belief that he wasn't good enough for his father—and that he wasn't good enough for me.

Tears welled in the corners of my eyes before streaming down the curves of my cheeks. How could I have been so blind? The redemption I'd been searching for all along had stood right before me and I was choosing to run away. "Dad . . ."

Sliding an arm around my shoulders, he pulled me in for a quick hug. "I was wondering when you were going to figure all of this out."

"I can't believe it took me so long," I cried.

"Better late than never."

Wiping at the smudged mascara covering my face, I

released a deep sigh. "What if he doesn't want anything to do with me?"

"I doubt that will be the case, angel."

"You can't know that."

"I have a good feeling about it. We all make mistakes. That's what it means to be human. If you can apologize and be upfront with him, I'm sure he'll forgive you."

"Thanks, Dad. Rain check on the movies?"

"Of course."

I pecked him on the cheek and took off for the stairs. Climbing them two at a time, I hurled myself through the door to my room. The entire space looked as if a hurricane had torn through it, but I didn't have time to care. There was somewhere I needed to be. Racing around the room, I tossed my clothes and painting supplies into the duffel bag I'd brought. Then I added my toiletries and makeup to the mess.

When I was done, the only things left untouched were the canvases I'd propped against my dresser. In all, I spent five minutes packing. Sliding my phone into my back pocket, I headed for the kitchen once more. Dad stood in the center of the room, holding my keys and a thick jacket. Taking them both, I pulled on the jacket and zipped up the front before rushing forward to hug him.

"Thanks again."

"Anytime. Be safe driving back to school." He held on to me tight for a few minutes before finally letting go. "I love you."

"I love you too."

Gathering up my things, I headed for the front door.

"And, angel, there's no need to be afraid anymore."

I smiled at him. He was absolutely right. "I know. I won't be."

Sprinting for my car, I tossed everything in the back

and slid behind the wheel. As I backed out of the driveway, I decided to call Wren.

"Hey, what's up? Have you finally decided to tell me what is really going on?" she questioned, sounding bored.

"I'm on my way back to school. Can you meet me later?"

"Of course."

"Awesome."

"Are you heading to his apartment first?"

I drove through my hometown, not daring to speed. The cops here had nothing better to do than hand out tickets. And I wasn't about to give them any more work. "Yeah."

"He may not be there. He told me earlier he was going to hang out with Logan."

"He did?"

"Have you tried calling him?"

I swallowed thickly. "I don't think he'd answer."

"Just how bad of a number did you do on him?"

"Do I really have to answer that question?"

"No," she answered. "All you have to do is fix it."

"Thanks. I'll call you once I'm back in Knox."

"Sounds good."

Turning up the volume on my radio, I took the fastest route for the interstate. Should I call him and attempt to explain my actions over the last three days, or should I wait and let it be a surprise? Both options had their own unique pros and cons. When I left, he'd begged me to talk to him, to trust him, and I could only hope he could be stronger than I was and actually do so when I asked.

Suppressing the doubt that was bubbling up from my stomach, I sucked in a deep breath and called him. An eternity elapsed between each unanswered ring. Silent prayers passed through my lips as I hoped above all else that he would pick up. Eventually, the call went to voice-mail. Not one to give up, I called him three more times.

But with each call, there was still no answer.

I couldn't blame his hesitancy. In the privacy of his bedroom, I promised to hand myself over to him. He tasted me, touched me, and just as he was about to give me more, I fled. If I'd continued to tread water, I'd been convinced I wouldn't be saved. Instead, I expected to drown.

Pine trees whirred by, blending into a smear of green as I barreled down the interstate. It would be dusk soon. Miles of road passed beneath the car as I continued toward my destination. The sky began to darken and I switched on my lights. There were only a handful of other cars out, and my foot pressed harder on the gas pedal, as if it were made of lead and not flesh. Anticipation swelled inside of me. What if he refused to see me? Should I keep trying, or should I give him peace? I chewed on my lip so hard I was surprised it didn't bleed. No matter what happened, the important thing was that I had to try to make amends. I needed to apologize for my actions and, at the very least, preserve the friendship Ry and I shared. Even if he refused any type of romantic entanglement, I was determined to have him in my life in some capacity.

Not only for me, but for Wren as well. In the past month, she'd come so far. After everything that went down, she hit rock bottom. But Ry helped me lift her up. He was there for her, for both of us really, and I didn't want to sacrifice a friendship she had come to rely on.

Usually, the drive between home and Knox takes around two hours, but I was turning on Volunteer Parkway after only an hour and forty minutes of driving. I tapped my fingers against the steering wheel. I'd be pulling into the parking lot of Ry's apartment soon, and there was too much nervous energy coursing through my body.

The moment I threw my car in park, I jumped out and raced for his apartment. I just needed a chance to explain everything. That's all I wanted. Slamming my fist against his door, I prayed for divine intervention.

Please let him open the door.

If I could talk to him right now, I'd want for nothing the rest of my life.

After three more knocks, I began to grow desperate. "Ry, please open up. It's me. I need to talk to you."

My plea was met with silence. Another three knocks and still nothing. Whipping around, I scanned the parking lot for his car. That should have been the first thing I'd done, but in a rush of adrenaline, common sense had failed me.

But his Jeep was here. It was parked four spaces to the left of my car.

"Ry!"

"I don't want to talk. You should leave." Even through the door, I could hear the harshness in his tone.

"But."

"I mean it."

Backing away from the door, I prayed this was all a figment of my imagination. And yet, there was no mistaking the hatred lacing his voice.

"Please, just—"

"Go," he shouted through the door.

Wren and my dad had both been mistaken. Ry didn't want to see me; he didn't want me anywhere near him. And I couldn't even blame him. I fucked up and betrayed his trust.

I ran for my car, tears pouring from my eyes at a rapid pace. This was what I deserved, what I earned. All actions have consequences. It's a universal truth you learn as a child. I had planted the seed of his anger, and the time had come for me to reap what I'd sown.

I barely remembered getting in my car, much less starting the ignition. My mind was in a state of utter terror. It recalled every touch Ry and I had shared as if the memories would be ripped away at any moment. Every fiber of my being was functioning on autopilot as I drove to Wren's. Relief filled my muscles as I parked my car next to hers. Grabbing my phone and purse, I sprinted for her apartment.

"Wren," I called out, beating my hand against her door.

Half a second later, I was face-to-face with my best friend. "Oh, Ter. What happened?" Sliding her arm around my waist, she led me inside.

"I went to his place to talk, and at first, I thought he wasn't there because he didn't answer the door." My sadness was all-enveloping. "But then he finally told me that he didn't want to talk to me and asked me to leave."

"I'm so sorry, babe."

There was no stopping my tears, so instead of trying to fight against the current, I let them fall. "His voice was filled with so much anger. I doubt he'll ever want to see me again."

"You don't know that. I bet he just needs some time to cool off."

"He hates me, and I can't even blame him for it. If I were him, I would hate me too." Collapsing on her bed, I immediately curled into a ball. Behind me, I could feel the weight of Wren's body settling on top of the comforter. She didn't say a single word as she wrapped her arms around me, hugging my body to hers. "I finally meet a guy capable of holding my interest and I bailed. What the hell is wrong with me?"

"There's nothing wrong with you."

"Hah," I replied with a hiccup. "I'm so screwed up that I can't even let myself fall for someone."

"See, that's where you're wrong."

"How so?"

"You did let yourself fall for him, and that's why this hurts so much."

"I'm glad you're not working tonight."

"Me too." Her arms squeezed me even tighter, and it reminded me of a night from many years ago. The day we'd buried my mother, I couldn't stop crying. Part of me believed it was all some kind of elaborate rouse. My mom had always been so healthy, so full of life that she couldn't possibly die before she was old and gray. I was adrift, lost in an endless sea of agony. But Wren was my anchor. She held on to me as I cried for hours on end. She had always been there to comfort me when I was at my worst, and it seemed she always would be. "It doesn't have to be today, or tomorrow, or even a month from now, but eventually, we do need to talk about everything."

"Okay."

"I'm sorry you're hurting."

"Me too, babe."

Me too.

chapter twenty-one

noir nights

I SPENT A WEEK at Wren's apartment. For three of those days, I refused to shower. Honestly, it was a miracle she didn't throw me out. She should have. At night, she would go to the hospital and work for twelve hours straight, and then in the morning, she would come home and listen to me cry. And to top it off, she didn't even complain. The woman was a true saint, because the majority of the human population wouldn't demonstrate so much compassion or tolerance. She didn't even try to pull me out of my depression. Instead, she allowed me to experience the multitude of emotions I was feeling. She understood my need to be sad. Life isn't a vacuum, and even though we try our best, it's impossible to be happy all the time.

I pushed off of Wren's bed and made my way to the kitchen. She stood in front of the refrigerator, dressed in a pair of light gray scrubs.

"You headed to clinical?"

"Yeah. I should be back around four. Would you mind meeting me at the Campus Grill around then? I was thinking we could grab a burger and some fries."

"Sure. It would be good for me to leave this apartment."

"I wasn't going to say anything, but I also think it would be good for you."

"I'm ninety percent certain I'm starting to smell."

"I was thinking more along the lines of ninety-five percent," she teased.

I poured myself a steaming mug of coffee and added a healthy splash of hazelnut creamer. "Ugh, I'm such a mess."

"There isn't some law stating that you have to be perfect every second of the day."

Taking a sip of the piping liquid, I sighed at the rush of caffeine entering my system. "I know."

"But I would also love you even more if you took it upon yourself to wash your damn hair."

"If this is supposed to be a pep talk, not gonna lie, you kind of suck at it."

"I love you, but there ain't no way you're going to get Ryan back looking like an extra who just walked off the set of *The Walking Dead*."

"Your confidence in me is astounding."

"It's one of God's little miracles," she countered. "Seriously, though, take a shower, borrow some of my clothes, and meet me at the diner later. That sound simple enough?"

"I think I can manage."

"Good!" I watched as she slathered two pieces of toast with strawberry jam and poured a glass of orange juice. "Well, I'm off. Love you, babe."

"Love you too."

I watched as she left, the deadbolt clicking into place as she locked the door from the outside. She was right, I needed to do something besides sulk in her apartment all day. I'd had plenty of time to soak in my despair, and to be honest, I was tired of feeling like a slug. Foregoing my usual bowl of cereal, I decided to carry my coffee into the bathroom and shower. At the very least, I needed to give this positivity thing a valiant effort. Otherwise, Wren would have my ass. She may have been pint-sized, but the girl was strong, and I didn't want to find myself on her bad side.

Cranking on the hot water, I waited patiently for the shower to heat up. After draining the last sip of coffee, I stripped off my pajamas and stepped beneath the scalding stream. Tranquility poured over my muscles as I simply stood there and enjoyed the feeling.

After I finished scrubbing every inch of my body, I emerged from the shower feeling like a new woman. And I didn't stop there either. Not only did I dry my hair and apply a full face of makeup, but I also slathered my body in lotion and dabbed on a bit of Wren's favorite perfume.

The show was next week, and I needed to finish a couple paintings before then. On Thursday, Wren had somehow managed to talk me into going to statistics class. I agreed only because I knew he would be there. Sure, I may have looked as though I'd walked through a hurricane to get to class, but I couldn't have cared less. The only thing that had mattered was getting to see him.

However, Ry had been nowhere to be found. Turns out he hadn't been lying.

He simply wanted nothing to do with me.

Wren was convinced he would be in class next week, but I wasn't so sure. The guy had aced every single test we'd taken. It wasn't like he needed to listen to the lectures or anything. His brain was hardwired for that shit, unlike mine.

I was already working on a backup plan for the show. Originally, I'd planned on painting Ry and Wren to represent my parents, but now that he wasn't even speaking to me, I decided to regroup. Instead of painting my parents, I would paint myself draped in chains and Wren would be covered head to toe in gold with angel wings decorating her back.

It wouldn't evoke the same emotions as my original idea, but I believed it would still be a beautiful display. And I hoped Jonas and my dad would both be proud.

I worked for hours on end. I painted until my hands were splattered with every color known to man. But this time, my muse wasn't the woman who'd given birth to me; it was Ry. I drew him standing outside, the dark night sky enveloping him. Technically, black wasn't a color. Instead, it absorbed every other color in the spectrum and reflected none of them back to the human eye. I surrounded Ry with an eerie black sky. In French, it was pronounced *noir*, in German, *schwarz*, but no matter what language was used, it still referenced an unending abyss.

The only dab of color I wanted on the entire piece was blue, for his eyes. When I finished, I took a moment to stare at the work. His expression said it all. I may not have been able to see his face when I stopped by his apartment a few days ago, but if I had, this is how I imagined he would've look.

Unmistakable pain was embedded into the lines of his face. That same emotion had been reflected in his voice when he asked me to leave. Maybe most people wouldn't want a visual representation of that memory, but I always wanted to be able to look back and remember exactly how I let Ry slip through my fingers. It's impossible to redo past mistakes, but if I tried hard enough, I could keep myself from making new ones.

Withdrawing from the creative daze I had been swept up in, I glanced at the clock for the first time. I only had a few minutes to spare before I needed to meet Wren. Cleaning up the mess I'd made on the floor, I washed all my paintbrushes and laid my painting on top of her dresser to dry. Then, I snagged a red sweater from her closet and slid it over my head. Luckily, my makeup still looked fresh. If I continued functioning like a zombie, she would never let me live it down. Combing my fingers through my hair, I slid on my brown booties and grabbed my purse.

When I made it to the diner, I realized I had beaten her here. I stepped inside and was immediately seated at a booth next to a window.

"What can I get you to drink?" the waitress asked.

"Oh, I'll have a sweet tea."

"And for the person you're meeting?"

"I'm sure she'll want one too, so just bring two teas if you don't mind."

"I'll get those right out," she replied, shoving her order pad back into the apron tied around her waist.

"Thank you."

Barely a minute had passed before the waitress returned with two plastic cups of tea. Grabbing the lemon wedged onto the rim of my cup, I squeezed its juice into my tea.

"Hey, I finally made it," Wren stated, sliding into the booth next to me. It was somewhat odd that she hadn't taken the seat across from me, but I quickly brushed the thought aside. She could sit wherever she damn well pleased.

"How was clinical?"

"Crazy." She stopped talking for a moment to take a

long drink of tea. "We had a code green on my assigned floor and it was like some *Jerry Springer* shit."

"What is a code green?"

"It's a security code."

"Oh, dang."

"Yeah."

"What happened?" I asked, unable to mask the curiosity creeping into my voice. I'd spent the past few days squatting in her apartment, so any kind of drama was extremely exciting.

"This man was admitted for pneumonia, and his wife was there in his room to help take care of him and stuff. Well, right as she's helping him to the bathroom, his girl-friend shows up."

"Holy shit!"

"That was my exact reaction too!"

"Apparently, neither of them knew about the other, so naturally, they're both pissed off."

I twisted my hair and laid it over my shoulder. "Yeah, I would be too."

"But the drama doesn't stop there."

"What else happened?"

"They started arguing about who should be taking care of him while he was in the hospital, and their argument progressed into a fist fight. They were pulling each other's hair and screaming so loud that the nurses on the floor had to call security to escort them off hospital grounds."

"Oh my God!"

"Yeah, it was insanity. That dude *so* didn't have a handle on his scandal."

"Sure sounds like it."

Our waitress then reappeared at our table. "Are the two of you ready to order or would you like me to come back in a few minutes?"

"I'm ready. What about you, Wren?"

"Me too."

I watched as she produced the order pad from her apron once more. "What can I get ya?"

"I'll have a cheeseburger and fries," I answered, handing over the menus we didn't even glance at. You only came to a place like this when you wanted to consume something dripping with grease.

"The same for me. Thank you."

"I'll get those burgers out to you as quick as I can."

As soon as she rushed to give our order to the cook, the bell on the door chimed. At the same time, our heads turned toward the sound. Ry stepped inside the diner and immediately locked eyes with us.

My body sank deeper into the booth. After our conversation the other day, I wasn't ready to see him.

"What the hell did you do?" I asked Wren.

"The two of you need to talk."

"Actually, I'm good. I've grown used to solitude."

"You've been at my apartment. That really can't be considered isolation."

"Good point," I agreed.

"Don't even think about bailing." Her hand fastened around my wrist as she held me in place.

"Judas Iscariot was also a traitor."

Her eyes rolled in the direction of the ceiling as she scoffed at me. "I'm going to do you a favor and pretend like you didn't just make that reference."

"What the hell is going on? You promised it would be just the two of us meeting to eat." Ry stood at the edge of our table, his hands balled into tight fists. He refused to make eye contact with me and, instead, focused his glare on Wren.

"Well, I lied. Sue me."

"I'm gone," he spat, turning on his heel.

"The hell you are. Sit your ass down or I swear to heaven above that the two of you will wake up drugged and taped together. We've got some shit to discuss, so you might as well get comfy."

Dropping into the empty booth across from us, Ry draped his arms over the back of the seat. "Pretty sure holding someone against their will is illegal."

"Pretty sure I remember you beating my ex to a bloody pulp on Halloween. It's not like you're a real stickler for the rules anyway."

"True."

She paused for a moment, and it was obvious she was hoping the two of us would strike up a conversation, but I hoped she was prepared to wait indefinitely. I could tell from Ry's body language that he wanted nothing to do with me. When she finally realized we weren't about to do anything of our own accord, she opened her mouth to speak. "I don't know what the hell went down, but the two of you need to sort it out. All I want is for both of my friends to be happy."

"That's easier said than done," he replied with a sarcastic laugh.

"What about you, Ter? Don't you have anything you'd like to say?"

Chewing on my lip, I played with my hair absentmindedly. I had a whole book of things I wanted to say to him, but that didn't mean I was brave enough to open my mouth and speak. Shaking my head, I prayed for my body to spontaneously combust.

Wren's gaze cut from Ry to me, her head shooting back and forth like the disc in an air hockey game. "Oh my God!" she cried.

"What now?" Ry questioned.

"You guys slept together!" Glee tugged at her features, her lips breaking into a wide smile. "I mean, I really thought you guys did, but I wasn't sure. But staring at the two of you right now, it's so obvious."

Ry and I glanced at each other for the first time since he'd sat down. A mixture of shock and embarrassment radiated from our flesh. "No," we immediately replied in unison.

"Yes, you did! I can tell. It's written all over both of your faces."

I squirmed in my seat. "You're imaging things," I countered with feigned confidence. I wasn't sure why my voice suddenly decided to make its appearance, but I was grateful all the same.

"Ryan?"

"Nothing happened."

"Bull fucking shit!" she cried, drawing the attention of more than one customer. "I'm right. Just fess up to it like a couple of adults."

"You're wrong," Ry countered coolly.

"You know what's amusing about the two of you?" Wren questioned. "You're both so similar. You both chased after the one thing you never wanted."

"What are you talking about?" Ry asked. His arms crossed over his chest, and his jaw clenched to the point I could almost hear his teeth grinding together.

"I'm talking about the fact y'all clearly have feelings for one another. Deny it all you want, but there has been an intense chemistry between the two of you since day one."

"No, we don't."

His denial cut deeper than any knife ever could. We did share an intense connection. In fact, it was like electricity, surging back and forth between our bodies.

Wren laughed slightly and shook her head. "The two

of you are the biggest cowards I've ever seen! You both use the pain your parents experienced as an excuse to avoid any kind of romantic relationship. Y'all care for each other deeply, and the looks you give . . ." She whistled loudly. "Looks that intense should be considered a sin."

"Interesting theory you have there," Ry commented, standing to his feet.

"The way you're acting just informed me that it isn't a theory at all."

"You don't know what you're talking about," I whispered. I shouldn't have opened my mouth. I should have kept quiet, because the moment I opened my mouth to speak, his blue gaze fixed on me. The intensity of his stare rendered me immobile. Pain, sadness, regret—it was all there, etched in every line of his face.

"I have an assignment I need to work on, so I'll see both of you around." He didn't even wait for a reply before stomping out of the diner.

My eyes registered every movement he made as he left. The moment he was gone, Wren rounded on me. However, before she could begin cursing me six ways from Sunday, our food arrived. Two plates laden with fries and cheeseburgers appeared in front of our eyes like magic.

"Is there anything else I can get the two of you?"

"No, thank you. This looks great," Wren replied sweetly. Once our waitress was out of earshot, she initiated her verbal assault on me.

"Girl, what the actual fuck?"

I cringed at her question. "I know!"

"How did it finally happen?"

Taking a giant bite of my burger, I mentally prepared myself to relive the sexcapades Ry and I had engaged in. "Well, we were at his apartment and I was working on my living canvas project. There I am, painting his body, and

Jesus, the man is a walking, talking work of art. I mean, every inch of him is utter perfection. As you can imagine, there was all this sexual tension hovering in the air around us, and then, it was like something in both of us just snapped. The next thing I know, I'm taking off my clothes, and the paint decorating his flesh is smeared all over mine."

"And?"

"It was hands down the most sensual thing I've ever experienced in my life."

"I'm not even surprised. The sexual tension hovering between the two of you was so palpable, so obvious, you could've cut it with a damn cheese spreader."

"That may be true, but you saw what just happened. We fucked, and it screwed everything up! We should've stayed friends. If we'd done that, none of this would've happened."

"Yeah, I don't want to burst your bubble, but I don't think staying friends was really an option for the two of you." She shoved a couple fries in her mouth.

All right, so she had a point there.

"Even if that were true, it's all fucked up anyway. There's no way to fix this."

"Babe, you don't know that."

"He didn't even want to look at me, and you know what? I don't blame him! I wouldn't want to be anywhere near me either. I mean, we spent an amazing few days together, and when things started to get serious, I bailed faster than men on *Maury* after they hear the paternity test results."

"You were scared. That happens to everyone. He won't be able to hold a grudge for long."

"I wouldn't be so sure about that. I think he'll hold this grudge for a very long time."

"Well, you can't avoid each other indefinitely," she replied, her voice soft.

"I've never felt this way about a guy before."

"I know, babe." She slid her arm around my shoulders, wrapping me up in a hug I hadn't realized I needed. "He feels the same way about you."

"Hardly. He can't even stand to be around me anymore."

"He's scared too. He's afraid you'll realize he's not enough for you and leave him behind, like his dad did."

"When I ran away, I wasn't thinking about that. The only thoughts running through my head were that one day I would lose him and it would be more pain than I was capable of withstanding. Not only that, but I believed that, by my leaving, he would be able to find someone truly deserving of his love."

"You need to be saying those words to Ryan, not me."

"I know, but as you saw, that's never going to happen."

"You made a mistake."

"A huge fucking mistake."

Setting her tea back on the table, she leveled me with a serious look. "Would you ever do it again?"

"No," I replied. "I wouldn't leave him again, not for the world."

She smiled sweetly at my confession. "You don't just care for him. You love him."

"I know."

"You need to make sure he knows that too."

"But how do I make him listen?" I questioned.

"Ter, look at me." I obeyed Wren's command, staring into her deep brown eyes. "If you want something, you go after it with every fiber of your being. Ryan is the person you're meant to be with—I have no doubts about it. And sure, things can change, people you think cared about you can rip you apart, but you have to tell Ryan how you feel. You have to take that chance, because if you don't, you'll always regret it."

I was already living with a huge regret, and I wasn't sure how many more my soul could withstand.

chapter twenty-two

a spectrum of colors

I'*LL STILL HELP YOU with the show, but after that, we're done.*
Wren read over the text message Ry had sent me at least a dozen times.

I was on the verge of tears, and the only thing keeping the metaphorical floodgates intact was the fact that I would be painting Ry for my art show within the hour. I should've been elated by the prospect of seeing him again, but his words left little room for celebration. This would likely be the last time we would ever meet.

A week had passed since our encounter at the diner, and although I had made numerous attempts to contact him, all of my efforts were in vain.

"Text message aside, you can't give up hope."

"Yes, I can. It's pretty much nonexistent at this point."

"Ter, this is your chance to tell him how you feel," she countered. "If he really wanted to be done with you, he wouldn't be helping you at all. He still cares about you. You have to believe that."

"Actually, I don't have to do anything."

"You are so damn stubborn sometimes, it's infuriating. You realize this, right?"

I shrugged my shoulders and continued pacing. "Maybe." Beneath the robe I wore, my body was completely painted. What Ry didn't know was that I was going to be joining him as the other living canvas in my display. A display which I had pretty much reinvented in the past week. Instead of focusing on the loss my father had suffered, I'd done a complete three sixty. Now, every piece decorating my wall of the art show would capture the central theme of love.

Some of the paintings were of my parents, like the one I had done to commemorate their wedding. Others included the three of us posing as a happy family.

But the majority of the paintings were of Ry.

He had infiltrated every cell housed inside my body. In the past seven days, I'd lived, breathed, and slept with the sole purpose of recreating his face hundreds of times. At my final meeting with Jonas yesterday, we spent the better part of two hours poring over each work of art. In the end, we'd selected twenty different paintings to display, and Jonas was completely enthralled with the work I'd done. He was astounded not only by the subject matter of my pieces but also by the spectrum of varying colors I'd used. Blue, green, gold, purple, red, yellow, silver, white, and black were used in stunning combinations. Some of the pieces were vibrant, while others were more melancholy. But each canvas was beautiful in my eyes.

Wren was also impressed by everything I had been able to pull off. She actually likened the crazed state I'd been existing in as a type of therapy. Whether or not that was true, I couldn't be certain. However, what did turn out to be true was that I felt better, lighter than I had in several weeks.

Tonight, I would make my confession to Ry. I didn't care what it cost me, I'd make him listen.

"So, let's go over the plan one more time, if you don't mind," I said.

"Ry comes in to be painted and I'll hover somewhere nearby in case you need help."

"And what about Dad?"

"I've got both of our tickets, so don't worry. I'll be sure to guide him around."

"Awesome. You're the best. Has anyone ever told you that?"

She pulled me into a quick hug. "Only a couple times."

"Seriously, I don't know what I would've done without you the past few weeks."

Her hold on me increased as we continued to stand there together. "You would have made it just fine by yourself. You're much stronger than you give yourself credit for."

Chuckling at her comment, I brushed it away almost as soon as the words left her lips. "Yeah right."

"I'm being completely serious, babe. You are so strong. I am constantly in awe of the strength you possess."

"Really?" I asked, my voice a bit shaky.

"Yes."

We separated from one another as another person approached us. Ry stood next to me, dressed in a pair of gym shorts.

"Are you ready?" he questioned, his jaw stiffening the longer he looked at me. "I'd like to get this over with."

"Of course." I reached for the palette I'd already prepared with an assortment of paints.

"I'll be out front with your dad if you need me," Wren said.

"Okay, thanks, babe."

Ry gave her a quick nod. I swallowed hard as I watched her walk away. The two of us were completely alone. At least a dozen different times, I tried to speak, but with every attempt I made, no sound ever escaped.

The silence was like a heavy weight lying across my shoulders. I was acutely aware of its presence, but there was nothing I could do to ease the burden.

"Wren isn't going to be in the show anymore?" he asked after eons of silence.

"No." My hands moved gracefully as I began to cover him in chains. The links wove around his limbs in heavy arcs. If I hadn't known it was all an artistic illusion, I almost would've believed Ry's body was tied up and wrapped in metal. "I'm going to be the other living canvas in the show."

"I see."

The tiny spark of conversation encouraged a false sense of confidence to invade my consciousness. "Ry—" His name was transformed into a plea as I uttered the first syllable.

"Don't," he ordered with an air of finality.

My initial reaction was to be discouraged by his request, but this was not a time to submit to fear. Wren was right, I needed to make him listen to me, no matter what. "Just hear me out for a minute."

"I can't . . ."

"Please," I begged, kneeling before him. My hand trembled slightly as I realized he was staring down at me. A dizzying mixture of emotions danced in the depths of his eyes. "I'm sorry I ran away. I'm sorry I betrayed your trust in the worst possible way. I knew about the pain your father caused you, and in a moment of weakness, I committed the same sin he did." My throat felt parched, but stopping wasn't even a conceivable option at the moment. The things

I wanted to say needed to be released into the universe, and once I finished my confession, I could only hope Ry would forgive me. "I realize I don't deserve your forgiveness, but I want you to know that I ran because of the way I felt about you. I've never cared for someone so much, and the moment I realized I was getting in over my head, I got scared."

"Being scared is understandable, but you should've talked to me about it. You have no idea how I felt when I got back to my apartment and read your note. It was like I was slowly being ripped apart," he explained. "You aren't the only one scared here. I'm just like you. I don't let myself get close to people because I'm afraid of getting hurt, and as it turns out, you only reaffirmed that belief."

"I'm so sorry. If I could go back and change it, I would."

He sighed heavily. "I begged you to talk to me, and you refused. What about that?"

"I know. I made a mistake."

He shook his head and averted his eyes. "I knew I never should have left the apartment that morning. If only I would have stayed and not gone to the gym, then we might not be here right now."

Minutes passed as I racked my brain, trying to think of the right thing to say. As I continued to contemplate, my hands left strokes of gray and black across his skin. The chains I was recreating today looked even better than the ones I'd finished at Ry's apartment. Burying myself in art was the only way I knew how to cope, how to exist.

"You can't think like that."

"Why not?"

"Because we still would've ended up right back here."

"And how do you know that?" he asked, his voice nothing more than a whisper.

Rising to my feet, I moved close enough for me to breathe in his exhaled breath. "I was too scared to admit how much I needed you."

"You say that like you aren't afraid anymore."

"I'm not."

"What changed?"

"I realized I wanted to be with you more than I wanted to be safe."

My heart raced with anticipation as I longed to hear his reply. But the words he would have spoken were never heard.

"Ten minutes until doors open!" Jonas called out.

Ry and I had been secluded in one of the classrooms of the Art Annex, but after the announcement Jonas made, bodies emerged from the other classrooms and began racing for the gallery. I was the only artist utilizing a human canvas, but everyone else seemed eager to put finishing touches on their creations.

I completed the chains and joined hearts covering Ry's flesh, and instead of revisiting our earlier conversation, I used the remaining few minutes to dry the paint. As soon as the task was finished, Ry slipped out of the room without a word.

If only I could get through to him and convince him that I was never going to run away again. I was the type of person who learned from my mistakes, and death was the only way I was ever going to leave Ry's side.

Discarding my robe on the floor, I placed a band of roses on top of my head. Like Ry, I only wore the most minimal amount of clothing. A glorified bathing suit and fake flowers covered the most intimate parts of my body, but I was tired of hiding just as much as I was tired of being a coward.

I was madly in love with Ry and I wanted the entire world to know it.

When I reached my display, I found Ry standing in front of a large painting I'd done of him.

"I thought you were supposed to be painted as your mother," he stated, turning to face me.

Removing my hands from my chest, I stepped closer. On the flesh above my heart, I'd painted a bloody, gaping hole. The carnage, however, stopped there, because every other inch of skin was covered by flowers.

"I changed the inspiration behind my show."

"To what?"

"Love."

"So . . ."

"If you look at your chest, you'll notice there are two hearts there."

His gaze dropped. The tips of his fingers outlined each heart I'd painted on his flesh. "Why?"

"Because," I replied, lowering my voice until he was the only one who could hear me. "It doesn't matter where you go or how many years pass, my heart will always belong to you."

"And what do the flowers symbolize?"

"The way I feel whenever I'm with you." My gaze faltered. Instead of staring into his eyes, I studied the roses I'd painted on my right arm. "Whenever we're together, I feel happy and excited and so full of life. This was the only way I could think of recreating that level of contentment."

"Ter."

I could tell he wanted to say more, but as he parted his lips, the doors to the gallery opened and a crowd flooded the empty space.

Moving at the speed of light, I positioned Ry and

myself in front of my paintings. Then, I intertwined our fingers together.

If this really was going to the be the last time I saw him, then I was going to make the most of it.

All around us, people flitted about, gazing at each display. After thirty minutes or so, Jonas arrived with a large gathering in tow.

"Here, we have a dazzling display exemplifying both the despair and beauty love can inspire," he announced. "As you can see, her heart has been ripped from her chest and painted on his. Would anyone care to guess what that symbolizes?"

"That I'm the sole owner of her heart," Ry said softly.

"Bingo!" Jonas shouted. "Everyone take your time to examine each painting in this building. You will be absolutely astounded by the amount of talent surrounding us." With his final instruction, Jonas winked at me before disappearing into the crowd.

People examined us with the scrutiny of scientists. They praised my work and that of my classmates as well.

Beside me, I could sense that Ry was growing more uncomfortable by the minute. Just as I was about to tell him to take a break, he took off. Following behind him, I sprinted as he made his way to the nearest exit.

"Ry!" I called out, hoping he would stop at the sound of my voice.

But his feet didn't stop until we were standing on the sidewalk outside the building. "Is what he said the truth?"

"Yes."

"And what do you expect me to say to that?"

"You don't have to say anything," I replied. "All I want is to ask you one thing, and if your answer is no, I won't bother you again."

Above us, the full moon illuminated everything in sight.

Stars twinkled in the night sky, complementing the light of the moon.

"Fine," he replied, crossing his arms over his chest. He looked as bored as a ten-year-old sitting through Easter Service.

"Will you go on a date with me?"

"Come again?"

I took a step toward him. This was all or nothing. The time had come for me to put it all on the line. If he chose to walk away, then he'd leave knowing how I really felt about him. My body was being drawn toward his, and I couldn't resist the temptation to touch him. My fingertips danced along the length of his arm as I met his gaze. "I love you, and I'd like for nothing more than to show you how much you mean to me. I know we did things a little out of order, but I don't care. All I want is to be with you. So, I'll ask you again. Ry, will you go on a date with me?"

"You love me?"

I nodded, unable to stop the smile spreading across my face. "More than you could ever know."

"Well, that's a relief," he began. "Because I feel the same way about you."

"You do?"

"Yes." Wiping a lone tear from my cheek, he bent to press his lips to mine. "I love you."

The effect of his confession was instantaneous. Flinging my arms around his neck, I jumped into his arms. The sensation of his hands fastening around my waist was second to none. My legs locked around him, and before I knew it, we were intertwined like ivy. His mouth claimed mine, kissing my lips with enough intensity to make us combust.

Eventually, we'd have to come up for air. But not right now, not this second. When his hand caressed the bare skin of my back, I gasped with delight. He touched me as if he never planned to let me go.

"Okay, I do have one request," he panted once we finally separated.

"And what might that be?"

"You're moving in with me."

"Come again?"

"Move in with me."

"You're being serious?"

"Absolutely."

"We still haven't had our first date."

He laughed and left a trail of kisses along the line of my jaw. "I thought you didn't mind that we were doing things out of order."

"I don't, but that's a pretty serious request."

"I know it is. So, will you?"

"May I ask why?"

"Because I want to wake up every morning to the most beautiful thing I've ever seen."

"Really?"

"Yes, because I never plan to let you go."

"Well," I replied, rubbing my lips against his. "In that case, I'll start moving my stuff in as soon as the semester is over."

"Sounds good to me." He set me back on the ground, but his hands never moved from my skin. "One day, will you tell me what it's like in here?" he questioned, kissing my forehead.

"Only if you promise to tell me what it's like inside your head."

"I can do that."

We both smiled at one another, and in that moment, time stood still. I was with the one person I loved more than anything. Ry was it for me, and I would happily spend the rest of my life making sure he knew it.

"Ry?"

"Yeah?"

"I just want you to know that I never plan to run away again. Wherever you are is home to me."

His grin widened mischievously. "Then after this show is over, I'm taking you home."

"And then what?"

"Oh, I'm sure we can think of something fun to do."

I giggled at his implication. There was nothing I wanted more than to be wrapped in his arms. "It has been a while since we covered your sheets with paint."

"I was hoping you'd say that."

"I said it because I love you, and because I happen to be a big fan of getting naked with you." His smile was infectious and I couldn't keep myself from kissing him again.

"I love you too." He stared down at me, and I couldn't help but be mesmerized by his eyes. "You know, you used every single color known to man in your display tonight. And as I was staring at it, I realized, I don't even know what your favorite color is."

"It's blue."

"Not pink?" he questioned.

"Nope."

"And why is that?"

"It changed to blue the day you walked up to me in statistics class."

End Book Three.

Playlist For Not Without You

1. Coma White by Marilyn Manson
2. Blue Jeans by Lana Del Rey
3. Amber by 311
4. Red Red Red by Fiona Apple
5. Gold by Kiara
6. Supermassive Black Hole by Muse
7. Silver by The Neighbourhood
8. Purple Haze by Jimi Hendrix
9. Green Eyes by Coldplay
10. White Blank Page by Mumford & Sons
11. Blackout Days by Phantogram
12. Damn Right I've Got The Blues by Buddy Guy
13. Black Mambo by Glass Animals
14. Yellow by Coldplay
15. Gold by Chet Faker
16. Nights In White Satin by Moody Blues
17. Blue Madonna by BØRNS featuring Lana Del Rey
18. Purple Rain by Prince
19. Gold Dust Woman by Fleetwood Mac

20. Red Eye by Kid Cudi featuring Haim
21. Vide Noir by Lord Huron
22. Spectrum by Florence and the Machine

Acknowledgements

To start, I'd like to thank my editor, Tamara, who stuck with me while I was writing this book. You are such an amazing editor and I am so grateful you push me to improve and hone my craft as much as you do. This book wouldn't be possible without your tireless support and efforts. I'd also like to thank my family for their unwavering support and love. Y'all mean the world to me, and I'm so lucky to have all of you rooting for me to succeed. To Tiffany, Brittany, and Lindsey I feel beyond blessed to have such wonderful friends by my side. Each of you shower me with encouragement and guidance and I can't thank you enough. To my beta readers, you guys seriously rock! I truly value your advice and input with every single story I send your way. Thank you so much! I also want to give a huge shout out to everyone taking the time to read Ter and Ryan's story. Writing this book was a struggle for me at times, but I'm so glad I pushed through it and was able to finish. I'm so appreciative there are souls out there who read my books. I feel beyond blessed!

Other Titles By A.P. Watson

<u>**Contemporary Romance:**</u>

I Know Better (By Your Side Series: Book One)

You Deserve Better (By Your Side Series: Book Two)

Burning Violet

<u>**Paranormal Romance:**</u>

Seeds of Eden (The Concilium Series: Book One)

About The Author

A.P. Watson grew up in the small town of Estill Springs, Tennessee. Living in a rural area allowed her imagination to run wild, and she began making up stories in her head at a young age. Being an avid reader furthered her love for storytelling. Her favorite books to read have almost always been heavily doused in romance, but she continues to enjoy a variety of authors—from Jane Austen and Charlaine Harris to Ayn Rand and Edgar Allan Poe. Finding herself immersed in unfamiliar worlds only inspired her to put pen to paper, and eventually, her love for reading transformed her into a writer.

While her reading preferences have no limits, she tends to write stories in the realms of contemporary and paranormal romance. Her stories are the culmination of her passions, combining her love for art, history, dance, and medicine. As she grows as a writer, A.P. would like to branch out into other genres while maintaining a central romantic theme.

When she isn't reading or writing, A.P. spends the majority

of her time dancing. She has been an avid pole dancer for several years and has performed in major cities all over the South. She is constantly enraptured by the athleticism, grace, and beauty of the sport and always looks forward to choreographing her next routine. A.P. has a Bachelor of Science in Nursing from East Tennessee State University, and in 2019, she obtained a Master of Science in Nursing with a Family Nurse Practitioner concentration from the same university. She has worked as a critical care nurse for over eight years and loves to incorporate her medical knowledge and experience into her writing. Her goal as an FNP is to combine her love for aesthetics and skincare by becoming certified to administer Botox and dermal fillers. She currently resides in Johnson City, Tennessee, with her adorable rescue pup, Elle.

FOLLW ME:

www.apwatsonauthor.com

Facebook: A.P. Watson Author

For giveaways, sneak peeks of cover reveals and new book material, join my Facebook reader group: Elementary My Dear Watsons

Instagram: @apwatsonauthor